M000169444

BONUS TIME

CLAIRE COOK

MARSHBURY
BEACH
BOOKS

Books by Claire Cook

Bonus Time

*Life Glows On: Reconnecting With Your Creativity to Make the Rest of Your Life
the Best of Your Life*

Shine On: How to Grow Awesome Instead of Old

Never Too Late: Your Roadmap to Reinvention

The Wildwater Walking Club (#1)

The Wildwater Walking Club: Back on Track (#2)

The Wildwater Walking Club: Step by Step (#3)

The Wildwater Walking Club: Walk the Talk (#4)

Must Love Dogs (#1)

Must Love Dogs: New Leash on Life (#2)

Must Love Dogs: Fetch You Later (#3)

Must Love Dogs: Bark & Roll Forever (#4)

Must Love Dogs: Who Let the Cats In? (#5)

Must Love Dogs: A Howliday Tail (#6)

Must Love Dogs: Hearts & Barks (#7)

Must Love Dogs: Lucky Enough (#8)

Best Staged Plans

Seven Year Switch

Summer Blowout

Life's a Beach

Multiple Choice

Time Flies

Wallflower in Bloom

Copyright © 2024 Claire Cook.

All rights reserved. No part of this publication may be reproduced, distributed
or transmitted in any form or by any means without the prior written
permission of the publisher, except in the case of brief quotations in a book
review. For permission requests, send an email to the author at
ClaireCook.com.

Publisher's Note: This is a work of fiction. Names, characters, places, and
incidents are a product of the author's imagination. Locales and public names
are sometimes used for atmospheric purposes. Any resemblance to actual
people, living of dead, or to businesses, companies, events, institutions, or
locales is completely coincidental.

Marshbury Beach Books
Author Photo: Deb Stelzer
Cover Photo: toa55
Bonus Time / Claire Cook
ISBN paper: 978-1-942671-36-7
ISBN ebook: 978-1-942671-35-0

Praise for Claire Cook

"Charming, engagingly quirky, and full of fun, Claire Cook just gets it."—*Meg Cabot*

"Cook's humor and narrative execution are impeccable."
—*Publishers Weekly*

"Claire Cook has an original voice, sparkling style, and a window into family life that will make you laugh and cry.
—*Adriana Trigiani*

"A beach tote couldn't ask for more."—*Kirkus*

"Claire Cook is wicked good."—*Jacquelyn Mitchard*

"Cook's poignancy and sassy humor resonate with readers; her theme of reinvention uplifts and inspires."
—*Savannah Magazine*

Claire Cook's wisdom, candor, and effervescent enthusiasm shine on in every word she writes."—*Book Perfume*

"The exuberant and charming Claire Cook is one of the sassiest and funnest creators of contemporary women's fiction."—*The Times-Picayune*

"Claire Cook (*Must Love Dogs*) has built a brand writing light-hearted women's fiction blending kernels of the absurd and comedic in compulsively readable combinations."
—*Shelf Awareness*

BONUS TIME

To old friends, the best bookends

"Find out where the joy resides,
  And give it a voice beyond singing.
  For to miss the joy is to miss all."

Robert Louis Stevenson

Bonus Time (the theme song)

Move to an island
So we could start a thrivin'
Step it up from merely survivin'
Paid our dues and done our overtime

Slide into flip-flops
Head out to start chillaxin'
Realize we're still too full of passion
Time to bend and stretch and find the light again

We've got bonus time
So how're we gonna use it
What a gift to find
We can choose it before we lose it

The world counts you out
But only if you let it
While they're looking right through you
Go for it, you won't regret it

Bonus time
Some get it and some miss it
It would be a crime
If we were to dismiss it

Three old friends

Who've stopped fakin' young

Earned our silver sprinkles and so not done

Not going gentle into that night

Don't have to flatter us but don't you dare diss us

The world's heating up and it's a crazy place

People call us elderly to our face

Now we're taking names and gonna kick some butt

Three old friends

Who've stopped fakin' young

Earned our wisdom crinkles and so not done

Not going gentle into that night

Bonus time

Some get it and some miss it

It would be a crime

If we were to dismiss it

We're talkin' bonus time

We're rockin' bonus time

Chapter 1

Heading to an island over a four-mile causeway is smooth sailing in a beachy blue EV named Evie. Like driving but not really driving. No sound of a motor running. None of those little transmission jolts pre-electric vehicles make as they jump from gear to gear.

The truth was Evie didn't need any gears. I was switching enough gears for both of us.

A soft canine snore reminded me that there were, in fact, three of us. I peeked in the rearview mirror just in time to see Chickpea, my chihuahua-pitbull rescue, stretch adorably in her faux fur-lined bucket booster seat.

Dogs were so much easier than husbands.

Evie, Chickpea and I had been traveling for almost sixteen and a half hours over two days, way too much of it spent on the nation's longest running north-south interstate, that gridlocked, ridiculously hazardous, tractor-trailer truckers' paradise I-95. I was pretty sure the *I* in I-95 stood for Interminable. Inexcusable? Idiotic? Or maybe just plain Ick.

The good news was I'd had plenty of time to work on my theme song. I was a firm believer that every stage in your life deserved a theme song, an anthem, a manifesto. And if you couldn't find one, you just had to make up your own. And then you had to keep belting it out at the top of your lungs.

Because when you sang in your car, or even in the shower, it didn't matter if you'd crammed a few too many syllables in, or if your hook wasn't very hooky and your bridge wasn't all that bridgey. It didn't matter whether or not you could hold a tune, or stay on key, or even if your voice wasn't one hundred percent sure what a key actually was.

All you had to do was sing it like you meant it. A theme song was a touchstone, a talisman. A theme song helped you walk through the world with purpose and intention and attitude, with spring in your step.

"We've got bonus time," I sang. "So how we gonna use it. What a gift to find . . ." I was going for little bit of an island sound in this rendition. Not quite reggae, but maybe more like Jimmy Buffett meets Gwen Stefani.

I'd originally planned to make an adventure out of the trip, frittering away time and miles, stopping to do fun things and visit family and friends in New York and Philadelphia and D.C. But in the end, I simply wanted to cut to the chase and drive straight through to the next stage of my life.

"The world counts you out," I sang. "But only if you let it. While they're looking right through you . . ."

This time I leaned a little more singer-songwriter, maybe Carole King meets Dolly Parton. It was a high bar, but I could see Chickpea's ears perk up in the rearview mirror when I tried singing it to the melody of *9 to 5*, so I thought I might be on to something.

"Go for it, you won't regret it," I roared. Chickpea jumped in at the end with a sleepy little howl.

At about the halfway point, somewhere around Richmond, Virginia, I'd checked in to a chain motel right off 95. The area was nice enough to feel safe walking a diminutive dog at night. The room was clean and had a small fridge and a microwave so I could zap the rest of last night's drive-through bean burrito for breakfast. The bed wasn't quite as comfortable as the one I'd carried in for Chickpea, but hey, you can't have it all.

In the morning, I'd pulled a fresh oversized T-shirt that said VIBES ATTRACT YOUR TRIBE over the same old yoga pants. I slathered all the skin that showed in copious amounts of broad-spectrum mineral sunscreen until I looked like a cross between a geisha and Casper the Friendly Ghost.

I was probably more concerned with dodging my fair share of skin cancer than avoiding more wrinkles. For the most part I embraced my wrinkles as the squiggly roadmap of a life well-lived. But I'd also seen that horrifying photo of the trucker with a dense jumble of deep lines carved into one side only from decades of driving.

So I'd paid extra attention to applying sunscreen to my left arm and the left side of my face, as well as the backs of both hands. By the time I stopped for the final bathroom break of the drive, my skin had even absorbed most of it.

"Marshbury, Massachusetts," I said, switching over to my best fake travel show host voice, "is now approximately one thousand one hundred and twenty-five miles to our north. Any future jaunts between the two locations will be conducted exclusively by air."

I gave Evie a quick pat on her dashboard screen. "Nothing personal. Think of it as you time, a chance to relax and recharge."

After yet another gulp of caffeine, I worked my blue stainless-steel tumbler back into the cup holder.

I sighed.

As lives go, it could be worse. I'd been around the sun enough times by now to know that it could always, always be worse.

And it could always get better. A lot better. And that part was pretty much up to you. You could sit around whining about what wasn't working, or you could shake things up and reinvent your life one more time. I mean, at this point, who's counting, right?

The truth was that life was going to keep getting all lifey on you whether or not you were actively living it, so you might as well slather on some sunscreen and jump back into the fray.

I pressed Evie's voice button on her steering wheel, asked her to find me the local classic rock radio station. While she searched, I watched a bright yellow sun pop out from behind some fluffy white clouds. A peek of blue ocean in the distance glittered in response. As if on cue, The Beatles broke into "Here Comes the Sun."

It felt choreographed just for me, a bit over-the-top maybe, but a good omen all the same. I belted out the sun, sun, sun, here it comes parts along with The Beatles. Chickpea's chihuahua genes kicked in and she barked along to the do-do-do-do parts.

Between the causeway and the sea, gold-hued marsh grass was blowing in the breeze as far as the eye could see. The Golden Isles, a group of small barrier islands south of Savannah, were named for the vast marshes that comprise a full one-third of the marshland along the entire Atlantic coast.

Up ahead, a pod of brown pelicans in V-formation led the way for us, then veered off across the marsh toward their next meal.

My stomach growled at the thought of food. As I rooted around for my last Larabar, I searched my memory banks for more names for a group of pelicans. A scoop, a squadron. A pouch. If they're fishing, you can call them a fleet.

For better or worse, I had the kind of brain that retained random factoids like these.

I resisted the gasp-worthy views that were like a siren's song daring me to take my tired eyes off the road for a millisecond too long. I smiled at the loggerhead turtle-crossing signs, made a mental note to track down an *I Brake for Turtles* bumper sticker. Wondered if I should ask Evie for approval since she'd be the one wearing it. Decided that while I fully supported giving human characteristics to cars, as well as all other forms of anthropomorphism for that matter, bumper sticker choice remained firmly in my domain.

At the end of the causeway, a carved wooden sign read: WELCOME TO SAINT SIMONS ISLAND.

Trees dripping Spanish moss flanked winding island roads. Glimpses of unspoiled beaches led the way to a sweet throwback village. I considered my food options, decided I couldn't handle one more takeout meal. Circled around to one of the island's two grocery stores.

I tucked Chickpea into her ultra-chic shoulder carrier. Gave my fake emotional support animal line a quick runthrough in case I needed it to keep from getting kicked out of the store. Grabbed some fresh provisions for both of us.

St. Simons is only about twelve miles long and not quite three miles wide at its widest point, so in no time we pulled into the charming townhouse community, perfectly executing the turn into my driveway.

I dug deep and gave my theme song a grand finale finish. "We're talking bonus time. We're rocking bonus time!"

When I leaned my head back against the headrest, I closed my eyes. It felt like they were lined with sandpaper. I opened them again, removed my oversized sunglasses and took a quick peek in the visor mirror. Tired hazel eyes peered back at me. Tufts of hair had escaped from the messy bun on the top of my head, and curly gray tendrils were dancing around like they were happy to finally be here.

I considered a brief EV nap so I wouldn't have to move. Instead I gave Evie a goodbye pat.

"Teamwork is the dreamwork," I said. Then I grabbed the groceries, hoisted Chickpea under one arm.

Before we reached the welcome mat, I stopped for a deep breath of salty, semi-tropical air, so thick I could feel my hair frizz.

"I can't believe we're actually doing this," I said to a palm tree.

I punched in my four-digit passcode, pushed the door open.

Four girls in disheveled, formerly cute outfits were sprawled across the open living area of my first floor, like a Gen Z version of the movie *Bridesmaids*.

Chapter 2

Keeping with the cinematic theme, my townhouse reeked of alcohol and vomit and the unmistakable scent of a recently opened bag of Lay's potato chips. A feeble attempt had been made to camouflage the smell cluster with a sugary vanilla air freshener. Either that or an unfortunate choice of perfume.

"Who are you?" one of the girls said.

"Glenda Gardner," I said. "The owner."

"Big yikes," another girl said.

I'd fully expected my rental property to have morphed into my new home-sweet-home in plenty of time to greet me. Professionally deep cleaned, fresh as a daisy. Short-term-renter-less.

I plopped my groceries on the kitchen island.

Chickpea jumped down from my arms, tail wagging.

"Aww," two of the girls said.

"Pupper," the other two said.

Then they all clutched their heads and groaned in unison.

"Just put it on our tab," one of the girls said.

"Put *what* on your tab?" I said, hoping they weren't quite entitled enough to mean Chickpea.

"Another night," the same girl said. Even with a hangover, she hadn't lost her ability to roll her eyes.

"How did you get back in here? Check-out time was 11 AM. Yesterday." At which point, I knew, their temporary passcode would have stopped working.

"We didn't leave," somebody said. "What a big brain we are."

"Squatters' rights," somebody else said. They all squinted up at me from raccoon mascara eyes.

"Why wasn't your car in my driveway?" I said. Somehow I seemed to have found myself in the role of convincing us all that they were still here.

One of them looked up from taking a selfie with Chickpea. "We got an Uber. Our moms won't let us drive with hangovers."

"I'm not your mom," I said.

"No cap," somebody said. "Our moms are way younger."

"Her silver hair is snatched though," another one said. "She understood the assignment."

"For real, for real," Chickpea's photographer said.

"Bet," somebody else said. "She's got good drip. For her age."

She glanced in my direction. "No offence."

"None taken." I crossed my arms over my chest. "Now get out. All of you."

"Okay, Boomer," one of them said.

"Wow, Glenda," Jan said. "So then what happened?"

"They just up and left?" Harmony said.

I shrugged. "I told them they had to help me clean the townhouse if they stayed. So they Ubered their way out of there in a nanosecond. Then I called the property manager, who charged them for two extra nights, kept their deposit, and put in an emergency call to the deep cleaners. And we all lived happily ever after."

The townhouse pool was nice but not over-the-top. Pool chairs and round tables were filled with a mix of residents and vacationers. Kids were splashing away. A fountain erupted discreetly from a golden marsh-encircled lagoon to one side of the pool.

On the other side, you could see a row of well-kept brick and tabby two-story townhouses, little metal roofs shading tiny front porches, pergolas framing the one-car garages and dripping with flowering jasmine.

"I thought Gen Z wasn't drinking alcohol," Jan said.

"Maybe they were alcohol curious," Harmony said.

"Maybe they ran out of CBD-infused beverages," Jan said.

We were stretched out side-by-side in lounge chairs at the edge of the pool, three ageless goddesses wearing statement sunglasses and flowy caftans. Not the kind of tongue-in-cheek caftans you'd see at a Mrs. Roper party or a Mrs. Roper pub crawl inspired by the resurgence of devotion to the classic *Three's Company* sitcom. But serious caftans, the kind that say this is who we are at this stage of our lives and we're claiming and embracing our hard-earned divahood. So deal with it.

For real, for real, as my Gen Z townhouse squatters would say.

Our caftans were definitely not paired with tributes, by dye or by wig, to Mrs. Roper's curly red hair. Instead, the three of us sported spectacular shades and funky styles of gray hair in all its splendor. And I liked to think my oversized turquoise beach hat took wide-brimmed to a whole new level.

"Well, hallelujah and lardy-dardy," Harmony said. "The golden pals finally living side-by-side in the Golden Isles."

"Knowing," I said, "that we'd eventually end up here together—you know, here for each other, come what may—got me through multiple misguided marriages."

"This. Was. The. Dream," Jan said. "And without it, my sons would still be passing me around like a free-babysitting fruitcake."

"So now what?" I said.

"We sip unsweet tea and enjoy the bejeezus out of the rest of our natural lives," Harmony said.

There was a beat of silence, followed by loud fake snores from Jan and me.

More silence.

"It's like," I said, "there's this ticking clock and it's us. I don't want to waste a minute."

"We'll figure it out," Jan said. "We just have to decide what we want our next chapter to be. And then rock the crapola out of it."

The three of us had connected a gazillion years ago, fresh out of college, working entry level jobs at a small suburban Boston company that printed local newspapers, supermarket flyers, towering forests of junk mail.

It was a time in the world when the smart girls avoided taking a typing class so we could fast-track to a real career instead of getting stuck as some grabby old guy's secretary.

Best laid plans and all, instead we all had to take turns at an actual switchboard whenever the switchboard operator went to lunch or took a break. When it was our turn, we'd put on the headset and sit at a big desk that filled a small room. Fully exposed by a huge plate glass window behind us, facing a daunting panel with rows and rows of holes, each one designated as either an incoming or outgoing line. On the desk were bunches of toggle switches and long cords that were like bungee cords without the stretch.

When a call came in, we'd hear ringing and a red light would flash. We'd have to put a cord into the flashing jack, push a key forward, greet the caller, and find out who they wanted to talk to. Then we'd have to look for the name under another set of holes and place a different cord in that jack and pull another key backward to ring that person. Another light would flash when they finished their call so we could unplug them.

The three of us were all horrible at it. We left some people hanging. We disconnected others. We connected our boss's girlfriend to his wife's extension. Repeatedly. We tangled up the bungee cords until they looked like a bad plate of spaghetti.

When it was one of our turns, the other two would sneak up on us and stand behind the glass window. They'd launch into their best imitations of Lily Tomlin doing Ernestine on *Laugh-In*. They'd stick their fingers down the front of their blouses. They'd press their pursed lips against the glass and mouth *One ringy-dingy* and *A gracious hello* and *Have I reached the party to whom I am speaking?*

The poor excuse for a temporary switchboard operator would try not to look, but it was impossible not to turn around and crack up. When the real switchboard operator finally came back, the three of us would sneak to the ladies' room to reconvene. We'd laugh hysterically, our tears too much for our blue Cover Girl 9-Hour Eye Polish, which was running in rivulets down our Indian Earth bronzed cheeks and into our Bonne Bell Strawberry Lip Smackers.

Sometimes we said we bonded for life over our shared switchboard ineptitude. Other times we said Lily and Ernestine brought us together.

All these decades later sitting out at the townhouse pool, Harmony reached for her lavender stainless steel water bottle.

Jan and I reached for our water bottles, too, as if hydrating were a team sport.

I turned my head in Harmony's direction. "If you hadn't talked us into buying down here ten years ago, we would have been priced right out of the market."

Harmony twirled a long lock of white-streaked hair. "It was a no brainer. Pre-construction prices. Good mix of year-rounders and washashores like us looking to ditch the snow and stay outdoor-active year-round. Rental management already in place. Plus FLETC pays top dollar for rentals which keeps all the rates high, so we were cash positive from day one."

I nodded. "*FLET-C*, so that's how you say it. I always forget what that stands for."

"Federal Law Enforcement Training Center," Jan said. "It's like this massive gated universe on the mainland. Pretty much everyone from state and local cops to federal agents train there at some point in their careers. FBI, CIA, TSA, MBA, PhD. You know, all the acronyms. Most of them stay on campus, but the special ones score an island rental."

I hoisted one side of my hat brim so I could look over my shoulder. "Ever had an actual sighting?"

"They keep a low profile," Harmony said. "But they all drive ginormous pickup trucks and back them into these tiny driveways for a quick getaway. It's such an obvious tell that it makes me a teensy bit nervous about our national security."

Chapter 3

Over the pool fence, we watched a massive white Chevy Suburban SUV roll slowly down the townhouse road. It stopped, rolled a little farther, looked like it might be about to turn into a driveway.

The SUV passed that driveway, and then the next one. It finally attempted a turn and covered the entire postage-stamp front yard of a townhouse.

A hefty reproduction antique streetlight at the front edge of the yard stopped the SUV with a loud slow crunch.

"In their defense," Jan said, "all these places *do* look pretty much alike, even in broad daylight. We just got here and I've almost walked into the wrong townhouse at least three times."

"Not with *your car*," Harmony said.

Hot FLETC federal agents materialized out of nowhere, some shirtless, some in tight T-shirts. They surrounded the SUV.

"Are those the good guys or the bad guys?" Jan said.

"Who cares?" I said.

A mom jumped out of her chair, looked over her shoulder, ran over to a group of swimming kids.

"Get out of the pool," she yelled. "Now!"

"Makes sense," Jan whispered. "I mean, the next SUV might roll right in there."

Back at the SUV, a FLETC agent yanked the driver's door open. Another agent grabbed a teenage boy by the scruff of his neck, jerked him out of the vehicle.

The barefoot teenager staggered forward, threw his arms around the nearest federal agent.

"Day drinking at the beach will do it every time," Harmony said. "Some of these foolish kids don't have the sense to pour pee out of a boot with the instructions written on the heel."

"I'm so relieved to be past that stage," Jan said. "Although if these FLETC people are reliable, it's a definite perk to living here. I'll have to file it away for when one of my grandkids gets old enough to be shipped down and scared straight."

We watched the FLETC agents sit the teenager down on the empty driveway, hover over him, give him a stern lecture. One of the agents backed the SUV off the postage-stamp lawn and pulled it into a driveway three doors down.

A Golden Isles police cruiser drove down the road, lights flashing, siren blaring, stopped next to the teenager and federal agents. A cop jumped out. The agents glared at the teenager while the cop handcuffed his hands behind his back, shoved him into the backseat of the cruiser.

Before the cruiser was out of sight, the FLETC agents had disappeared into thin air.

"Huh," I said. "It almost makes me want to stand up and faint just to see what happens."

"A good case of the vapors couldn't hurt," Harmony said.

"The vapors?" I crossed my arms. "I'm fine with owning my age, but nobody puts Baby in the Victorian Era."

"Why?" Jan said. "Are you on the lookout for a federal boyfriend?"

"No way," I said. "Done. Finished. I've shut the front door. And the back door. All the doors. You know beyond a shadow of a doubt you're completely done with men when you start naming your vibrators."

"Studley," Harmony said in a deep voice.

"B-O-B, aka battery operated boyfriend," Jan said in a vibrating voice.

I put my hand over my heart. "Buzz LightKnight."

"I'm with you," Jan said. "One husband who died on me and left me with three teenage boys to raise by myself. One wife that bailed to have kids with a younger woman who still had the bandwidth for babies. And just in case you've always wondered, wives aren't any easier than husbands, although it does double your wardrobe. Over. It. All. Although in a weak moment, I might take a stab at a non-binary relationship."

Jan and I looked at Harmony.

"What can I say?" Harmony said. "Richie likes it just fine where he is, doing some consulting, hangin' out with his buddies, playing in an extreme pickleball league."

Jan and I waited her out.

Harmony shook her head. "If the first wedding anniversary is paper, and the 25th is silver, and the 50th gold, I guess the 38th is giving each other space. And grace."

We looked out over the pool, lost in our thoughts.

I reached over and patted Harmony on the arm. "Don't worry. He'll call you any day now to say he's on the way."

"Or," Jan said, "that he can't find the ketchup."

When I turned my head, my wide-brimmed turquoise hat hit Harmony in the face.

"You're gonna knock me into the middle of the week looking both ways for Sunday, Honey," Harmony said. "You need to register that hat as a lethal weapon. Either that or get it its own zip code."

"Sorry about that." I pulled the massive brim down past

my shoulders. When I let go, it popped back up. "This hat has triple UV protection, which on top of being thoroughly plastered in SPF three million means I'm almost not feeling the lack of an ozone layer."

"I know, right?" Jan said. "Don't you just miss the days when we slimed ourselves all over with baby oil, wrapped a double album cover in aluminum foil, angled it under our chins and fried our faces to a crisp?"

We all shuddered, reached for our tubes of sunscreen.

"I'd be onboard for a belated attempt at minimizing further sun damage," Jan said. "I can't believe our key fobs won't unlock the pool gate until 8 AM. Ridiculous. I sent an email to the entire HOA Board. Crickets."

I took a long sip of water, leaned over and angled my blue stainless steel water bottle into my enormous beach bag. I put the water bottle down, swung my legs off the lounge chair, bent over and fished out Chickpea.

Using my hat brim as camouflage, I walked over to the nearest planter, put Chickpea down and let her pee her tiny bladder out on the dune grass. I scooped her up, kissed her, popped her back in the beach bag.

A 30-something woman with highlighted bobbed hair, her phone bulging a thigh pocket on her leggings, walked over to us, crossed her arms.

"Hi there," she said. "No dogs allowed. Pool rules."

"Thanks, Karen," Jan said.

"Actually, it's Paige," the woman said. "I'm on the Board."

"Dog?" I gave her my best faux-puzzled look.

"I said NO DOGS ALLOWED IN THE POOL AREA," Paige yelled.

"That's so cute," Harmony said. "She thinks you're deaf."

"Or moderately demented," Jan said. "You know, the louder she talks, the better the chances you'll understand her. I do that with the landscapers who don't speak English."

Jan raised her voice to a roar. "CAN YOU TRIM MY BUSH A LITTLE TIGHTER?"

Everybody in the vicinity turned to look at us.

Chickpea chose that moment to emerge from the beach bag and jump up on my lap.

"What *is* that?" Paige said.

Chickpea lapped my face.

"I've never seen it before," I said. "but my guess would be a chipit. You know, half chihuahua and half pitbull. You can also call it a pithuahua. Or so I've heard. From people who actually have one."

Harmony pointed. "You don't think those sweet little kids are peeing in that pool as we speak? At least Chickpea here had the good manners to fertilize the dune grass."

"Out," Paige said. "Now."

"Listen, Karen," Jan said. "We'll cut you a deal. Program the pool lock to open at 5 AM and we won't sue you for ageism."

"And dogism," I said. "Wait. Is that a single-use water bottle you're holding?" I held out my hand. "Guzzle it down and hand it over so I can at least make sure it gets recycled."

Paige ignored me. "The rules are the rules. You can take it up at the annual HOA meeting. Next year." She raised her voice. "That's HOME. OWNERS. ASSOCIATION."

The three of us sighed, shook our heads, started gathering up our stuff.

Paige walked away, talking on her cell as she looked over her shoulder at us, clearly reporting our canine infraction.

Harmony shook her head. "Some folks would stumble up on a river flowing chocolate and gripe because there was no whipped cream."

"I feel kind of bad for the Karens of the world," I said. "They didn't all deserve to get cancelled."

"It is what it is," Jan said. "If your name is Karen, you just have to buck up and do a full rebrand. I'd suggest dropping the first syllable, adding a W, and going with Wren."

Jan tweeted like a bird. Chickpea's ears popped up.

"We don't have to think of her as a Karen," I said. "Pool Patrol Paige works pretty well. Although Dog Doo Donna has a nice ring to it."

We single-filed it to the exit, heads held high, opened the pool gate, walked through.

I waved Chickpea's paw at the people who were staring at us. Harmony and Jan waved, too.

"Adopt don't shop, y'all," Harmony yelled.

"Come on," I said as we did the hop, skip and jump to our townhouses. "Let's take a ride. I still have to teach you our theme song."

"Fine," Jan said. "But only if you're open to collaboration."

Harmony swung an arm around my shoulder. "Get ready, Honey. They don't call me Harmony for nothing."

Chapter 4

Back in the day, Harmony was the first one to give her two weeks' notice at the publishing company to take a job at a local radio station. Jan and I followed her like she was the Pied Piper.

Jan was pretty sure she was on the way out anyway, since she'd missed a little something while proofreading a supermarket flyer. Instead of twenty-five cents a pound, the entire supermarket chain ended up having to honor the mistake and sell whole chickens for twenty-five cents each. So far nobody had asked Jan to pay for her big oops, but she knew she was skating on thin ice.

I was ready to go, too. Thinking I might stumble on an actual path to career advancement, I'd been trying to learn as much as I could about offset printing. It was still fairly new, a big step up from the labor-intensive hot type machines that had been used for centuries, basically since Gutenberg, where you pressed a page of paper directly onto a block of type.

We used a cold type process where an image was etched onto thin aluminum plates, with extra plates for colored photos or type. A positive image was developed in the camera room from a full-page negative, before going to another department for mounting on the plates. The plates would transfer their inked image to a rubber roller, which would then print the page. At least, I was pretty sure that was how it worked.

One day a camera guy offered to show me how the images were developed from the negatives. As soon as he closed the darkroom door and turned out the lights, he grabbed me and shoved me up against the wall, kissing me, hurting me.

I froze, my heart beating a mile a minute. Then I kneed him in the balls and got out fast, slamming my hip into a hunk of machinery in the dark. And I never told a soul. It was too cringey. Nothing really happened. I was stupid to fall for it.

Until a few years later, somehow it came up and Jan told me he'd done the same thing to her. And when we asked Harmony, it turned out that it wasn't just a *me, too* but a *me, three*. Back in the days before we had words for these things.

All by way of saying Harmony quit the publishing company, and Jan and I were right behind her.

It was a time in the world when we were crouched under a glass ceiling so low that we didn't happen to have a lot of cutting-edge female role models spinning around in our orbit. We knew we'd be horrible nurses and teachers and dental hygienists, and we knew there were other options out there, but we weren't exactly sure what they were.

Harmony had an in because she was dating a pharmacist from a dusty old family pharmacy that advertised regularly on the radio station. He was cute, a few years older than us, and definitely one of the better boyfriends of that era. Not only did he give us free diet pills, but he let us all use his name as a reference.

We told ourselves and one another that the radio station job was a rung up on the career ladder, a resume builder, a giant step toward this cloudy concept of fame and fortune we were all sort of chasing.

The real draw was that the radio station had a swimming

pool. A nice pool even. The station was a barely converted house, an expanded Cape perched high on a hill with a sprawling backyard and extensive vegetable gardens. Even if the job didn't turn out to be that great, how cool would it be to be able to change into a bikini at lunch and catch a few rays?

The owner was an old guy who had to be at least 50. He spent most of his time sitting behind an enormous dark wood desk deep in the bowels of his office. The rumor was he lived with his wife in another house and kept his girlfriend handy in a motel nearby. His girlfriend ran the radio station. She was a former weather girl on an actual television station, which somehow made her an irrefutable expert on everything and undeniably the boss of us.

Harmony answered phones. Jan sold ads. I wrote staggering piles of snore-worthy thirty- and sixty-second advertising copy. We took turns reading the radio spots into a microphone while one of the guys who played boring music and gave the traffic and weather reports recorded them. Once while the three of us were standing in line at a little convenience store, my voice came on the transistor radio sitting on the counter saying something stupid about a bank. And we laughed so hard that when we got back to the car and opened them, our Tabs fizzed over.

The radio station dress code required dresses or skirts for female employees. So for a quick change we wore our bathing suits as underwear with sleeveless blouses and dungaree wrap skirts. Stretched out in our bikinis on lounge chairs around the pool at lunchtime, we practiced holding in our stomachs to make them as flat as possible. I pulled in extra hard, hoped my extra little pooch didn't show as much as I was afraid it did.

We passed around a shared bottle of Hawaiian Tropic Dark Tanning Oil, which we took turns buying, and which would forever after be the smell of summer. When we were out of Hawaiian Tropic, we switched to less expensive baby oil with a few drops of iodine in it to get us through to our next paychecks.

I had the fairest skin of the three of us, so I never once achieved anything close to a dark tan, Hawaiian Tropic or otherwise. I went from Snow White pale directly to boiled lobster red. When I started to peel, Jan and Harmony would each pick a shoulder and pull off long cellophane-like strips of skin. And then I'd oil up and start all over again.

Our theme song of that era was definitely Queen's "Don't Stop Me Now." It played constantly on every radio station, except unfortunately the boring one we happened to work at. We blasted it on Jan's tinny little radio. We sang along at the top of our lungs when the station manager was out, whisper-sang it when she was in. We were all about having a good time. Having a ball.

Motor-mouthing from diet pills, drinking Tab and nibbling at warm cucumbers and hunks of cantaloupe we'd pilfered from the gardens, we pooled our gossip. Apparently, the station owner not only kept the former weather girl-slash-current station manager in a motel down the street, he grew just enough vegetables to get tax-exempt farm status. And he hired disabled adults to weed the gardens so he could get some kind of additional kickback. Or at the very least, cheap labor.

The three of us knew from personal experience about the cheap labor part.

Occasionally one of the Kennedy cousins would show up at the radio station. He was about our age and he'd been kicked out of two boarding schools and yet still mysteriously ended up going to Harvard. Somewhere in the mix, he and another cousin got arrested just over the bridge on Cape Cod for marijuana possession and put on probation. And nobody else would take him in, so he lived with the owner of the radio station.

Even to us, it might have seemed like there were a few knots in this yarn, except that we had proof. Every once in a while when Harmony answered the phone, a woman would identify herself only as Ethyl and ask to talk to the owner. I mean, what more do you need?

No one ever introduced us to the Kennedy cousin. He'd walk right in like he owned the place and we should know who he was. Which was probably fair, since we were pretty sure we did. Sometimes he'd stay around, smiling a toothy smile and flirting with us for a few minutes, and then he'd head for the boss's office.

Harmony was getting sick of her pharmacist, and Jan and I were both between boyfriends, so we started fooling around with the idea of one of us setting our sights on him.

One day the three of us were huddled in the station's kitchen, which was just an ordinary kitchen. We were hiding from the station manager and giggling about whether we should buck up or play rocks/paper/scissors to decide which one of us should hit on him first. And he walked right in.

And then he crossed over to the refrigerator, opened the door, and started rifling through our lunch bags. In front of us. He grabbed a Twix bar from Jan's bag and a Mug-O-Lunch from mine. He pulled one of our precious Tabs out from under the loop that attached it to the rest of its six-pack. And then he walked out the kitchen door without even looking at us.

Our food had been disappearing from the radio station fridge off and on since we'd started working at the station. We figured it was the disabled adults, so we cut them some slack, especially since they helped us steal vegetables from the gardens. And since all those free diet pills meant that we hardly ever ate our lunches anyway.

But this. This. THIS. We were making exactly $125 a week. Before taxes. No sales commissions. No extra pay or residuals for voicing radio spots that might play for decades, and who knew, could even go on to win an Emmy for the station. And this obnoxious rich guy walks right in and *steals our lunch?*

"Unbelievable," I said.

"What's his is his," Harmony said. "And what's ours is his, too."

"Maybe," I said, "he's so spoiled that he thinks the refrigerator fairy magically replenishes whatever he eats."

"Let's get real," Jan said. "He expects the maid to do the grocery shopping after she finishes ironing his button-flap briefs."

"None of us is ever going out with him," I said.

"Ever," Harmony said. "Even if he begs."

"Especially if he begs," I said.

Jan clapped her hands together. "That's it. That's the sound of a crush being crushed."

Decades later, when this particular alleged Kennedy outed himself as more than a bit of a wingnut, the three of us would devour the news coverage, sharing links in our group text chain. *Can you believe it?* we'd type. *And to think we almost dated him.*

In the end, it wasn't possible farm tax fraud or disabled adult kickbacks or a maybe Kennedy stealing our lunches that did it. Summer simply turned into a picturesque but brisk fall. And the last of the vegetables withered on the vine. And the disabled adults pulled a blue plastic cover over the pool. And Harmony broke up with the pharmacist. And winter weather blew in with a frigid vengeance as it does in New England.

And that was almost the end of our radio days.

Chapter 5

"Three old friends," I sang, "who've stopped fakin' young."

Even though it was still dark, Harmony and Jan jumped right in. "Earned our silver sprinkles and so not done," we belted. "Not going gentle into that night."

Evie carried us smoothly over the short East Beach causeway and looped us around the roundabout. I found a spot in the practically empty Coast Guard Station parking lot.

Since we were early, we stayed in the car and sang a few more lines of our theme song. I squirted a big glob of sunscreen on one palm, passed the tube to Jan, who was riding shotgun.

"Do we really need to put that gunk on this early?" Harmony said from the backseat.

"Yes, we do," I said. I took a feeble stab at singing the sun will come out tomorrow line from *Annie*.

"Hack of the day," Jan said, possibly to make me stop singing. "You can mix your own ten percent vitamin C serum for pennies. It just takes a second. It degrades quickly once you mix it, so I make mine daily. A quarter of a teaspoon of ascorbic acid powder mixed with a little over a teaspoon of water."

lly?" Harmony said.

lly," Jan said. "After you wash your face at night, just .. ⌄ıı your face and neck and chest and rub it in. Then pour the rest on your palm, rub your hands together and rub what's left over the back of your hands and your arms. Just make sure you put it on evenly and give it time to absorb into the skin before you glop on anything else. And don't overdo it, because it can oxidize and act like those fake tanners. Unless you like that orangey-tan look."

"You can use vitamin C serum in the morning instead," I said, "but it can make some people's skin more photosensitive. So you definitely need to follow it up with lots of sunscreen with daytime use. Topical application of vitamin C makes a big difference though. It can brighten your skin, heal surface damage, boost collagen. And it helps the skin repair itself from UV damage and the antioxidants can even help protect the skin from further sun damage."

Harmony stuck her hand out for the sunscreen from the backseat. "If you can make it for cheap, then how come vitamin C serum has such a fancy-pants price? I've seen those C serums for well over a hundred dollars an ounce."

"Ascorbic acid is unstable in creams," Jan said. "So they add all these ingredients you don't need, and even use more stable but less effective vitamin C derivatives. So we're paying more and getting less. Overcharging women like us is big business, in case you haven't noticed. Anyway, I've got plenty of ascorbic acid powder to share. One of you can place the next order when we run out."

"Thanks," I said.

"Maybe," Harmony said. "But I might just keep overpaying because it's easier. And because I've worked hard my whole life to be able to afford getting overcharged."

"Okay," I said. "*Bonus* hack of the day: niacinamide. It's a form of vitamin B3 and really gentle. It's great for reducing age spots, blotchiness, wrinkling and yellowing, and it keeps your skin from losing water. I haven't tried making my own yet, but I found an inexpensive five-percent cream online that's just niacinamide and moisturizer."

"I mix my own," Jan said. "It's stable so I store it in an eyedropper bottle and just use a few drops morning and night. To make a five-percent serum, you mix one part niacinamide powder to twenty parts water."

"I knew I should have stayed awake in math class," I said. "I've also started taking 500 milligram niacinamide capsules twice a day. This study in Australia found that it works well for people with a history of a basal cell or squamous cell carcinoma, and/or extensive skin damage from sun exposure, so dermatologists are just starting to recommend it."

"Good to know," Harmony said. "I'll check in with my dermatologist. Or at least Dr. Google."

"These days," I said, "my morning skin ritual is wash, niacinamide cream, moisturizer, sunscreen. At night, it's wash, vitamin C serum, niacinamide cream, moisturizer. I used to alternate the vitamin C with retinol cream every other night, but it was too harsh for my skin."

"Try making a retinol sandwich," Harmony said.

"Yum," Jan said.

"Moisturizer-retinol-moisturizer," Harmony said. "Calms that reaction right down. Stay away from alpha hydroxy acids though. They work, but they make your skin more vulnerable by increasing skin sensitivity."

"This is why women should run the world," Jan said. "The sun isn't even up and we've already hacked our entire skincare regimen."

"So where were we?" I said once I'd patted Evie goodbye and the three of us had climbed out and taken a deep breath of salt air.

"Sipping unsweet tea and enjoying the bejeezus out of the rest of our natural lives," Jan said in her best Harmony imitation.

"Bless your heart," Harmony said.

Even though Harmony had mostly lived in the Boston area for decades, she'd grown up in the South. Over the years I'd noticed that her Southern accent reasserted itself during moments of laughter and anger and stress. And especially whenever there were other Southerners around.

Her accent was practically in full bloom since we'd repossessed our St. Simons townhouses.

In the almost dark, Jan, Harmony and I walked across the beach parking lot toward the ocean in our yoga pants and flip-flops. We used our cellphone flashlights as backup to the gorgeous band of pink pre-sunrise light at the horizon.

We each carried a rolled-up beach towel under one arm. I'd slung a big unbleached cotton bag over my shoulder.

"We were figuring out our next chapter," Jan said.

"I'd like to help save the planet," I said. "And since we've landed on an island, it seems only fair that we start with the ocean."

"Just once," Harmony said, "I'd like to be able to walk the beach with you and not have to pick up trash."

"And I'd like to believe that someday there won't be any to pick up," I said.

"I think," Jan said, "what I really want to do is be a super-hero. Or supershero."

"Superhero is gender neutral," I said.

"Good to know," Jan said. "But I'd prefer to double down on feminine traits. You know, empathy, sensitivity, intuition, superior intelligence. Humility. Plus, supershero has a nice ring to it."

"I'd prefer badass," I said, "but fine, I can live with supershero. Just promise me I won't hear the words *waitress* or *actress* coming out of your mouth. Or *authoress*."

"Deal," Jan said as our flip-flops made the transition from paved parking lot to packed sand.

"And what would a day in your life as a supershero look like?" Harmony said in her humoring-Jan voice.

"Saving the world," Jan said. "Following clues. Solving mysteries. Driving around with my special friend Ned in his snappy blue roadster."

I shined my cell flashlight at her. "I think you just made a sharp turn at Nancy Drew. I'm not sure she counts as a supershero, but she was definitely my hero. And/or shero."

"We'll need skills though," Jan said. "Hard skills. Might take a while to pull all the pieces together. In the meantime, I'm contemplating pottery. Or poetry. Or possibly popsicle-stick crafts."

"Or beach trash art." I pointed my light at a tall metal post at the beach entrance. At the top of the post, a huge chicken-wire manatee sculpture filled with beach trash looked like it was swimming without an ocean.

"Upcycled statement art at its finest," I said.

"Admit it, Honey," Harmony said. "You could go for a good-looking manatee right about now."

We sat cross-legged and barefoot on our beach towels. A shockingly beautiful round ball of orange sun was coming up over the ocean now, doing its part for sunrise yoga at the beach. A hint of full moon was still visible overhead.

I had to admit I'd been paying more attention to the sunrise than the yoga part. Still, I felt practically mellow and a lot less stiff than I'd been at the start of class.

Our young nimble yoga teacher faced the mixed bag of yoga students clustered around, winding things down.

"Inhale up," the yoga teacher said as she raised her arms.

We raised our arms along with the rest of the class.

"And exhale down," the yoga teacher said.

Everybody exhaled, lowered our arms.

"Thank you for allowing me to lead you in practice," the yoga teacher said. "Do good. Shine bright. Have fun."

"Maybe we could work that into another verse for the extended version of our theme song," I whispered.

"Or it could be our first tattoo," Jan whispered.

"*Your* first maybe," Harmony whispered.

The yoga teacher gave us a knock-it-off look before she pressed her hands together in prayer position and closed her eyes.

"Namaste," she said as she bowed her head.

"Namaste," we all said.

Harmony and Jan pushed themselves up from the sand, never a graceful move for anyone who used to be younger. They each reached out a hand to me. I considered blowing them off, decided to take the free ride.

"Thanks," I said when I was fully vertical again. "Not that I needed a lift."

We brushed off our sand-covered backsides, gently wiggled the accumulated sand off our beach towels, started rolling up the towels.

Clueless, a buff young couple across from us picked up their towels and vigorously shook the sand off them.

Their sandstorm blew right into our faces.

All three of us rubbed our eyes, opening and closing our mouths like a trio of fish.

Rolled up beach towels tucked under one arm, we walked the beach, still brushing sand from our faces.

The sun was up high enough now that our oversized T-shirts were readable.

Jan's said PEACE LOVE YOGA.

Harmony's said NAMASTE, Y'ALL.

Mine said F*CK PLASTIC.

"I'm madder 'n a wet settin' hen," Harmony said. "That sand couple didn't even see us. When it comes to ageist kicks in the teeth, invisibility takes the red velvet cake."

I shook my head. "We should have laid into them. I guess I figured, why bother, they wouldn't even hear us."

Jan put one hand behind her ear. "Huh?"

"Let's not forget Pool Patrol Paige," Harmony said. "And what about that server at the coffee shop the other day who ignored us? Ageism, pure and nasty."

"It was fine," Jan said. "I got up and grabbed the pot and poured our coffee."

"Just like a supershero," I said.

I reached into my shoulder bag and handed out reusable net ocean cleanup bags and compostable food service gloves all around.

Harmony and Jan groaned, but they slid on the gloves.

We picked up pieces of trash as we splashed along the edge of the water, dropped them into our bags. A plastic fork, a fishing lure, a piece of Styrofoam cooler, cigarette filters, a deflated balloon with a dangling string.

Jan picked up a set of Dracula teeth, started to put them in her mouth. She reconsidered and dropped the teeth into her bag.

"And to think this is one of the beaches people take care of," Harmony said.

Jan picked up a crushed beer can. "Unless you just raided your parents' beer stash before you drove their SUV into a streetlight."

"Most of the trash washes in with the tide," I said. "There are twenty-one thousand pieces of plastic in the ocean for each person on earth."

"Dial it down, Sunshine," Harmony said. "I can't be invisible and sad for the ocean at the same time."

"If we were supersheroes we could," Jan said.

"Come on," I said. "Let's take this stuff back to our place so we can be sure it gets recycled."

I turned to Jan. "Unless you want to use it for a dolphin trash sculpture?"

Jan shook her head. "Pass. But I might keep the teeth. A quick run through the dishwasher and they'll be good as new."

As soon as we got back to the townhouse complex, we headed straight for the recycling area. In a small fenced-in area behind the pool restrooms, we sorted our beach trash into trash barrels marked Cans, Bottles, Paper, Cardboard, Plastic (#1 & #2), Glass.

I held my empty net bag over my heart. "'How far that little candle throws its beams! So shines a good deed in a naughty world.'"

"Herman's Hermits?" Harmony said.

"Shakespeare," I said. "Portia says it in *The Merchant of Venice*. The candle is a metaphor for looking ahead to a brighter future. I think the rest of the play is pretty much about racism, revenge and money."

"How random is it," Jan said, "that you can still quote your high school Shakespeare, but we couldn't for the life of us remember—"

"—whose car we took to the beach and where in tarnation we parked it." Harmony said.

Chapter 6

I waved my key fob in front of the lock. The three of us, dressed in exercise clothes and sneakers and clearly on a mission, power-walked into the pool area.

A man about our age was strutting around the pool deck, puffed up with self-importance. Knuckle-bumping the men, hugging and cheek-kissing the women, holding court.

The remaining strands of his hair appeared to be super-glued to his scalp. He was wearing a pink tucked-in golf shirt with the collar up. Blue, silver and neon green argyle-patterned golf shorts. His belt was lost somewhere under his belly.

"That's him," Harmony said. "That's the HOA president."

"Ya think?" Jan said.

We watched as a trio of 50-something women closed in on him, flirting away.

I shook my head. "Oh, that's so, so sad. All the smart, kind, interesting women in the world, and that's the best they can do. And there are at least ten of them for every creepster like that. Let it go, ladies. You're buyers stuck in an eternal seller's market."

"No projection happening here," Jan said.

The HOA president noticed us watching him, gave us a big wink.

"Yuck," Harmony said.

"Gross," I said.

"Grody," Jan said. "To the max."

He strutted over to us.

"Beaufort K. Butts the third," he said. "Fourth-term HOA president." He threw his arms open wide. "I'm a hugger."

"Aaaand we're not." I said.

All three of us took a step back.

He laughed. "Love me some hard to get. You little ladies can just call me Beau. Or Mr. President. Up to you."

"Or Butt," Jan said under her breath. "Butt could work."

"What can I do you for?" Butt said. "Or was one of you lookers just working up the courage to ask me out on a date? Spoiler alert: answer's yes."

Harmony batted her eyes. "We'd just like to ask you for an itsy-bitsy teensy-weensy favor, Beau."

"Anything for you, Doll," Butt said, speaking directly to her breasts.

"We'd be tickled pink," Harmony said, "if you'd repro-gram the remote keyless entry thingamajig on the pool gate to open at 5 AM, just for little ol' us."

"So," Butt said. "You're the dog ladies."

Jan pointed to me. "She is. The two of us barely know that dog lady. So if you can do us a solid and get this pool open early for us—"

"No can do," Butt said. "I gotta tell you, everybody's fees are up, trash and recycling, landscaping, pool maintenance. I just finished paying for a brand-new accessible pool lift that's fully compliant, and those don't come cheap, ya know. You can bring it up at the next annual meeting, but we're not looking to blow the whole pool budget on frivolities."

Harmony tilted her head, stuck out her lower lip in a pout.

"What's the rush?" Butt said. "You broads got all day. Take your time, get your beauty sleep before you grease up and try to wiggle into a tight little bathing suit."

"How would it cost more to open the pool early?" Harmony said. "I mean, it's not like the pool's got other plans between 5 and 8 AM. It's sitting right here anyway."

"Don't you worry your pretty little heads about the arithmetic," Butt said, "but the more hours the pool is open, the more it costs me to keep it clean."

"That's ridiculous," I said. "We probably won't even get in the water. And I wouldn't dream of breaking the dog rule again, if that's what you're worried about."

The three of us tried to stare him down. Then we side-eyed one another, assessing our next move.

Butt waggled his eyebrows. "However, I can be bought. Sex. Drugs. Casseroles. Pick your poison."

He pointed to a row of townhouses down the road from ours. "I'm easy to find. Third one from the right. Sign on the door says AFTERDUNE DELIGHT."

Our row of townhouses was softly lit by reproduction antique streetlights, one a bit crooked now, and overhead porch lights. Each door was painted a coastal shade of ocean blue or turquoise or minty green. Instead of numbers, the doors were marked with beachy name plaques.

I opened my door and stepped out on my cute front porch with Chickpea. When I closed my door again, my beachy door sign read PORPOISE OF LIFE.

The sign on the door to one side said FANTASEA. It opened and Jan stepped out on her porch, pulled the door closed behind her.

The door to the other side of mine said REST

ASHORED. Harmony stepped out and pulled it closed behind her.

"This is so much fun," Jan whispered. "It's like being back in college but with better dorms."

"And singles," Harmony whispered. "Which is a huge upgrade since I spent my entire freshman year pretending I couldn't hear my roommate having sex with her boyfriend."

"I know, right?" Jan said. "At least we only share walls and not rooms with Glenda. If she starts having loud sex with her next boyfriend, we can just knock three times."

"Funny," I said. "So funny I forgot to laugh."

Jan never knew went to quit, so she started singing "Knock Three Times."

Harmony jumped in on the part about knocking on the ceiling if you want me. I resisted until they got to the twice on the pipes if the answer is no part.

"Was that Tony Orlando and Dawn?" Harmony said when we fizzled out.

"If I say yes," I said, "will you promise me you won't launch into 'Tie a Yellow Ribbon Round the Old Oak Tree'?"

Of course they did, but at least they only whisper-sang it. In sleep T-shirts, exercise pants and flip-flops, coffee mugs in hand, we crossed the almost-dark road to the pool, more streetlights and the barely lit pool area giving us just enough light to see.

We leaned two dark objects against the darker pool fence. Took turns waving our key fobs in front of the sensor at the pool gate. The sensor flashed red. And red. And red.

Jan sighed and reached for one of the objects, a four-step stepladder with tall curved senior safety handles at the top. She opened the ladder, locked it into place.

We hoisted the ladder over the fence and lowered it to the pool deck on the other side.

Harmony reached for an identical ladder. She opened it

and locked it, positioned it on our side of the fence, across from the other ladder.

Jan swung her arm around my shoulder. "Age before beauty."

"Age IS beauty, bitch," I said.

"Is that term-of-endearment bitch or basic bitch linguistic shaming?" Jan said.

"You started it, Girlfriend," I said. "And if bitch is good enough for Chickpea, I don't think we need to get lost in the weeds here."

An early dog walker shined a flashlight in our direction.

"Shh," Harmony said. "Keep it down. We're about to get ourselves kicked out before we even get in.

"Maintenance," Jan sang to the dog walker. "It never ends."

We waited until dog and walker were out of sight.

"Fine," Harmony said. "I'll go first. *Bitches.*"

Chickpea stood guard over our coffee cups. Jan and I held the stepladder steady while Harmony kicked off her flip-flops and climbed the ladder.

"Be careful," Jan said. "You don't want to fall and break a hip."

"Maybe I should go first," I said. "Mine are titanium. The rest of me will break before they do."

Harmony ignored me, held onto the tall handles as she stepped over the fence to the other ladder, turned around, eased herself down to the pool deck.

We passed the coffee mugs over like a bucket brigade. Jan climbed over the fence. I handed Chickpea over and followed.

We turned and stubbed our toes on a hulking object at the edge of the pool, covered in something tarp-like. Coffee splashed everywhere.

"Ouch/damn/shit on a shingle," we said all together.

"Holy guacamole," Jan said. "What *was* that?"

"Must be that new fully compliant accessible pool lift Butt-face was talking about," I said.

"Maybe we can find a way to strap him in," Harmony said, "and see if there's a button to get it to buck Butt like a bronco."

Chapter 7

Jan, Harmony and I dangled our feet in the water, pant legs rolled up, stars twinkling above us, a barely waning moon. Chickpea chilled in the middle of the pool on a huge pink flamingo float.

"What a pain in the butt that was," I said.

"Pun intended," Jan said.

Harmony blew out a puff of air. "I've got a mean hankerin' to hog-tie that Beaufort K. Butts with telephone wires, just like they did back in the day in *9 to 5*. We watched that movie together so many times over the years, I bet we could do it blindfolded."

"Everything's pretty much wireless now," Jan said. "Makes it more complicated."

"Plus," I said, "you can't really get away with hanging someone from the ceiling with a garage door opener for a month like you could back in 1980."

"A month?" Harmony said. "I think it was longer than that. But you're right. Nobody's got that kind of attention span anymore."

"And shooting at people in a public place is a lot less palatable now," Jan said. "Someday they might actually even do something about it."

"I mean, it's not like she was really aiming," I said. "At least I don't think so. Memory's a funny thing."

"What I remember most," Harmony said, "is the three of us with our feet up on somebody's coffee table, rewinding the DVD so we could watch the good parts over and over again, while we fantasized about doing the exact same thing to our own bosses or clients."

"Or boyfriends," I said. "Or husbands."

Jan sighed. "Women get way too few opportunities to live vicariously through the movies."

"Remember?" Harmony said. "We called it our mastermind group."

"I wish we'd had the guts to actually go through with it," Jan said. "Instead of going back to work the next day and kissing up to some idiot."

"I don't know, prison or paradise." Harmony gestured around us. "I'd say we masterminded our way to the right choice."

We sipped our coffee, lost in our memories. Chickpea floated around on the pink flamingo some more.

"What burns my butt—" Harmony said.

"You're doing it again," I said.

"Low-hanging fruit," Jan said. "It's a butt-joke world."

"What dills my pickle," Harmony said, "is that nobody even sees us anymore. It really is like we're invisible. And did you hear that hostess at the restaurant when we were pouring our own coffee? 'Can somebody wait on those three elderly ladies before they break something?' *Elderly?* Come *on*. We're not even elderly adjacent."

"By definition," Jan said, "I think elderly starts at 65."

"Then somebody better come up with a better definition," Harmony said. "Or a more optimistic word. Or both."

"No kidding." I shook my head. "Some idiot article I just

read even said that the senior demographic begins at 55. Ridiculous. You're practically still in diapers at 55."

"All this ageism is getting really old," Jan said.

"It sure is," Harmony said. "It's like ageism is the new sexism. Except they haven't fully eradicated the old sexism yet."

"It's better," I said. "We've come a long way, baby."

"And we've got a long way to go, baby," Jan said.

"Imagine," Harmony said, "if we could mush sexism and ageism together and flip the whole damn script."

"Sage-ism!" Jan said.

"Exactly," Harmony said. "We could make everybody go around spouting our hard-earned wisdom."

"Be the change," I said.

"Eat plenty of fiber," Harmony said.

"Don't be a dick," Jan said.

We sipped our coffee and thought some more. Chickpea floated around on the flamingo.

"Life isn't that stupid bell curve they've fed us," I said, "where you peak in the middle and it's all downhill from there. We can keep growing and changing and stepping it up."

"It's fear-mongering," Jan said. "They want to make us more afraid with each passing year, so they can sell us anti-aging this and brain-enhancing that. It's a total racket."

"The focus should be on health-span," Harmony said. "Not looks-span or age-span or lifespan. Eat healthy. Stay hydrated. Keep moving."

"Try new things," Jan said. "Keep learning. Use your acquired wisdom to make a difference. Have fun. Connect. Stay current so you don't turn into a dinosaur. It's not exactly drone science."

Jan looked at Harmony then at me. "See what I did there? Updated it from rocket to drone?"

"Totally un-dinosaury," I said.

"I say," Harmony said, "we just tell 'em all to stick it where the sun don't shine—"

"Or go fuck themselves," Jan said. "I mean, how much older do we have to be before we can drop an occasional f-bomb when we feel like it?"

"Swearing," I said, "is actually a sign of intelligence. And it's an excellent exercise in word retrieval."

One by one, we all dropped our heads back and lit up the sky with the most colorful words we could think of. I was pretty sure cartoon swear bubbles actually came out of our mouths.

"Maybe we just let it all go," Jan said. "Rise above the negativity. Do our own thing. I mean, other than being irritated by the whole stupid world and wanting to go to bed at 8 o'clock, I've never been happier."

"I've been thinking about taking up painting," I said. "You know, set up an easel on the sand after I finish picking up trash. Find the perfect beachy berets for Chickpea and me."

"I've been thinking about learning to play the ukulele," Harmony said. "Oh, wait, I already did that."

"Then can I borrow the ukulele?" Jan said.

"Sure," Harmony said. "When I dig it up, I'll bring it over to you."

"Thanks," Jan said, "I'll let you know. I'm also considering carpentry and video game design."

The sky was lightening and a breathtaking pink band began to glow low on the horizon, peeking between palm trees.

"Wow," Jan said. "Just wow."

"It's called the Belt of Venus," Harmony said. "Named after the Roman goddess of love."

"Love," I said. "Ha. I don't spend much time looking backward, but if I have one regret, it's that I never had that gut-punching, fireworks-lighting-up-the-sky kind of love. You know, the soulmate, the one you can't live without."

"I didn't know that," Jan said. "Getting married three times, you'd think the odds would have been in your favor to hit the soulmate jackpot at least once."

"Four times, if you count marrying the first one twice." I realized I was fiddling with a non-existent ring on my wedding-ring finger. I leaned over and wiggled my fingers in the pool water instead.

"Hindsight 20/20," I said, "I don't think I ever really felt seen by any of them. I always felt more like an accessory, you know? Like I was what they needed for the season. And then when it changed, they moved on to something newer and fresher."

"It's hard to believe anybody's fresher than you, Honey," Harmony said.

"Thanks, Honey," I said. "I resemble that remark."

Harmony splashed her feet in the water. "That one-true-love-of-your-life song and dance isn't much more than a steaming pile of mule manure we've been fed. Marriage takes a bunch of work, a ton of letting things go. And some days you still can't stand the damn sound of them breathing. Or chewing."

"Or brushing their teeth," Jan said. "Or blowing their nose. Or cracking their knuckles. Or whining. And whining. And whining."

"I don't want to try anymore," I said. "I don't want to be one of those women pining to get the last man standing to ask her to dance. I know it sounds hokey, but after a lifetime of hopping from man to man, I finally feel whole. I just want to have a nice no-drama unconditional relationship with myself."

"And with your friends," Jan said. "You have spectacular friends."

"True that," Harmony said.

The Belt of Venus had faded away and the sky was in that brief intermission when the sun was getting ready to rise. Movement caught our eyes.

On the other side of the pool fence, a man was jogging with perfect form across the road that ran through the town-house complex. Maybe 40ish, tall, muscular, shirt off, sweat glistening under the soft light.

His head stayed straight ahead as three women and one small dog watched his every move.

His running appeared to turn slow-motion, and I was pretty sure we could hear the barefoot running-on-the-beach music from *Chariots of Fire*.

He lifted one hand up and then put it down again. Maybe a wave, maybe an aborted head scratch.

"But," I said, "there's not a damn thing wrong with a little hot federal agent watching."

Chapter 8

On the weekend *9 to 5* was released, the three of us went to the movies together, cheering along with the rest of the mostly female audience. I kept casting and recasting myself in all the roles. I was Violet, so smart and promotion-deserving and so unfairly overlooked. Then I was Doralee, who couldn't help being beautiful and didn't deserve to get sexually harassed for it. Then I was sweet Judy as she made her first tentative foray into the working world.

Everything in me wanted to gang up with them to take care of that dirty rat of a boss of theirs.

Afterward, we stood outside on the sidewalk, shivering on a cold, dank November night.

"Stellar," I said. "I mean, far freakin' out."

"To the max," Jan said. "That was not just a funky workplace comedy."

"Off the hook," Harmony said. "Holy statement of female empowerment."

We noticed a few people marching back and forth in front of the movie theater, holding picket signs that said BOYCOTT 9 TO 5 and HANOI JANE.

"Oh, take a chill pill," Jan said. "So Jane Fonda got tricked into making a huge mistake. Can you imagine being blamed for the rest of your life for one dumb thing you did?"

"The poor thing wasn't that much older than we are now," Harmony said. "You're supposed to make stupid mistakes when you're young. That's why they call it young and foolish."

"She's probably blaming herself enough for everybody." I stared straight ahead. "It's a lot to have to live with something you can't take back."

That movie hit us hard. Our minds were blown. It was validating and comforting, and yet also a warning siren, a cautionary tale.

We could have used that film-fired energy to take over the radio station. We probably would have been running the place within a year. Or we could have spring-boarded to somewhere bigger together and been running *that* place within a couple of years. At the very least, we should have checked the job listings in the classified section and updated our resumes before we quit.

Instead, we marched into work on Monday, stood side-by-side in front of the former weather girl-slash-current station manager and gave our two-weeks' notice.

We waited for her to beg us to stay. Maybe even bump up our weekly salaries to a cool $150.

She looked right through us, shrugged. "Pack up your things and leave now."

We scooped up last week's tattered brown paper lunch bags and what was left of our six-pack of Tab from the fridge in the kitchen. We grabbed the dregs of our Hawaiian Tropic Dark Tanning Oil from the kitchen cabinet we'd stashed it in. Harmony held up our baby oil with the drops of iodine in it.

"We are not that desperate," I said. "We're moving onto bigger and better things."

The reception desk Harmony sat at was community property. Jan spent most of her time on the local road trying to sell ads. So I was the only one who had an actual desk. I opened my desk drawer and pulled out our zippered makeup bags. Mine was covered in avocado green daisies with pink centers on a beige background with a turquoise grid. I loved that little bag so much that when it disappeared years later during some move or another, I'd never completely get over it.

On the way out, we circled around the pool, walked through the gardens. Jan detached the last remaining pumpkin from a withered vine. It was small and frostbitten and misshapen, a Charlie Brown's Christmas tree kind of pumpkin.

"I think," Jan said, "we should leave it in the fridge for the next time you-know-who is looking for a lunch to steal."

"That'll teach him to buzz off," I said.

"Imagine," Harmony said, "how heartbroken he's going to be when he comes back to steal our lunches and ask us out."

We did one more lap around the pool for good luck. We left the pumpkin in the fridge, even though it was already starting to feel like we were the ones who'd just turned into pumpkins.

"Catch you on the flip side," we said as we stood in the parking lot, trying to be brave.

For a while, we kept in touch. I got a job working the front desk at a dance aerobics studio while I looked for a real job. When the owner wasn't around, I let Jan and Harmony in for free. I danced in the back of the room with them so all three of us could sneak in a workout together.

With our final paychecks, we splurged on shiny lycra thong-back leotards and footless tights to wear with our leg warmers and wristbands. We wore matching headbands that bisected our foreheads and dented our heavily crimped hair.

Finally, I got an entry-level job at an advertising agency in Boston. Jan moved to New York to live with a cousin and hunt for a job there. Harmony moved home to the South where she could live rent-free and work on getting her master's while she figured out her next step.

And then we didn't see one another for years.

In our defense, it was so much harder to stay in touch back then. It was a time in the world when every Sunday night college kids would stand in long lines snaking through the dorm hallways to the row of payphones so they could call home at the lowest rates. They'd dial, let it ring once, then hang up and wait for their parents to call them back to make it cheaper than calling collect.

Reach out and touch someone ads were everywhere, trying to convince you that it didn't matter how much it cost to call someone important to you. But money was money, especially when you didn't have any. It was a huge hassle, a mind-numbingly confusing and financially stressful game.

Once you were out of the same area code, phone calls were ridiculously expensive, and when you crossed the state line, they were astronomical. You could fill your tank up with gas for the price of catching up with a friend. And that was on the weekend. If you absolutely had to make a long distance call on a weekday, it would have to be late at night and you'd have to make it fast. Like three minutes fast.

So we sent Christmas cards. We wrote the occasional letter, filled with promises to come visit. And then we just didn't.

When you're younger, you think friendships like ours will just keep on coming, one after another and another. They'll be a dime a dozen. Over time you realize what a rare and beautiful gift they are. And if you're smart, you go back and do your best to scoop them up. You let them ebb and flow, as all good friendships do, but you treasure them. And you never, ever let them go again.

We were stretched out side-by-side in lounge chairs, bathrobes over nightgowns this morning, flip-flops kicked off, coffee mugs in hand. Chickpea was ensconced in the middle of the pool again on the pink flamingo float.

"All this sneakin' over the fence in the dark is getting on my last nerve," Harmony said. "We're going to have to come up with a workaround at some point."

"Sneaking over the fence *is* the workaround," I said.

"It's pretty magical once we get in here though," Jan said. "Like having our own secret clubhouse before the rest of the world even wakes up. Maybe we need to make a clubhouse sign for the gate."

"NO BOYS ALLOWED," Harmony said.

"KEEP OUT," Jan said.

"AND THAT MEANS YOU," Harmony said.

A flash of robe dropped to the pool deck. A nightgown followed. There was a splash.

"Glenda?" I heard Jan and Harmony say.

"Come on in," I said. "The water's fine. Well, more like pre-fine, but I'm warming up already."

In no time, three robes and three nightgowns were piled at the edge of the pool.

In the almost dark, our heads and shoulders bebopped above the water. An occasional flash of silver hair shimmered as it caught the soft glow of a streetlight.

We each rested one hand on the enormous pink flamingo float, used our other hand to paddle the flamingo around in a circle.

Chickpea enjoyed the free ride, occasionally leaned over and lapped my face.

"I can't believe we're freaking skinny-dipping," Jan said.

"Take that, world," I yelled. "We're not elderly. We are ageless freaking goddesses who do a mean water ballet."

We switched arms, circled the flamingo float in the opposite direction.

"Water ballet might be a teensy bit of a stretch," Harmony said. "But when I was growing up, I used to spend hours and hours splashing around in the little swimming hole behind our house pretending I was Esther Williams."

We'd been friends for so long that I didn't even have to ask to know we'd all jumped into the same Esther Williams fantasy. In our minds we wore an explosion of brightly-colored flowers on our swim caps, the straps of our 1950s swim dresses peeking above the water. Flesh-toned bodysuits underneath the swim dresses were like a forgiving camera-ready second skin.

Harmony, Jan and I looked at one another. One hand resting on a magnificent movie-set pink flamingo with real feathers, we extended our opposite arms gracefully overhead, then out to the side, in practically perfect unison. I imagined Chickpea standing on her hind legs in the middle of the flamingo, wearing a tiny floral Esther Williams swim cap, too.

"We've still got it," Harmony said, bringing us back to skinny-dipping in the pool, one hand on a vinyl pink flamingo.

"We sure do," Jan said. She dove under the dark water, flipped her hair back as she broke the surface again.

"For me," I said, "it was Busby Berkeley. That intricate water ballet choreography of his—you know, like looking into a kaleidoscope—gave me goosebumps all over. When some relationship or another was coming apart at the seams, I'd sneak downstairs in the middle of the night and turn on the classic movie channel. I could picture myself in those kaleido-scope scenes so clearly. And I never missed a move."

Harmony and Jan joined me in my Busby Berkeley fantasy. We wore elaborate gold headdresses and long-sleeve sparkly gold bodysuits. We floated on our backs, our heads resting on the elegant pink flamingo like a pillow. Treading water with both hands, silver and gold streamers floating out in front of our bodies on the surface of the water.

Chickpea started wrestling with her imaginary tiny elabo-rate gold headdress in the middle of the flamingo.

"Chickpea," I said. And suddenly we were skinny-dipping

again. We pushed away from the blow-up flamingo, started treading water.

"*The Little Mermaid*," Jan said. "All day long. The original. The sequel. The prequel. The TV series. The new sequel. I've been singing 'Daring to Dance' in the shower since the early '90s. It might even be the overarching theme of my life so far."

We dove right in to Jan's fantasy. We even started singing "Daring to Dance," taking a stab at the melody and embellishing it with bits and pieces of half-remembered lyrics about something inside and taking a chance and daring to sing and to dance and to dream and to sing and to live.

I knew we were all wearing long red Ariel wigs over our silver hair as we kicked our feet and pushed the pink flamingo in laps around the pool. Our mermaid tails floated out behind us, and Chickpea was wearing a tiny red Ariel wig, too.

"I needed that," Harmony said.

"You and me both, sistah," Jan said.

And we were skinny-dipping again.

"Do you know," I said, "that I can't remember the last time I was in a pool? It's like my whole life has been driven by this unrelenting body hatred, body hiding. I was even in a full body suit in our water ballet fantasies."

"Me, too," Harmony said.

"Me, three," Jan said.

"Sometimes," I said, "I look at old pictures and I think how could I not have known how beautiful I was? I had absolutely no idea at the time. All I could see were an unflat stomach and jiggly thighs. I mean, how old do we have to be to let all that crap go, you know?"

"We're stark naked in a swimming pool," Harmony said, "so I'd say we're takin' a pretty good run at it."

"I don't give a rat's ass what anyone thinks about how I look anymore," Jan said. "It's freeing. I don't even let them weigh me at my doctor visits anymore. I just tell them that I'm a conscientious objector to the whole ritual and I reject being weight-shamed."

"You can do that?" I said.

"Sure you can," Harmony said. "What are they going to do, hog-tie you and strap you to the scale?"

Movement outside the fence caught our eyes. Somehow the sky was almost light. The same man was jogging by, same perfect posture and steady stride, same muscular build, same shirtless, sweat-glistening torso.

We watched his every move, mesmerized. I was pretty sure I heard the *Chariots of Fire* music begin to play.

He lifted one arm up in a definite wave.

We all waved back.

"Maybe he's not that young," I said.

I shook my head. "He's that young."

We all leaned sideways in the pool so we could keep watching him.

"You've got to admit," I said, "it's the perfect fantasy though. You know it's never going to happen, so you don't even have to shave your legs."

We watched him until he disappeared like a mirage.

"Holy moly cannoli," Jan said. "You don't think he noticed we're skinny-dipping in here, do you?"

Our eyes went to the pile of discarded clothing on the edge of the pool.

Chapter 9

Almost exactly a decade after we quit the radio station, little dots of kismet brought the three of us back together. It seemed amazing then, and it would only grow more and more magical through the lens of hindsight.

Jan and Harmony were both married with kids at that point and my second marriage had just unraveled. We'd mailed one another wedding invitations over the years, although I was pretty sure I'd only sent them one to my first marriage. They weren't serious invitations, more like the kind of invitation that says I know it's too far away and would be too expensive, but even though we're barely in touch, I wanted you to know I thought of you.

We sent wedding gifts though. I sent Harmony and Jan each the same wooden cutting board etched with a hanging disco ball and the bride and groom's names and the date of the wedding. Part of me was trying to be funny and another part thought it was a very cool present.

Jan sent me a SodaStream machine and an empty can of Tab. Harmony sent a framed cross-stitch of a few lines from Queen's "Don't Stop Us Now." I cried when I opened both of them.

Long story as short as possible, my first husband was one of the principles at the Boston advertising agency where I worked. He was handsome and too old for me and all about the chase. I was so thrilled when he set his sights on me that I got pulled right into his web.

As soon as I fell in love, he'd pull back. As soon as I walked away, he'd come after me. It circled around and around, endless loops of pain and pleasure. The drama was intoxicating and addicting, and somehow we stayed together long enough to get married.

He didn't want kids because he said it wasn't fair to the teenage kids he already had. Who hated me. We separated and got back together again and then they hated me more. Cliché that he was, one day a colleague told me in the break room that he was screwing around with one of the interns. When I confronted him, he left me for her.

Massachusetts follows equitable division rules in divorce, so only the assets we'd acquired during the marriage, which were pretty much nonexistent, were divided. The judge also factors in the length of the marriage and the age and employability of each spouse. In short, even though he cheated on me and left me, equitable division meant he kept both his Boston house and his Plymouth lake house getaway.

My second husband was a nice guy. We met at the job I took next, writing for an inhouse ad agency at a shoe company in South Boston. It was so boring and regimented that a bell would actually ring to announce the beginning and end of break time, even for the creative team. He was so different from my first husband that when he asked me to marry him, I said yes.

At night, we'd cook dinner together and then curl up on the sofa and watch movies on his brand new state-of-the-art VCR. He even wanted kids. And then after a year of trying, he wanted us both to get checked out or adopt or something, anything. Commercial sperm banks had been around for maybe a decade and donor eggs were just becoming publicly available.

A friend of his had recently adopted a beautiful baby from Korea. We weren't getting any younger but we still had options, he said. At the library, I found something called "Seven Core Issues in Adoption" which outlined the lifelong issues experienced by all members of the adoption triad: loss, rejection, guilt and shame, grief, identity, intimacy, and mastery/control.

I bailed. The shoe company wasn't big enough for both of us, and it seemed only fair that he should keep his job. And since he'd owned the house we were living in before we met, I knew he'd get it anyway. So I quit and moved out.

And that's when I bumped into Jan.

We were wearing terrycloth hoodies and sweatpants this morning. It wasn't like we texted each other before every clothing change to synchronize our outfits. It wasn't as if we were losing our separate identities and merging into one person.

It was just that after a while your clothing choices tended to sync up with those of the friends you hung out with the most. The way your periods used to back in your pre-menopausal days.

In the almost dark, Harmony and Jan held the stepladder on the pool side while I climbed over the fence and made my way down to them.

We turned, took a couple of steps.

All three of us kicked the covered-up hunk of the accessible pool lift.

"Ouch/damn/shit on a shingle," we said.

"We need to get rid of that thing," Harmony said. "It's a

hazard. Maybe we could sell it on eBay. Or Facebook Marketplace."

"Don't disrespect the pool lift," I said. "We might be needing it someday."

"Why?" Jan said. "If it comes to that, I'm counting on the two of you to do the heavy lifting."

"Okay," Harmony said. "What will it be? Poolside? Lounge chairs? Or just cut to the chase, strip down to our birthday suits and jump right in?"

"Come on," Jan said. "I've got a better idea."

Jan wove her way through the shadowy poolside tables, chairs pushed in, umbrellas closed, and over to a bench pushed up against the side wall of the restrooms and adjacent to the outdoor showers.

"*Psst*," Jan said. "Over here."

"*Psst?*" I said. "Really? Who actually says *psst?*"

Harmony, Chickpea and I started weaving our way over to Jan, the humans bumping into tables along the way.

"Chickpea doesn't happen to have her seeing eye certification, does she?" Harmony said.

"No," I said, "but I'm pretty good at pretending she's an official emotional support dog. So if we break a shin, she can probably stay with us in the hospital."

We finally made it over to Jan. She was sitting on a bench under a soft halo of light from the restroom door.

"Sit," Jan said.

Chickpea sat.

"I meant the other bitches," Jan said.

"Why?" I said.

Jan ignored me. Harmony and I sat down on the bench on either side of Jan.

"Guess what I found last night when I was looking for my popsicle sticks?" Jan said.

"Don't keep us in suspense too long, Honey," Harmony said. "I'm on tenterhooks."

"And this is what our lives have come to," I said. "Sitting in the dark by the Gulls and Buoys rooms, waiting to see what's more exciting than popsicle sticks."

Jan pulled a small metal tin out of her hoodie pocket, opened it.

"My stash," Jan said. "It hasn't been replenished since recreational marijuana was legalized and my sons stopped giving me joints on Mother's Day to be funny."

Harmony and I crossed our arms, considering. Chickpea tilted her head.

"I only smoke every decade or so, which pretty much makes me the poster child for moderation," Jan said. "But there's still at least one big fatty in here somewhere."

Jan started pulling out items. "And I've got some blue raspberry edibles. A gift from my friend Mel for driving her to chemo."

Jan held an edible up to the sky. "Rest in power, Mellie!"

Harmony held her hand over her heart. "Bless her sweet soul."

"I don't want to rain on your parade," I said, "but marijuana still isn't legal in this state."

Harmony pulled up something on her phone. "'Possession of one ounce or less of marijuana is a misdemeanor punishable by up to one year imprisonment and/or a fine up to one thousand dollars, or public works for up to twelve months.'"

"Okay then," Jan said. "I guess we'd better smoke up the evidence fast. I can stash the edibles in with my old menopause gummies. What a scam that was."

"Hold your horses," Harmony said. "If we're going to go for it, I think I'd be more comfortable in an enclosed space. With the doors locked. And the refrigerator. And we'll need one of those guides. Or a straight person. Or at least a list of restaurants that do DoorDash."

Jan shook her head. "We don't want to chance setting off the smoke alarms in our building. Fresh air will blow the incriminating smoke out to sea." She gestured to the restrooms. "Plus I've chosen the location carefully so we can flush and run if we need to."

Jan reached for a small retro cooler. "And I brought snacks." She flipped open the cooler and pulled out a long fireplace lighter.

"You're going to burn off what's left of your eyebrows with that thing," I said.

"It's all I could find. And don't you dare jinx me." Jan ran her index finger along one eyebrow and then the other. "Oh, to be well-embrowed again."

"That's why they invented those thick-framed statement glasses," I said. "So nobody can see your eyebrows. And don't stress about them—they're fine. Eyebrows should be sisters, not twins. Plus, think of all the time we save barely plucking."

"Thanks, Pollyanna," Jan said.

"Rosemary oil twice a day," Harmony said. "It tests as well as minoxidil for age-related hair loss and it smells great. I mix rosemary essential oil with a little bit of coconut oil or leave-in conditioner and use it on my eyebrows and on my scalp, especially those tricky little places around my temples where the hair is starting to recede."

"Thanks," I said. "And did you know rosemary oil repels mosquitoes, too? Talk about a win-win."

"Back to hair removal," Jan said. "Nobody told me my eyebrows were going to start migrating to my chin—I definitely didn't sign up for that. So here I am, brutalizing my poor face with everything from plucking to waxing to laser—"

"Remember electrolysis?" I said. "I mean, pure torture. Like letting yourself get electrocuted on purpose—"

"And then," Jan said, "somebody told me that you can just shave your face. It blew my mind. I mean, think about it. That's why men's skin looks so much better than ours does at this age. They've been shaving since puberty. It's like free exfo-

liating, and here we are getting all ripped off buying exfoli-
ating scrubs and mitts and acids."

"I'm all in on selective facial shaving," I said. "Just don't
try it on your eyebrows or you're going to end up with sisters
from another mister."

Jan gave the fireplace lighter a test flick.

"Wait," Harmony said. "I've got a couple of conditions.
Nobody drives a car. Nobody climbs a ladder. And nobody
gets in the pool. With or without clothes. For . . ."

Harmony checked her phone again. ". . . one to three
hours after inhaling. Possibly shorter given the age of the
stash, but if I had my druthers, we'd stick to three. Richie will
kill me if he has to drive all the way down here to bury me."

"Let's think this through," I said. "Isn't it kind of early for
getting high?"

"You know that old saying," Jan said. "It's 5 o'clock
somewhere."

"I'm pretty sure they mean PM, not AM," Harmony said.

"Or maybe," I said, "we wait for the weekend so people
are sleeping in?"

"We're doing it," Jan said. "Right here, right now. We
could be around for thirty more years or thirty more minutes.
We just don't know. So we can't put anything off. We've got to
seize the day. Grab the gusto."

Harmony nodded. "Make hay while the sun shines."

"Speaking of," I said. "How 'bout we wait for daylight?"

Jan sighed.

"Fine," I said. "Carpe the freaking diem."

Chapter 10

Jan licked her fingers and pinched out the last of our joint. She found her phone, pulled up a playlist.

"I had to download some of the good songs again," she said. "Most of my mix tapes had disintegrated."

Jan pushed play. We rocked out with Brewer and Shipley to "One Toke Over the Line."

When Willie Nelson started singing "Roll Me Up and Smoke Me When I Die," we really got into it. We danced our hearts out, twirled our cares away. Occasionally we *shh*-ed one another, trying to keep the noise level down to a dull roar.

We were free as birds, high as kites. I couldn't tell if it was real, or if it was as much of a fantasy as our water ballet had been. Even if it was the placebo effect and Jan's stash had lost its magic decades ago, it didn't matter. The longer I lived, the less I cared about drawing a hard line in the sand between fantasy and reality.

We sang along with Grace Slick to Jefferson Airplane's "White Rabbit."

"When the mushrooms on the chessboard get up and tell you where to go," Jan sang.

"When your doormouse is walking backwards," Harmony sang.

"Something-something about logic and proportion falling sloppy dead," I sang.

Pretty much the only parts we got right were *Call Alice* and *feed your head*. But Grace Slick and Alice in Wonderland would have been proud of us. Because we sang that song like we felt it, which is all that really matters in pre-dawn stash-fueled dance parties.

And in life.

Finally we slid down to the pool deck and leaned back against the restroom building. Chickpea shot us a judgy look from her perch on the bench.

We took turns reaching into a silicone food container for a perfectly cut square of watermelon, popping it into our mouth.

"It's like this entire universe of a juicy watermelon-flavored party in your mouth," I said.

We all dissolved into laughter.

"We've gotta write this stuff down," Jan said. "It's genius."

We ate some more watermelon cubes. Closed our eyes as we savored every square inch of them.

"What was I saying?" Harmony said.

"Nothing," I said.

We laughed even harder.

"Heavens to Betsy that's good pot," Harmony said. "It really held up to the ravages of time and tin storage."

"Wow," Jan said. "The ravages of tin and time storage. That's so, so beautiful."

"You can't call it pot anymore," I said. "The dinosaurs will come and take it away from you."

"Weed," Jan said. "It's weed now. The way to remember it is to think of this cute little garden and you're pulling up all the plants that aren't weeds and throwing them away."

"Heavy," I said.

We ate some more watermelon.

Harmony sighed. "No offense to the watermelon—"

"None taken," Jan said as she moved her watermelon cube like a puppet.

More uproarious laughter all around.

"Remember those good old munchie days?" Harmony said. "Chocolate syrup on a pile of chocolate chips with chocolate sprinkles on top?"

"Peanut M&Ms dipped in peanut butter," Jan said.

"Mystic mints," I said. "An entire row. No less and no more. Well, sometimes more."

Harmony pointed. "Do you think we can get that accessible pool lift over there to pick us up and drop us at our front doors? Or should we wait until we're stepladder-worthy? You know, like seaworthy but with steps."

"Like seaworthy but with steps," I said. "So good. And you're a poet and you don't even know it."

Jan threw a watermelon cube up in the air and actually caught it in her mouth. "How did we get so healthy?" she said once she stopped choking on it. "Whole food-plant based-water-water-exercise-water-exercise-water. We almost never even drink wine anymore."

"I guess," I said, "I have this crazy idea that if we play our cards right, we might hit triple digits."

"What's the prize?" Jan said.

"Chocolate syrup on a pile of chocolate chips with chocolate sprinkles on top?" Harmony said.

Jan stretched her arms over her head. "I don't think the goal is triple digits. I think it's more like enjoy the shit out of life, and the minute you can't anymore, you go to sleep that night and just don't wake up."

Harmony picked up her phone. "I wonder if there's an app for that."

We dissolved into laughter.

"When did it happen?" I said. "*How* did it happen? We're freakedy-weadedy, fuckedy-wuckedy, practically-wackedly OLD."

There was a long beat of silence

"Nobody's perfect," Harmony said.

We all cracked up.

It was getting lighter now.

"Uh-oh," I said. "It's getting lighter."

There was a movement over by the fence.

"Did you see something?" Harmony said.

"Where?" Jan said.

"There," Harmony said.

"What?" I said.

"A person," Harmony said.

"Who?" Jan said.

"No," I said, "who's on second. What's on first. My fourth husband used to do that routine all the time. I think it was some kind of sports ball thing. It got really old really fast."

Our jogger was standing at the pool gate. Shirtless. Glistening with sweat. I heard the faint notes of *Chariots of Fire*.

He waved.

"It's *him*," I whispered.

"His lips are moving," Jan said.

"I think he's talking to us," Harmony said.

"*Is* he talking to us?" I said.

"What would Nancy Drew do?" Jan said.

He flashed his key fob at the gate scanner and walked through.

"He's coming," Harmony said.

"*Is* he coming?" I said.

"Are *we* coming?" Jan said.

As we watched him weave his way through the tables and over to us, Jan fumbled with her stash tin, finally got it into her hoodie pocket.

We all blinked up at him.

"Good morning ma'ams," he said. "My name is Dash."

"Dash," I said. "Dash. It's so, so perfect."

"Down girl," Harmony whispered to me.

Chickpea jumped down from the bench, sashayed over to Dash.

Dash laughed, squatted to pat Chickpea while she wagged her tail like crazy. "Walter's my real name. But I was fast in middle school and Dash stuck."

"Good pivot," Jan said. "Much more brand appropriate."

Dash stood up again, reached into his shorts pocket.

He flicked his head in the direction of our stepladders. "Pool key not working?"

"Glenda/Jan/Harmony," we said, dodging the question.

"Nice to meet you, ladies. I'm down a ways in the next-to-last building. Door sign says A WAVE FROM IT ALL or some ridiculous thing. Anyhow, I was just thinking if you're having key fob issues, you can borrow one of mine. I've got two."

"Aren't you sweet," Harmony said. "Actually, ours work fine. We're just waiting for the HOA president to come around to our way of thinking about opening the pool at 5 AM for us."

"And allowing dogs in," I said. "At least well-behaved dogs. Although why should dogs have to be polite, obedient, cordial with everyone, soft-spoken, just because they're girls. I mean dogs."

I realized the weed was still talking. "I'll stop now. But not because I'm afraid of voicing my opinion."

"Wait." Jan checked her watchless wrist. "How did you get the pool lock to open before 8?"

"Oh," Dash said. "I work at FLETC. I think they've got a

deal where our key fobs are programmed to work 24/7. You know, just in case we want to hop in the pool at odd hours."

"Seriously?" the three of us said.

Chapter 11

Ten years after I'd last laid eyes on Jan and Harmony, I drove
through some open gates and walked into a great big factory-
like building in the middle of nowhere for a job interview. By
the time I walked out again for the last time, the company had
grown to the size of a small college campus. An entire office
park had built up around it and upscale suburbs had spread
like a giant glob to envelope the office park.

But right now it was seriously out in the sticks. Career-wise
it felt like a huge backslide to even consider working in a
nothing place like this, but I'd weighed this against the higher
priority of never crossing city paths with either of my exes
ever again. Plus, I'd been watching the classified job listings
and sending out resumes for a month now, and pitiful as it
might be, this company had actually called to set up an
interview.

Before I approached the reception desk, I ducked into the
restroom to pee. And to fluff my hair high and touch up my
magenta lips. And mostly to give myself a pep talk in the
mirror.

Just as I started to push the door of a stall open, Jan came out of the one next to it. She looked like a cross between Jan and a soccer mom.

We looked at each other. And then we screamed.

"Cut the shit," Jan said.

"Unfreaking believable," I said.

We gave each other a big hug.

"I swear I just smelled Hawaiian Tropic Dark Tanning oil," Jan said.

"I always wear it for job interviews," I said. "It brings me luck."

Jan looked me up and down. For what it was worth, I was wearing my go big or go home power suit. Gray pinstripe jacket with serious linebacker shoulder pads and matching trousers with a crisp white blouse plus a flounce of a black tie. And black pumps over sassy striped knee-high nylons. Even though I would have much preferred my red high-top Reebok Freestyles with slouchy pink socks.

"Too much?" I said.

"Never," she said. "Maybe they'll subconsciously think they have to pay you more money for your dry-cleaning bills."

And then Jan gave me the scoop for my interview.

"The place sucks," she said. "But I was losing my mind at home all day with three wild boys and they have great child-care that goes right through preschool and the discount gets bigger with each kid and it comes right out of your paycheck."

I was ready to turn and run, but I made myself nod politely.

Jan clapped her hands together. "Okay, don't use me as a reference because they'll think we'll socialize too much, which of course is true. Take whatever they offer you. I'm in Human Resources so we'll sort it out from there. Say you're a quick study and you want to build a long-term career with a fast-growing company. Tell them how impressed you are with the research you've done about them and that you're the kind of person that takes ownership of difficult challenges, works well with people, and wants to learn and grow. And you always brush your teeth and never have B.O."

"Got it," I said.

And I did.

The sun was shining as Harmony drove Ms. Daisy, her bright turquoise electric forward-facing, street-legal, 4-seater golf cart.

Jan was riding shotgun. Chickpea and I were buckled up in the backseat.

"Slide into flip-flops," we sang. "Head out to start chillaxin'. Realize we're still too full of passion. Time to bend and stretch and find the light again."

"Wow," Jan said. "We almost sounded good that time."

"Why do you think," I yelled from the backseat, "we never started a garage band back when we first met?"

Harmony made eye contact with me in the rearview mirror. "Because we didn't play any instruments and none of us could hold a tune?"

I leaned forward so they could hear me better. "But that never stopped the boys. They just found a guitar or a set of drums and taught themselves to play and sucked at it until they didn't. I mean, I guess I'm saying why didn't we even see that world as a possibility?"

"You mean," Jan said, "beyond being groupies or singing and playing the tambourine for some stupid guy band?"

"Heavens to hockey sticks," Harmony said. "Remember that Elvis impersonator one of us dated?"

"He was so not an Elvis impersonator," I said. "He graduated from Berkeley College of Music and was offered a perfectly respectable gig as a tribute artist. They even gave him his own tour bus."

"We didn't know how to be three-dimensional women in a

two-dimensional society," Jan said. "Nobody could even grasp the concept of an all-girl band back then. The only one out there was Fanny, who paved the way for the Go-Go's and the B-52's and everybody else. I mean, come on, a Filipina American lesbian garage band? Truly ahead of their time."

Jan found a YouTube video on her phone and the three of us did our best to sing "Charity Ball." We muddled our way through most of the lyrics, coming in hard for the lines about stand and move and deliver and you've got my number and giving it everything you've got. Chickpea chimed in on the woo parts.

"I loved that song," Harmony said, "but I had no idea Fanny played all their own instruments. I'm mean, The Monkees didn't even do that."

"I'm just saying," I said. "We could have been the female Rolling Stones."

"Sure," Jan said. "And then think how many more wrinkles we'd have."

Harmony put on the radio and we started singing at the top of our lungs and seat-dancing with Cyndi Lauper to "Girls Just Wanna Have Fun." It was one of Chickpea's favorite songs so she yelped her accompaniment.

Harmony leaned her head out and shook her fist at a vehicle driving way too close behind us. "Get off my butt, y'all," she yelled. "And that golf cart you're driving better not be a gas guzzler."

The driver of the other golf cart gave us a dirty look.

"Come on, Ms. Daisy," Harmony said. "Let's leave that poor excuse for a golf buggy in the dust."

Jan reached a hand out and casually circled her middle finger around in the air as we sped up.

Even with time out for minor golf cart altercations, we were at Sea Salt Healthy Kitchen in no time. It was our favorite place to stop for the occasional fake-baked gift.

Chickpea and I waited outside, Chickpea lapping at a

water bowl. A server came out and handed her a doggie treat.

Through the plate glass window, I watched Jan micro-managing the young girl behind the counter.

Jan pointed. "No," I was pretty sure she was saying. "Not that perfect cookie. The one to the right that's shaped more like an amoeba."

I didn't have to be much of a lip reader to know the young girl said, "Are you sure?"

Jan nodded. The girl shrugged and finished boxing up the cookies.

"One day you'll understand, Sweetie," I heard Harmony say as they walked out of Sea Salt.

The truth was that the three of us no longer cooked anymore, or at least we avoided it as much as possible. Instead we assembled.

Over the years we'd each slowly pivoted away from SAD, a fitting acronym for Standard American Diet. We'd learned to ditch those calorie-dense and nutrient-poor ultra-processed foods, full of added sugar and salt and bad fats. We swore off dieting forever.

We turned to real, whole, fiber-rich, unprocessed ingredients, heavy on leafy greens and beans and whole grains and berries and colorful cruciferous vegetables. We felt healthier, lighter, happier, sharper, less stressed. Most of it was eating well, and the rest was probably reaching the point in life where you've learned to shrug off most of the annoying stuff.

My diet was exclusively whole food plant based these days. Harmony ate the same way maybe eighty percent of the time. Jan did the best she could.

I believed you could divide the entire world into moderators and abstainers. Moderators can enjoy a decadent artery-clogging treat every once in a while, and then flip the switch and go back to eating healthy. Abstainers like me would immediately start backsliding. Before I knew it, I'd be rolling around in a McDonald's parking lot scarfing down supersized cartons of fries.

In all aspects of my life, I seemed to have two gears: all in or all out. I completely got it when Yoda said, "Do or do not, there is no try."

The good news was I felt so much better eating this way that it was easy to stick to it. For breakfast I loaded my Vitamix with handfuls of fresh or frozen spinach and kale and arugula and any other greens I had kicking around, plus lots of frozen berries. Then I'd sprinkle in some steel cut oats and broccoli sprouts. And beans or lentils or legumes. Sometimes I'd throw in some leftover sweet potato or a few dates or a chunk of a lemon.

After that I'd add amla, which is Indian gooseberry powder, plus turmeric, black pepper, cacao powder, ginger, cinnamon, cardamom, a dash of cloves. I'd add water and soy milk powder and anything else I felt like adding. I'd blend it until it was completely pulverized and smooth. If it didn't taste that great, I'd had a heaping spoonful of peanut butter, which always makes everything better.

Sometimes I'd drink the whole thing for breakfast and have a huge salad for lunch. Other times I'd save half for lunch and have a mid-morning snack of an apple and a handful of nuts or maybe hummus and orange pepper slices.

Harmony and Jan did their own thing for breakfast and lunch. But whether we ate together or separately, the three of us were big into buddha bowls for dinner. It was both fun and efficient to get together and batch assemble them for a week.

Buddha bowls are the perfect one-bowl or plate dish. They consist of colorful dollops of greens, grains, protein, veggies and fruits, artistically arranged and then stockpiled in the fridge. Before eating them, you just add anything else you want, then drizzle with sauce and sprinkle on toppings.

Chapter 12

Jan's place smelled great as we walked in. The downstairs of her townhouse had an open layout, bright and beachy and newish. And cookie cutter enough to be basically identical to Harmony's and mine.

A glass bowl filled with popsicle sticks was centered on the table in the middle of the dining area. Starfish-printed throw pillows decorated a white slipcovered sofa.

A faux-weathered sign over the sofa said LIFE IS BETTER AT THE BEACH. Photos of Jan's three sons, their families and her grandkids were everywhere.

Harmony and I placed the inner pots of our Instant Pots on potholders on the kitchen island. Harmony's was filled with a cooked mixture of steel cut oats and sorghum and purple barley and rye. Mine was filled with steamed black lentils, which look like caviar and have a subtle earthy taste. I'd also brought a couple of rinsed and drained cans of chickpeas.

Jan removed two cookie sheets of roasted vegetables from the oven—sweet potatoes and broccoli and tri-colored carrots and red onions and orange peppers and deep red beets—and placed them next to our contributions.

She placed one metal sheet on some potholders and the other on the wooden cutting board etched with the hanging disco ball I'd given her for her first wedding.

My eyes teared up. "I can't believe you still have that."

"I still have mine, too, Honey," Harmony said.

"You both better still have the SodaStreams I gave you," Jan said. "And those empty cans of Tab are probably collectors' items by now."

We covered the dining room table and every inch of available space with empty square glass batch-cooking containers. Then we lined up our spinach and kale and berries—sometimes we used fresh and sometimes frozen—as well all the toppings we could dig up, from goji berries and prunes and barberries and moon drop grapes to almonds and pumpkin seeds and ground flaxseed and wheat germ.

And then we got to work creating our buddha bowls. We plopped little piles of each ingredient in each glass container, starting at one end and working our way through. It was like a factory assembly line, but it was also creative, like painting with food. By the time we finished, we each had a week's worth of dinners that were as beautiful as they were crazy healthy.

After that we made a big batch of dressing to drizzle on top—lemon juice and minced garlic and miso and mushroom powder and nutritional yeast and almond flour and ground flaxseed and date sugar and water. We taste-tested it until we liked the proportions, and then we divided it three ways.

We each left one of our buddha bowls on the counter. Jan put the rest of her stuff in the fridge while Harmony and I ran home and did the same with ours.

When we came back, Jan was standing at the kitchen counter eating a Devil Dog.

"*What?*" she said. "Life is all about balance."

I shook my head. "Don't expect Harmony and me to

come visit you when you're in the hospital getting your arteries roto-rooted."

Harmony grabbed a Devil Dog out of the cardboard box, held the cellophane to her nose.

"Don't worry," she said. "I just want to smell it for old time's sake."

We were sitting side by side on Jan's sofa. We'd sliced up an apple and an avocado, worked them into our early-bird dinner buddha bowls, drizzled on the dressing, sprinkled on our toppings.

"Delish," I said. "Way beyond just basic, every day, run-of-the-mill good."

"*Shh*," Harmony and Jan both said. Because we were also streaming *The Golden Bachelor*.

"Oh, my eyes, my eyes," I said. "I'm not sure how much of this I can watch."

"It's actually pretty deep for this franchise," Jan said around a mouthful. "I mean, you have to admit it's not lowest common denominator reality programing. It's by far the least cringe-worthy of the Bachelor shows."

"There's a high bar." I took a big bite of sweet potato, let it melt in my mouth.

The golden bachelor was a 72-year-old widower, and 22 potential rest-of-his life female partners between the ages of 60 and 75 were vying for his attention. The only upside I could see was that most of the women seemed to be wearing the bridesmaid dresses they never thought they'd get a chance to wear again.

"Personally," Harmony said, "I'm tickled pink at seeing women our age getting a second chance at love. And I think it's great that they're not afraid of stepping out of their comfort zones and onto the TV screen to go for it. Look at them: they're smart and vulnerable and real."

We watched for a while in silence, munching away on our buddha bowls.

"Why are they making some of the women sleep in bunk beds in a mansion?" I said.

Nobody had an answer. I speared a hunk of red onion, followed it up with a scoop of chickpeas and whatever.

In a bad birthday suit joke, we watched a woman open her trench coat and flash the golden bachelor. Then we watched the golden bachelor take a bite of her birthday cupcake and ask her to lick the frosting off his mouth.

"Yikes," I said. "And I thought I've had some tragic birthdays."

"I'm kind of fascinated by all the nips and tucks," Jan said. "Holy fake hair, fake faces and fake boobs. I mean, I respect their rights to do whatever they want to their own bodies, but it's not exactly understated. And that chicken dance. Not a good look."

"I think they're beautiful," Harmony said. "Inside and out."

"But," Jan said, "there are only a few of them we'd actually want to hang out with."

"It's the desperation," I said. "I hate seeing women our age subjected to the whole meat market thing. And I don't like the odds. It feels like too much of a one-time chance. If the sultan of swing doesn't pick me as his concubine, I'm totally screwed. Or I guess not screwed. I mean, who needs that?"

"But look how much fun they're having with the other women," Harmony said. "It's refreshing to see women our age encouraging other women."

"Sure," I said as I stabbed a blood-red beet. "Until they don't get a rose and the knives come out."

"And who wouldn't want to get all dressed up?" Harmony

said. "And stay in a luxurious mansion and have a photo shoot with professional hair and makeup and good lighting?"

"We're not doing it," I said. "No matter how hard the producers beg, we are not doing Season 2 of *The Golden Bachelor*."

Our buddha bowls and *The Golden Bachelor episode* finished, the three of us stood in Jan's kitchen area eating hunks of dark chocolate for dessert and staring into the open bakery box we'd moved to Jan's kitchen island.

"Isn't fake-baking just the best thing since sliced bread?" Harmony said.

"Sensuous even," I said. "The smells, the textures, the tastes."

"So relaxing," Jan said. "Even though I still think a box of Devil Dogs would have worked just as well."

We all leaned in and sniffed the bakery box.

Jan started opening cupboards and placing an assortment of items next to the box. A muffin tin. A mailing tube. A Tupperware container. A little beach pail with an attached shovel. An assortment of mason jars.

"I say let's go with the mason jar," Harmony said. "I've seen that on Pinterest."

"Just one?" Jan said. "If we stretch the cookies, we might be able to fill three jars. You know, one from each of us?"

"I think that's overkill," I said. "We don't want him to think we've got nothing better to do than stand around all day fake-baking."

"Plus," Harmony said, "we don't want to be responsible for the demise of his abs. That six-pack of his is a thing of beauty."

Jan shoved everything but a single mason jar out of the

way, unscrewed the top, put the lid and ring down beside the jar.

We took turns picking up cookies, pinching and poking them, then stacking them on top of each other in the jar.

Harmony mangled a cookie a bit too enthusiastically.

"Wait," I said. "Don't mess it up that much. We want them to look homemade, not like we went dumpster diving."

Chapter 13

The sun was just beginning to set as the three of us walked along the tree-lined road past the townhouse buildings, groupings of five and seven and ten townhouses clustered together.

"In Italy," I said, "they call a leisurely walk at this time of day a passeggiata. It's from the verb passeggiare, which means to walk. It's supposed to be a short walk taken purely for pleasure and the joy of socializing with your neighbors."

"Happy passeggiata, y'all," Harmony yelled as we waved at a car rolling by.

She turned to me. "Like that?"

"Exactly," I said. "You even sounded Italian."

We passed postage-stamp front yards decked out with tiny walkways and short driveways and overflowing planters.

Every third driveway or so had a massive pickup truck backed into it, facing out toward the road.

I was walking Chickpea on a silver leash made from recycled plastic bottles and dotted with a few upcycled gems from old costume jewelry. If I could have ordered a matching bracelet for me, I would have been wearing it.

Harmony held the mason jar. We'd placed a little square of pinking-shear-cut gingham fabric between the lid and the ring, wrapped a loop of jute twine around the jar and tied it in a bow. A cute little handmade tag we'd all signed was attached to the twine.

"Every time I think about it," Harmony said, "I'm still so mad I could chew up nails and spit out a barbed-wire fence. I can't believe Butt lied about not being able to let us into the pool early. He can reprogram it for some people and not for us?"

"I mean, he only came right out and asked us to try to bribe him," I said. "That cheat. That lying, self-absorbed, lecherous cheat."

"The more hours the pool is open," Jan said in her best Butt imitation, "the more it costs me to keep it clean. Don't worry your pretty little heads about the arithmetic."

"I say we show up at his place with those pinking shears and cut his family jewels into fractions," Harmony said.

"Listen," I said. "We've got Dash's key fob, so we don't even have to lug the ladders now. And Chickpea doesn't mind having to sneak in. Maybe we should just quit while we're ahead."

Jan turned her head in my direction. "Do you think Butt is taking dirty money from FLETC and pocketing it?"

I shrugged. "I'm kind of thinking keyless pool entry bribery might be beneath FLETC's pay grade."

"Agreed," Harmony said. "Butt probably just found a way to tack an extra charge on to their HOA fee. But it's not like FLETC's going to hand him a personal check made out to Beaufort K. Butts, so how does he get his hands on the moolah?"

A couple rode toward us on beach cruiser bikes. We said hi all around.

Three hot shirtless men in shorts with FLETC insignias jogged by.

"Good evening, ma'ams," they said as they passed us.

We good evening-ed them back, turned to catch the rear view.

"I love this place," I said.

We started walking again, passed another big truck backed into a driveway.

A few townhouses later, a door opened and two women stepped out on the front porch. Butt stepped out behind them and gave them both a way-too-lengthy hug.

"Yuck," Harmony said.

"Gross," I said.

Jan pointed two fingers at her eyes and then at Butt. "We're watching you, Buttman."

We stood on Dash's front porch, looking at his door sign.

"A WAVE FROM IT ALL," Jan read. "Dash deserves better than that."

"HUNK LIVES HERE?" I said.

"Let's not objectify the poor thing," Harmony said. "How 'bout THE STUD MUFFIN IS IN."

Jan rang the doorbell.

Dash opened his door in jeans and a tight T-shirt.

Harmony held up the mason jar.

"We baked them ourselves," I said. "To thank you for your chest. Key fob. That's on the chest of drawers in my entryway as we speak."

"Takes some time," Harmony said as she handed Dash the cookies, "but always worth it for homemade."

"The mason jar was mine," Jan said. "And the pinking shears."

"Why thank you, ma'ams," Dash said.

"No need to ma'am us," I said.

Dash smiled. "My mother would disagree. She brought me up that ma'am's a non-negotiable sign of respect."

"It's a sign of courtesy and deference where I come from, too," Harmony said. "But one minute you're this hot young miss ma'aming other people. And then you get a few miles on you. And wham, bam, you're a ma'am."

"Yeah," Jan said. "It always feels kind of benevolently ageist to me. Like let me jab you with a quick reminder that you're no spring chicken."

"Fine," Dash said. "I'll drop the ma'ams. But you're going to have to write a note to my mom for me."

Dash's townhouse was almost identical to ours. A lack of family photos and personal items make it look like the rental it was. Beiges and whites with nautical accents, pops of turquoise and coral. A weathered sign that said SEA THE BEAUTY.

One half of a kayak cut in half vertically hung over the white slipcovered sofa.

Harmony, Jan and I sat side-by-side on the sofa. Dash sat in a chair across from us. We all munched away on cookies.

I closed my eyes. "So good."

Jan gave me a look. "If we do say so ourselves."

"Enough about us," Harmony said. "Tell us how you ended up here, Dash."

Dash swallowed a bite of cookie. "Not much to tell. Ten years as a US Marshal. It took over my life and I let it blow up my marriage. I needed a reset. FLETC hired me as a training instructor, set me up in this place."

"Good for you for knowing it was time for a change," Harmony said.

"The thing that got to me the most," Dash said softly, "was when we'd have to track down some fugitive and take him out, and some of the other guys would cheer when he went down.

Like it was a goddamn video game. I never did that. Not once."

Dash shook his head. "I guess I figure it'll be time well spent if I can help a couple of my knucklehead students get it through their thick skulls that these guys might be scumbags, but they're human, you know? They have *mothers*."

"We didn't really bake your cookies," I said. "We bought them. We're sorry."

Dash burst out laughing.

Jan shook her head.

Harmony turned and looked up at the kayak to make sure it wasn't about to fall on our heads.

"You're fine," Dash said. "First thing I checked when I moved in. It's attached to a stud."

"I used to be attached to a stud," I said. "Sorry, that just came out."

Harmony ignored me, smiled at Dash. "FLETC's lucky to have you, Sweetie. What's it like there?"

"The Federal Law Enforcement Training Center is massive," Dash said. "More than ninety federal law enforcement agencies train there with a goal of consistency of training quality and interagency cooperation. CIA, FBI, CDC, DIA, DOCOS, FAA, TSA, ICE, USAI, USMS, USSS, VAOIG, NPS, NIH . . ."

"All the acronyms," I said.

"All the acronyms," Dash said. "Sixteen hundred acres. Twelve hundred permanent employees. Five thousand students at once."

"So it's like a big college campus?" Jan said.

"More like its own world," Dash said. "There's Danis City, kind of a mock urban area. Residential homes, apartment building, pawnshop, coffee shop, shopping center, police station, courtroom, meth house, biker bar with a stripper pole."

"Huh," Jan said. "I haven't even contemplated pole dancing yet."

I was totally mesmerized. "What else?"

"Let's see," Dash said. "There's an amphitheater inspired by the Twin Towers with two small towers on the roof and a memorial display of the stuffed pink bunny that belonged to the youngest victim of 9/11."

The three of us put our hands over our hearts.

"Rest in peace, baby girl," Harmony said.

There was a long beat of silence.

"What else," Dash said. "A full mock airport terminal for air marshal and TSA agent training. Counter-terrorism building. Forensics is pretty interesting. Staged scenes with dummy cadavers, the whole nine yards."

Jan made her fingers explode from her head in that mind-blown gesture. "I wonder if there's a senior center tour we can take."

"Or maybe," Harmony said, "you can get us in for a quick peek on your day off, Dash?"

"We'll fake-bake you more cookies," I sing-songed.

"If you want the whole experience," Dash said, "you can always apply for jobs as role players. FLETC uses them in training exercises for everything from innocent bystanders and passengers to shopkeepers and criminals. Money's good and the exercises usually only run a few hours."

"But we worked our whole lives to stop working," I said.

"Plus," Harmony said, "it sure sounds like breaking more than a nail could happen in one of those exercises."

"Come on," Jan said. "This might be the closest we ever get to being full-fledged supersheroes."

Dash stood up, walked his phone over to us. "Type in your numbers and I'll text you the link to apply online. If you decide to go for it, before you press submit, print out your applications and I'll also hand-deliver a hard copy and put in a good word for you."

He waited while we typed in our numbers. Jan handed him back his phone.

"You'll have to pass a full federal background check," Dash said.

"No problem," Jan said.

Dash looked us right in the eyes, one after the other. "And, you'll have to pass a pre-employment drug screening."

He raised his eyebrows. "Just saying."

Chapter 14

Jan, Harmony and I finished rolling our trash barrels out to the end of our driveways for trash day pickup.

We crossed over to the pool, stood in front of the pool gate in our bathrobes, sipping our coffee and breathing in the salty pre-dawn air. You could almost imagine a cool breeze was blowing if you hadn't been up north to feel a real cool breeze for a while.

Chickpea yawned and stretched out across my feet as if they were pillows.

"Of course he could smell the pot," Jan said, jumping right back in to where our last conversation had left off as if no time had elapsed. "I mean weed. Weed, weed, weed."

"The way to remember is to think of this cute little garden and you're pulling up all the plants that aren't weeds and throwing them away," Harmony said in a spot-on Jan imitation.

"That wasn't me," Jan said. "That was the grass talking. Weed."

"But the smell could have been coming from anywhere," I said. "I mean, it's not like we were *acting* high."

Harmony patted my shoulder. "You keep telling yourself that, Mary Jane."

I wiggled my feet out from under Chickpea and swiped Dash's key fob in front of the scanner. It flashed green. I pushed the gate open and we all walked through.

"It's no fun this way," Jan said. "The stepladders were part of the risk, the excitement, the adrenaline rush."

"Cool your jets, Super Ma'am," Harmony said. "And thank your lucky stars that Dash got us full access to the pool without having to go within ten feet of Butt to get it."

We took a few careful steps in the almost dark, still managed to kick the covered-up hunk of the accessible pool lift.

"Ouch/damn/shit on a shingle," we said.

"That's it," Jan said. "We need to get this thing out of here before one of us loses a toe. Maybe we can roll it over to Butt's driveway. If anybody needs his stupid new accessible pool lift, we can tell them he delivers."

Jan leaned over, grabbed a corner of the brand-new-looking tarp-like cover, whipped it off.

"Wait, *what?*" I said.

"If that's a new pool lift," Harmony said, "Beaufort K. Butthead needs to work on his shopping skills."

We swiped our phone flashlights on to get a better look. The pool lift seat had a big crack right down the middle. The stand was spotted with rust.

A big blue trash truck rolled down the townhouse road, its arm reaching out and scooping up each barrel, dumping the contents into the back of the truck.

Under the glow of the streetlights, we watched the truck stop in front of the recycle area. The driver got out, opened the fence gate, climbed back in the truck.

The trash truck arm grabbed the recycle barrels one after another, dumped their contents on top of the rest of the trash.

"Shut the fence door," I said.

"What?" Jan said.

"The trash guy?" Harmony said. "I don't see it, but maybe he cleans up nice."

I closed my eyes, shook my head.

"The recyclables," I said. "They're not really being recycled."

Chickpea tucked under one arm, I shoved the pool gate open, marched straight to the recycle area, opened the fence. Lifted the hinged covers of the recycle barrels one at a time. Sure enough, they were all empty.

I slammed the fence closed. I turned, saw a 40-ish woman dressed in business attire rolling her empty trash barrel past her car and back toward her open garage.

As the woman rolled her trash barrel into the garage, I marched across the street to her.

"They're not really recycling!" I yelled. "The HOA is charging us for it, but they're just dumping the recyclables on top of the trash. We can't let them get away with it!"

The woman turned to face me.

"It's all right," she said slowly. "You're just a little bit mixed up. Is there someone I can call for you? Do you want me to check your phone address book?"

"What the actual fuck are you talking about?" I said.

Harmony and Jan walked up the driveway. The woman gave them a sad smile, walked past me, got into her car. She pointed the remote at her garage. The garage door creaked closed as she backed out of the driveway.

"You okay?" Jan said.

"Other than shamed, degraded and humiliated?" I said. "She wasn't even that much younger than we are. Well, maybe twenty or thirty years, but whatever happened to 40-to-forever camaraderie? You know, all for one and one for all, everybody sticking together?"

"I was chatting with this woman I knew at a party once," Harmony said. "I don't remember how it came up, but I said something about us being the same age. And she said, 'No we're not, I'm two years younger.' I mean, we're both lookin' at the half-century mark in our rearview mirrors, and we're going to quibble about her being a freshman in high school when I was a junior?"

"It's like this stupid who's the youngest, who *looks* the youngest contest," Jan said. "*Oh, you haven't changed a bit* crappola. Maybe it's a way of feeling superior, or of distancing themselves from the inevitable."

Jan paused. "Although to be fair, you did sound fairly demented. Next time you try to rally the troops, you might want to bring it down a few decibels."

"Thanks," I said. "I needed that."

"What are friends for?" Jan said.

We sat at one of the round pool tables, trying to make eye contact around the strapped-down umbrella.

Jan stood, pushed the umbrella open, sat back down.

"By all that I stand for and if it's the last thing I ever do," I said, "Beaufort K. Buttbrain is going down for this. I'm spitting mad. No, I'm madder than that."

I looked at Harmony. "Help me out."

"So mad you want to knock Butt's teeth so far down his throat he'll spit 'em out in single file?" Harmony said.

"Thank you," I said. "I mean, fake baking is one thing, but fake recycling? Who does that? And now we've got to figure out how to recycle everything here along with all the beach trash."

"We?" Jan said.

"Okay," I said. "Let's recap. We know that the HOA is charging us for recycling but not actually doing it. We also know that Butt refused to reprogram our key fobs, but does it for FLETC. We surmise that money is involved and that Butt pockets it."

"In his butt pocket!" Harmony said.

"Stay focused," I said.

"Okay," Harmony said. "So we know that Butt didn't really buy a new accessible pool lift. Instead he just covered the old broken one with a new cover. And we surmise that money was withdrawn from the HOA fund to pay for the non-existent new lift and that Butt pocketed it."

"In his butt pocket!" Jan said.

Harmony and Jan fist bumped.

"Grow up, you two," I said.

"Never," Jan and Harmony said at the same time.

"Owe me a Coke," they both said as fast as they could.

"So the question becomes," Jan said, "what do we do about it? We could A, do nothing. We could B, confront him."

"Which will only make him A, lie," I said.

"Or B, hit on us," Harmony said.

"Or C," I said, "both A and B."

"Let's take a step back," Jan said. "What exactly would we like to accomplish here?"

"I'd like to show Buttwit he can't mess with us," I said. "Or our recyclables. If we let a jerk like that get away with it, it's going to ruin this whole place for us."

"I agree," Jan said. "The stakes are a lot higher than they look. If we don't turn the tables, it's like we're handing over our superpowers before we've had a chance to fully develop them."

"But the good news is," Harmony said, "I think we've got our first actual case."

"And we know who the criminal is," Jan said. "Nancy would be so proud of us."

"I'd like to protect the other townhouse owners, too," Harmony said. "He's messing with their pool hours and money, too."

"While we're at it," I said, "I'd like to make some other positive, eco-friendly changes around this place. The Butts of the world are all thinking about themselves, not the environment."

"And I'd like to be supersheroes," Jan said. "So basically, we're all on the same page."

Harmony squinted. "How do you figure?"

Jan ignored her. "So, after much deliberation, the obvious solution is to get ourselves hired as FLETC role players."

"I suppose it would be a good story to tell one day," Harmony said. "Assuming we lived through it."

"I guess," I said, "it does sound a little bit like being an extra on a Hollywood movie set. And maybe once we get a foot in the door, we could work our way up to advising federal agencies on policy. But how will being FLETC role players help us kick Butt's butt?"

"While we're on the job," Jan said, "we pick up some hard supershero skills. We give ourselves time to formulate a brilliant plan to get Butt to play by the rules, to start recycling for real, to pay back everything he's stolen, to order a new accessible pool lift, to reprogram our key fobs."

Harmony and I gave each other doubtful looks. Chickpea tilted her head.

"And then," Jan said, "once we've put all the intricate puzzle pieces together, we leap."

"Leap?" I said. "We're not talking supershero capes here, are we?"

"Not necessarily," Jan said. "We can work out the details as we get closer. Okay, you'll both sail through that federal background check, correct?"

"Not even a speeding ticket," Harmony said. "I'm pretty good at talking my little ol' way out of things."

"I've got this one shoplifting charge from second grade," Jan said. "You don't happen to know the statute of limitations on penny candy theft, do you?"

"Do political protests count?" I said.

"Of course they do," Harmony said. "Every voice matters."

"And don't worry," Jan said. "I won't even look at my stash tin until after we pass the pre-employment drug screening."

Harmony scrolled on her phone. "It says THC only stays in the blood for twelve hours and in the saliva for twenty-four hours. However, THC can show up in the urine for up to thirty days, depending on frequency of use."

"Does it say anything about once a decade?" I said.

"We've got this," Jan said. "We'll hope for blood or saliva. And if they ask us to pee in a cup, we'll say we reject the concept of peeing on demand and they'll simply have to wait until we're feeling it."

Chapter 15

Back when Jan and I started working together again, I pictured us eating leisurely lunches in the company cafeteria together every day, going out for drinks and long decadent dinners after work.

Human Resources, where Jan worked, was even right around the corner from Marketing, where I worked. Marketing was kind of an umbrella for Advertising and Merchandising and Public Relations and Sales and Development.

The big boss was a jerky old guy, but the man I reported to directly was okay, and he was thrilled I didn't have kids or a husband, because none of the women who did have them wanted to travel to trade shows. Or possibly they did want to go, but their husbands didn't want to have to pick up the slack in the parenting department.

So I traveled to trade shows, set up booths, piled them high with samples and thick merchandise catalogs. Sometimes in exciting places like New York and Chicago, sometimes not. Even back then, there was a trade show for everything. Hotels and restaurants, consumer technology, concrete, contractors, health services, dentists, toys, footwear, fitness, food, beauty, education, weddings, chickens, candy, coal.

The company had started as a screen-printed T-shirt business. They added monogramming and moved into personalized uniforms and accessories. They started making branded hotel items like robes and slippers, toiletries and welcome bags, as well as political bumper stickers and campaign buttons. Then they added personalized disposable water bottles and hotel keycards, which were cutting edge at the time.

Eventually we could print your logo on everything from beer and soda cozies to Rubik's-Cube knockoffs to slap bracelets to scrunchies to sweat wristbands to metal lunchboxes to Silly-ish Putty. When I started working there, we were just beginning to print logos on gel pens and water bottles with straws and light-up yo-yos and pinhole lens glasses and fanny packs.

Years later a recurring nightmare would sometimes wake me up in the middle of the night. I was sailing on the ocean in a storm and one of our personalized items after another would come crashing over the deck on a wave.

But at the time, I never once thought about the impact of what we were doing. I just kept trying to come up with the next imprintable thing I could suggest.

When I wasn't traveling, I wrote advertising copy and press releases and rewrote template letters for the sales team and even weighed in on products and logo design and slogans for clients. The company was growing so fast it was all hands on deck. I said yes to everything and soaked up as much knowledge as I could. I had no idea where I was heading, so who knew what I might need down the road to survive.

Jan was just as busy. Human Resources was absolutely slammed trying to find enough decent hires to keep the company boat afloat.

Lunch with Jan was out because she ate in childcare with

her three boys. Lunchables, those pre-packaged trays with lunch meats, cheese and crackers arranged in individual compartments like kiddie charcuterie boards, were all the rage. Jan's kids were obsessed with them. She offered to bring an extra one so I could eat with them, too. I passed.

Drinks and dinner were out, too, since Jan headed straight home right after work to cook dinner and do family stuff. So instead we hung out in the restroom as often as we could sneak away, catching each other up on company gossip and making plans for the adventures we were going to have together once things slowed down.

"London," Jan would say. "We're going to stop by the palace first and scoop up Diana and get her to show us around. She looks like she needs to get out as much as we do."

"Miami," I'd say. "We're going to rent a convertible and drive all twelve miles of South Beach. And then we'll walk the Art Deco district and then we're going to conga till dawn at the clubs on Ocean Drive. And I'm going to accidentally on purpose bump right into a guy wearing a linen suit that never wrinkles who looks like he just stepped off the set of *Miami Vice*."

Instead, when we thought we could get away with it, we'd casually sneak out in the afternoon, taking separate cars so we wouldn't get caught, and meet up at Marshalls. We'd figured out a shortcut, so it was practically right down the street.

Marshalls was our happy place. Even though it was a discount retailer that sold clothing and seasonal and out-of-season items below retail prices, it felt glamorous to us. It straddled the perfect line between high-end fashion and maybe we could actually afford this, especially if it had a bright red clearance tag on it.

So we'd each grab a shopping cart and start at one end and cover every square inch of real estate. We'd dash into side-by-side cubicles to try things on, do a fast fashion show in the middle of the dressing room aisle to get a thumbs up or down from each other.

Our plan was that if someone from work showed up, I'd say I was doing research for promotional product ideas. Jan would say she was trying to scoop Marshalls employees to work for us. It never once occurred to us that if one of our coworkers showed up at Marshalls on a weekday afternoon, they'd be skipping out on work, too.

Jan would fill her cart with marked-down holiday decorations for next year, as well as gifts to hide away for her sons and her husband for birthdays and Christmas. I'd fill mine with stuff for my barely decorated new apartment. Plus clothes, clothes and more clothes.

Once I found myself putting a pastel pink men's polo shirt in my cart because it was marked down. And because I thought my next boyfriend would look great with a popped collar. And he wouldn't be afraid to wear a pink shirt with his khakis and boat shoes.

Jan pulled her cart up next to mine and raised her eyebrows. "Someone you want to tell me about?"

I grabbed the shirt, held it out to her. "I thought you might want it for your hubby. Great price."

"He's not a pink guy," Jan said. "Let's see if we can find him one in mint green."

When we'd finished making the rounds of the whole store, we'd reverse direction and put almost everything back where we'd found it. We mostly wanted the mood lift, the dopamine hit of recreational shopping. We wanted the tactile and visual distraction, the bright lights, the smell of something new, the thrill of the hunt.

Somehow it felt like we were adding not just items but possibilities to our carts. As if maybe if we ever actually went anywhere exciting, we could wear this. Or that. We might have also liked that we could control what we put in our carts and what we took out, at a time in our lives when, for very different reasons, it didn't feel like there were all that many things either of us could control.

Sometimes we'd realize we'd spent way too long at Marshalls. And we'd panic and leave our full carts in the aisle. As we sprinted to our cars, I'd say something like, "I feel so guilty we just did that."

"Don't be ridiculous," Jan would say. "The stock clerks are probably grateful they don't have to keep standing around trying to look busy. We probably even saved their jobs."

Harmony's townhouse was practically identical to Jan's and Dash's and mine.

A vase full of flowers sat on the middle of her dining room table. I peeked at the card: *Love, Richie.*

A bright orange ukulele rested against sunny yellow throw pillows on the white slipcovered sofa. A weathered sign over the sofa said HAPPILY EVER AFTER AT THE BEACH.

The three of us were sitting on stools at Harmony's kitchen island, laptops open in front of us.

"Wowzer," Jan said. "It says a normal training day uses an average of one hundred and eighty role players to support thirty exercises and multiple scenarios at FLETC."

"'Must be physically and mentally capable,'" Harmony read, "'of portraying an assigned role, staying in character, applying independent judgement within a scripted scenario, and/or ad-libbing if directed. Must utilize creativity to make the situation real in a training environment.'"

"This is so us," I said.

"'Must dress in costume appropriate to the role,'" Jan read. "I can feel the supershero energy already."

"'Must practice acceptable personal hygiene,'" I read, "'present a neat appearance and wear appropriate clothing.' Piece of fake-baked cake."

"Honey," Harmony said. "I've been meaning to mention this. That nontoxic deodorant you're using doesn't always do the trick."

"Fine," I said. "I'll switch back to the charcoal magnesium musk one, even though the patchouli in it gives me flashbacks to a former boyfriend I'd prefer to forget."

"We're going to knock this out of the park," Jan said. "Come on, let's get these federal clearance forms and job applications filled out."

We hunched over our laptops, half-full glasses of unsweet iced tea beside us. In front of us was a picked-over plate of broccoli florets, baby carrots, celery sticks, grape tomatoes and cucumber slices surrounding a little bowl of hummus.

Next to that were three squares of stoneground 94% cacao Taza Wicked Dark chocolate, which tasted amazing if you hadn't had a KitKat bar in a few months. Or maybe a year. Your palate really did change when you stopped eating sugar and salt and crappy ingredients long enough to let it.

"What should I put for marital status?" Harmony said. "Not technically separated but currently not living in the same house seems like it's none of their damn business."

"How much space do you get?" I said.

"He's not living with me," Harmony said. "How much more space *can* you get?"

"Just check n/a for not applicable," Jan said.

We all leaned over our laptops, typed some more.

"Do you think all your references have to still be alive?" I said.

"Just put it down," Jan said. "By the time they find the obituary, you'll be so valuable they won't want to lose you."

"Holy baloney," Harmony said. "I forgot what an aggravating pain in the neck the working world is."

"Think skills," Jan said. "Hard skills. Supershero skills."

"It's all about the Butt," I said. "We're taking him down."

Harmony, Jan and I walked purposefully down the road. Jan carried our printed-out FLETC role player applications. Harmony carried another mason jar, this one filled with fake-baked brownies. I walked Chickpea on another eco-friendly leash, a little nautical number made from recycled sails.

Every third driveway or so had the usual massive pickup truck backed into it, facing out toward the road.

A bright red sporty-ish car drove up beside us and stopped. It was the kind of car you drive when you don't have the money to buy a flashier sports car, but you're still a narcissistic jerk.

The tinted passenger window rolled down. Harmony hid the mason jar behind her back.

"Well, if it isn't the Bobbsey Twins," Butt said.

"Huh," I said to Jan and Harmony. "Apparently one of us really is invisible."

"FYI," Harmony said to Butt, "there are three of us, so you're going to have to find a better literary reference."

"Flicka, Ricka and Dicka could work," I said.

"I'm fine with Flicka or Ricka," Jan said to Harmony and me, "but somebody else is going to have to be Dicka."

Harmony squinted at Butt. "We already know," she said under her breath, "who the real Dicka is in this scenario."

Butt tore his eyes away from Harmony's breasts long enough to look at the papers in Jan's hand. "What's that you got there, girlies? Love letters for little ol' me?"

We ignored him, started walking again.

Butt rolled his car along with us, leering out the window. "Stop over any time if you want to discuss me getting that pool open early for you."

We kept walking. Butt kept rolling.

"A little AFTERDUNE DELIGHT, ladies?" Butt said. "I had that sign changed up myself. Get it?"

"Get this, darlin'," Harmony said under her breath.

Harmony started to flash her middle finger. I grabbed her hand.

"Stay cool," I whispered. "Just keep walking."

"We don't want to tip him off," Jan whispered, "until our superpowers are fully activated."

"That poor excuse for a Butt," Harmony whispered, "thinks the sun comes up just to hear him crow."

By the time we got to Dash's townhouse, Butt had either pulled into his own driveway or found someone else to harass.

Harmony rang Dash's doorbell.

Dash answered, smiled, squatted down to pet Chickpea.

Jan handed him our role player applications. Harmony gave him the mason jar.

Dash opened the door wider, inviting us in.

We shook our heads no, said our thank-yous.

He gave us a thumbs up and closed the door.

"So that's that," I said.

"Don't think about it," Harmony said. "It'll happen or it won't."

"Oh, it'll happen all right," Jan said. "When you're in touch with your inner supershero, the magic always happens."

Chapter 16

Once Jan and I were working at the same place again, it didn't take us long to track down Harmony. She'd been back in the area for a few years, practically right under our noses. She was married with two young kids, a girl and a boy.

We rendezvoused for a quick cup of coffee on a Saturday morning at my sad little apartment in Marshbury. That way Jan and Harmony wouldn't have to try to talk and wrangle kids at the same time.

"Reunited and it feels so good," Jan sang as she opened my door without bothering to knock.

Harmony and I jumped right in. We all roared the line about how me minus you is such a lonely ride.

"Who was that anyway?" Harmony said when we ran out of lyrics a few syllables later.

"Peaches and Herb," Jan said.

My eyes welled up. It really had been a lonely ride without them. I blinked the tears away so things didn't get sappy.

Jan gave my little living room a onceover. "I don't know whether to feel sorry for you or Kermit the Frog green with envy that you have basically nothing in this whole place."

"You should have seen it before I found the hot pink bean bag chairs," I said.

Jan and I tried hard to get Harmony to come work with us. Jan pitched the childcare situation, said she could move her resume to the top of the pile, pull her in to pretty much any department she wanted.

I shook off an image of the two of them and their bevy of kids eating lunch together in childcare while I sat alone at my desk working my way through lunch.

"Come on," I said. "Do it. It'll be just like old times."

But we couldn't talk her into it. Harmony and her husband had worked it out. He went to a day job with great benefits while Harmony did day-at-home-mom duty with the kids. She'd have dinner in the oven and hand him the kids as he walked in the door and she walked out.

What Harmony did for work was constantly evolving. Over the years she'd take on side hustle on top of side hustle, before we'd even heard of the expression, although years later I'd find out it had been around since the '50s.

"I do a little bit of all of it," she'd say instead, "and a whole lot of some of it."

She bought antiques at estate sales, restored them and sold them at flea markets and auctions. She stenciled cute designs on baby clothes and bibs and sold those, too. Then she started running the estate sales.

Harmony and her husband used the equity in their house to buy a beach shack and fix it up on weekends. Long before VRBO was a thing, they rented it out for big money by the night and the week during tourist season, with Harmony doing the booking and most of the cleaning. Then she'd put a longer-term winter-rental tenant in place at a lower rent, and do it all over again when beach season started up again.

The Equal Credit Opportunity Act had been around since the '70s, but Jan's husband's name was on her credit cards. I was still using a single credit card from my second marriage.

Since I'd just quit my job, he let me keep the card as long as I changed the billing address and paid the bills, and he took out another one. Harmony made Jan and me apply for cards in our names to build our own credit, something that neither of us had ever really thought about.

Jan and I didn't know the first thing about stocks, but Harmony talked us into buying a few shares in Hasbro and Boston Beer that we really couldn't afford. The stocks soared over time, and later she talked us into selling them. Even our tiny piece of the pie was enough for the down payments on our island townhouses.

"It's a great investment," Harmony said years later when we bought the townhouses. "Plus we can use them for our own vacations any time we have a break between renters. And one day way down the road we'll be able to ditch the cold winters, live side-by-side—"

"And raise the roof!" Jan said, pumping her palms toward the ceiling the way people did back then.

"Not literally," Harmony said. "Trust me, the HOA will never approve it."

When we finally moved to the island and into those townhouses, Harmony was the only one who didn't have to sell another home first. Which was both a good and a bad thing, since it also meant her husband could stay up north and leave their marriage at least temporarily in limbo.

"I know what you are," Jan would say to Harmony when she first heard the term. "You're a serial entrepreneur."

"And we're lucky to know you," I'd say.

Harmony smiled that big smile of hers that never changed. "That's what friends are for. To fill in the blanks."

Back when Jan and I first reconnected with Harmony, she'd just added installing and maintaining plants for office buildings and hotels and rich people's houses to her repertoire.

"Professional installation," she said. "If you call it professional plant installation instead of just going to a nursery and buying plants for them, you can charge enough money to make it worth the aggravation. You also have to call it full-service plant maintenance instead of watering. The trick is to present yourself as a specialist, a plant service expert who will take full ownership of their indoor and outdoor landscape."

"Wow," I said. "Who are you and what have you done with our old friend the radio station receptionist?"

"You go, girl," Jan said. "That Kennedy cousin must be kicking himself that he missed his chance."

I basically didn't have a life outside of work at that point, so lots of nights I'd ride around with Harmony for something to do. I'd help her water Boston ferns and lug in huge planters filled with bird of paradise and anthurium and Ficus trees and Norfolk Island pines.

She'd offer to pay me and I'd turn her down. Once when I got home from work, my front door was decorated with a grapevine wreath wrapped in bittersweet. A couple of months later it was neatly changed out to an evergreen wreath with a bright red bow.

"Thanks for giving me hope," I said when we were driving around on an icy night. "It's good for me to be out here with you. As opposed to home in bed with my Marimekko snow flower comforter pulled over my head."

Harmony reached over and patted my hand. "Life is long. At least if we're lucky. You've got plenty of time to figure it out, Honey."

Chapter 17

A gazillion years later, we opened our townhouse doors in plenty of time to hit the beach before sunrise.

Jan took one look at me. "Who are you and what have you done with our friend Glenda?"

I spun around so they could get the full effect. "I woke up with an overwhelming urge to channel Diane Keaton in *Something's Gotta Give.*"

Playing dress-up as an adult is an underappreciated form of creativity. Plus a great way to not feel guilty about hanging onto the clothes you couldn't bear to part with in your last decluttering session.

"Off to shop my closet." Harmony turned around and pushed her door open again.

"I'm in," Jan said.

"Make it fast," I said.

We were all in full coastal grandmother garb in no time. Beige wide-legged ankle-length trouser pants, untucked white boyfriend shirts, relatively clean white canvas sneakers.

Jan wore a tan bucket beach hat. Harmony a white one. I'd even found a floppy beige coastal grandma scarf and tied it in a bow over Chickpea's collar. Sun safety won out over cine-

matic authenticity, so my bright turquoise hat with the ridiculously oversized brim was our only flash of clothing color.

When we got to the beach, the pink light at the horizon
was gone.

"Bummer," I said. "We missed the Belt of Venus."

"Life's a tradeoff," Harmony said. "Nobody gets it all,
Honey."

Jan yanked up her wide-legged pants. "Speaking of belts,
the next time we decide to do coastal grandma, remind me to
wear one."

We walked along the water's edge, picking up trash and
dropping it into our net bags. We stopped occasionally to
scoop up beached sand dollars, too, so they wouldn't die
waiting for the next high tide. Careful not to break their
fragile flat circular skeletons, we returned them gently to the
ocean if they were still alive.

"Multitasking at its finest," I said. "Rescuing sand dollars
is magical. Think about it—they could live another six to ten
years just because of us. It makes me feel like a cross between
Wonder Woman and a mermaid."

"Or a supershero." Jan bent down and scooped up a sand
dollar, walked to the edge of the water. "If it's brown, put it
down," she said as she carefully tossed it in.

"If they're purple or brown or gray, they have to stay,"
Harmony said while she rescued another sand dollar. "If
they're white or light, you can hold on tight."

Just so you know, unless a sand dollar is white or the palest
gray, it's probably alive. A live sand dollar will be some shade
of purple or brown or dark gray and have tiny bristles like
little hairs on the underside and around the edges. It has kind
of a velvety feel.

If a sand dollar is dead, it will be smooth all over because
its bristles have fallen off. The skeleton that remains is called a
test. And just like when you were back in school and had actually studied, it's okay to take the test.

I was walking in the middle, so Harmony and Jan spread out to keep a safe distance from my hat. Chickpea darted off to frolic with some other beach dogs, galloped back to check in, darted off again.

"Look," Harmony said. "A pod of dolphins."

Sure enough, a pod of dolphins dancing in our direction was just visible in the ocean.

"A group of dolphins leaping out of the water and diving back in can also be called a display of dolphins," I said.

"They're in full display mode, for sure," Jan said.

Behind the dolphins, a spectacular orange ball of sun was growing larger and larger at the horizon.

Low tide had created the perfect blank canvas of packed sand for us. It was also a good seashell morning, which didn't usually happen on St. Simons Island because most of the shells got blocked by sand bars on their way from the sea to beach.

Spontaneously, we put our stuff down and started getting creative. Harmony found a knobbed whelk, which looks like a small conch shell, at the edge of the water.

"Don't worry," she said as she placed it on the sand. "I already checked to make sure a sea critter wasn't using it for a house."

The beautiful spiraled shell became the centerpiece of our sand mandala. We circled out from there with sand dollars we found up by the high-tide wrack line, bleached silvery white and long past saving. Then we added a circle of cockle shells, then a circle of angel wing shells. After that we filled in with broken pieces of marsh grass that had washed in on the last tide. We added a whelk egg case, which looks like a tiny Slinky. Then an oyster shell and more cockle shells.

With each tide, the beaches of the Golden Isles change radically. Sand shifts, sandbars and tidal pools appear and disappear and reappear. And the next time you walk it, it could look like an entirely different beach from the last time you walked it. The average change between high and low tide in terms of water depth at a given point is approximately seven feet, and depending on weather and the moon, as much as ten or twelve feet.

All by way of saying that our sand mandala didn't have a snowball's chance in St. Simons of surviving the next high tide.

And that was the point of sand mandalas.

"So incredible," Harmony said. "So zen."

"Those Tibetan Buddhist monks have it right," I said. "They spend days creating a colorful sand mandala and then they don't even wait for nature to take it away. As soon as they finish it, they sweep away the colored sand. The message is supposed to be that everything at some point comes to an end. And yet the monks believe that everybody surrounding the mandala is blessed by seeing it and experiences profound joy and peace."

Jan looked at our mandala. "I don't know if we're quite there yet, but I like to think the people who see ours before the tide erases it will at least smile."

Chickpea dashed over, grabbed a piece of marsh grass from the mandala like it was a bone, dashed off again. I found another shell, filled in the space.

"It's a good lesson in letting things go," Harmony said as we started walking again.

We breathed in the salt air, stretched out our legs.

I stopped. "I can't do it."

"Those were really good shells," Jan said.

We turned and jogged back to our shells, stuffed the best ones into our coastal grandma pockets.

"It's fine," Jan said. "We don't have to do everything the monks do."

"May we always have shells in our pockets and sand between our toes," I said when we started walking again.

"If you don't factor in beach trash patrol and having to

drive the townhouse recyclables to the recycling center along with all the crap we pick up here," Harmony said, "I could do this all day every day. I don't care if we ever hear from FLETC."

"We will," Jan said. "I can feel it in my burgeoning super-shero bones."

I turned my head at the thud of sneakers on sand behind us.

Two over-achieving 30-something female walkers in sports bra tops and lycra shorts, both with belts around their waists that held multiple single-use water bottles, came up behind us.

Instead of passing on the left, or even on the right, the walkers strode aggressively through the two small spaces between the three of us.

My hat went flying. Jan nabbed it in the air.

The two women kept walking, oblivious, pumping their arms, giant-stepping away.

"Just wait till you find out that all that pushing gets you absolutely nowhere, y'all," Harmony yelled.

"And you end up right back where you started," I yelled. "Because no matter where you go and who you go with in this life, there you freaking are."

"Don't come crying to us," Jan yelled, "if you need to borrow a senior discount card for your skinny lattes."

Chapter 18

Ten and a half years after we first saw *9 to 5* together, the three of us went to the movies on opening weekend of *Thelma and Louise.*

"It's my Mother's Day gift," Harmony said. "Not the movie ticket, just getting out of the house for a few hours without having to work. Richie's watching the kids and getting the beach house ready for new renters."

"I got time off for good behavior, too," Jan said. "Although Mother's Day was almost two weeks ago, so now it's merely a distant memory for my guys."

I excused myself to go to the ladies' room, made it back just as the final preview trailer was wrapping up.

"Take your time, why don't you," Jan whispered. "You almost missed the beginning."

The packed mostly female audience hung on every scene, every line. It was a movie that showed how much fun we have with our best girlfriends, just how far we'll go for them, how little we need men. There was horror and trauma. There was love. And Brad Pitt.

It was a movie that also wasn't afraid to be funny and silly and sarcastic. The whole theater exploded with laughter when

Thelma told Louise to shoot the cop's radio and she blew out the one playing music in his car instead.

When the movie ended, the stunned audience observed a moment of silence. And then everybody burst into applause.

"That was the da bomb," Jan said as we stood outside the theater on a warm spring night. "The best girl power female friendship road trip movie I've ever seen. Wait. Have there been any others? Anyway, there will be. The floodgates are going to open and women will be starring in all the good friendship road trip movies from now until eternity."

"It was definitely all that and a bag of chips," Harmony said. "I just don't know about the ending. I feel like Louise would have shoved Thelma out of the car in the nick of time."

"I think they both would have jumped out and found their way to Mexico and assumed new identities." Jan said. "They could have run an underground railroad to get other women out of tight spots."

"Maybe the point," Harmony said, "is that they got to write their own story, choose their own destiny."

"'You've always been crazy,'" Jan said. "'This is just the first chance you've had to express yourself.'" Her Louise imitation was in serious need of refinement.

"'You get what you settle for,'" Harmony said, almost sounding like Thelma. "I think that's the message everyone's going to remember about this movie," she added in her regular Harmony voice.

"'My husband wasn't sweet to me,'" Jan said, switching from Louise to Thelma, "'and look how I turned out.'"

They turned to me, waiting.

I took a deep breath. "'Everything looks different now,'" I said. "'You feel like that? You feel like you got something to live for now?'"

And then I burst into tears.

I was wedged into a corner of my secondhand couch, my Marimekko snow flower comforter pulled up to my chin. Jan was rifling through my kitchen looking for something for us to drink. Harmony had just called her husband's pager with my shoebox-size cordless phone and was waiting for him to call her back so she could tell him she'd be a little bit late.

"I feel like we could all use a good stiff Appletini," Jan said. "But this is the best I could come up with."

I reached my hand out from under the comforter to take one of two etched Arby's promotional Christmas wine glasses filled with warm white wine and ice cubes.

"Nice glasses," Jan said. "Ho, ho, ho."

I sniffed. "Yard sale."

"Okay, dish," Jan said when Harmony walked in with another Arby's promotional glass and found a seat. "We need the 411."

I closed my eyes, swallowed hard. There had to be at least a dozen ways to say this and I couldn't come up with a single one.

I hugged the wine glass to my chest with one hand, pointed to a Hallmark card on my coffee table with the other.

Harmony jumped up from her hot pink beanbag chair, slid the card out of the pale purple envelope, opened it, read it, handed it to Jan.

"Happy Mother's Day," Jan read. "To someone who's just like a mother to me. Kimberly."

I waited for the sky to fall. Instead, hot tears rolled down my cheeks and plopped into the icy wine.

"I don't get it," Harmony finally said. "Who's Kimberly?"

I'd dreamed about saying it out loud for so many years. Still, it took everything I had to get the words out. "My daughter."

"No. Way," Harmony said.

"Seriously?" Jan reached for the card again, gave it another read.

"She turned 18 in November," I said softly. "She must have filed a request to get her original birth certificate unsealed."

"And she waited six months until Mother's Day so she could send you a card?" Harmony said.

I nodded.

"It's hard to read subtext in a Hallmark card," Jan said, "but the kid sure knows how to make an entrance."

"When will you meet her?" Harmony said.

"Wait," Jan said. "We want the whole story first. And then we can figure out when we're going to meet her."

I was pretty sure I didn't feel a thing as I told Harmony and Jan the whole story. It felt like I was floating above us, just below the yellowed popcorn ceiling, watching some poor pathetic person I didn't even know.

"Junior year," I said. "At this stupid party. Somebody's parents were away for Valentine's weekend and we were all drinking this disgusting punch made from Coke and Mateus rosé and little bits from all the bottles in their liquor cabinet. Bread was blasting on the stereo and some of the boys were singing *get naked with you* instead of *make it with you*."

"I think I went to high school with those boys," Jan said.

"*Shh*," Harmony said.

"And," I said, "this popular kid told me he'd had a crush on me since freshman year and he was going to break up with his girlfriend so we could be together."

"So he wasn't even your boyfriend?" Jan said.

I closed my eyes. "We ended up under a pile of winter coats in one of the bedrooms. I told him to stop and he laughed. And we were both really drunk and then it was over."

"Oh, Honey," Harmony said. "Then what happened?"

"Nothing." My fingers were getting numb from holding the wine glass. I took a sip I couldn't taste and switched hands. "When he passed me in the hallway at school on Monday, he didn't even look at me. His arm was around his girlfriend's shoulders."

"Sleazeball," Jan said. "When did you realize you were pregnant?"

"I made it through the rest of the school year." I tried to smile. "Denial really is more than a river in Egypt. I mean, I guess I knew but I didn't know. I locked it away in a little box in my head and just kept hoping it wasn't really true. And peasant blouses and long oversized vests were in style and I stopped snapping the top of my bell-bottoms."

Harmony and Jan looked at me, remembering the bell-bottoms they were wearing when I couldn't snap mine.

I closed my eyes, opened them again. "I was supposed to have this summer internship at a local newspaper. At the end of the last day of school, my mother called me into my parents' bedroom. And my life blew up."

"He raped you," Harmony said.

"Yeah, he did," Jan said. "I hope you at least blew up his life, too."

I shrugged. "What was the point? More shame and humiliation than I was already feeling? I didn't even know him. I was stupid to let it happen."

"No," Jan said. "He was a predator and an asshat."

"So you didn't tell anyone who the father was?" Harmony said.

"Nope," I said. "My parents didn't push. I think they might have been relieved they could run the whole show. Or maybe it didn't seem quite so real to them if they didn't know who the sperm donor was."

"He had to have known," Jan said. "Do you still have your yearbook? I'd really like to see the whites of that slimebucket's eyes."

"Cut it out, Jan," Harmony said.

"I'm serious," Jan said. "I think we should hunt him down and make him suffer. Maybe he's still in the area. Can you imagine if there was a way you could just tap a button and instantly find anybody and everybody you went to high school with?"

"I never got a yearbook," I said. "I didn't even have a picture in it. Just my name on the camera shy page."

"Then what happened?" Harmony said. She and Jan were both leaning forward, their own lives temporarily forgotten.

I blew out a puff of air to see if I could still breathe. "My mother kept telling me how much I'd embarrassed my father and how he wanted to send me to a convent to have the baby. And my father kept telling me how much I'd embarrassed my mother and how she wanted to send me to a convent to have the baby."

"Did they?" Jan said.

I shook my head. "Title IX had just gone into effect our junior year, which I guess was a lucky break after the unluckiest-suckiest one of my life. Title IX meant that even if you were pregnant, the school had to allow you to continue to participate in classes and extracurricular activities."

"Like if you were a cheerleader, they would have to give you bigger pom poms to camouflage your belly instead of kicking you off the squad?" Jan said.

Harmony glared at Jan. "Knock it off."

"Eat my shorts," Jan said. "I was just trying to add a little levity."

"And," I said, "they also had to let you choose to participate in a special instructional program for pregnant students instead. And also excuse any absences due to your pregnancy.

And once you had the baby, allow you to return to the same academic and extracurricular status."

Harmony and Jan took sips of their wine. I chewed my bottom lip.

"I had this fantasy," I said, "that I'd hold my head high and go back and that everybody would be there for me. We'd read *The Scarlet Letter* at the beginning of junior year, and I thought, you know, sin, forgiveness, redemption? Owning your actions without letting your mistakes dictate your future?"

Harmony nodded. Jan raised her eyebrows.

"I was so far along by fall," I said, "that I stayed home. The one friend who stuck by me brought my assignments to and from school. I spent a lot of time at her house because being at mine was so bad. She and her mom were the only ones who treated me like I was the same old person."

I fished an ice cube out of my wine, put it in my mouth. When I spit it back into the glass, it created a mini tidal wave. "Everybody else completely shunned me. My parents and my older brother never let me forget for a second how much I was embarrassing them. And then my friend accused her mother of paying more attention to me than to her own daughter, so there went that friendship."

"Ah, high school," Jan said.

"That must have been so, so painful," Harmony said.

I shrugged. "This woman came to the house one night and my parents told me she was handling the adoption."

"Wait," Jan said. "This was like the year before Roe v. Wade, right? Do you think that might have made a difference?"

"I don't think so," I said. "I was incapable of making any kind of decision. And I think on some level I thought that I deserved to go through all this. Who knows, maybe with better parents, it would have at least been part of an actual discussion about options."

"You caught the tail end of what they call the 'Baby Scoop

Era,'" Harmony said. "I wrote a paper on it for a class in grad school. It was an unfortunate time in the history of U.S. adoptions that started following World War II and ended in the early '70s."

Harmony tapped her wine glass with one fingernail as she remembered. "An increase in out-of-wedlock pregnancies and the social pressures of being an unwed mother led to a peak number of adoptions arranged by adoption agencies, many of them not-so-voluntary since the birth mothers couldn't really make the choice to keep the baby. Shame is a powerful driver."

I closed my eyes, opened them again.

Jan disappeared, came back with the wine bottle.

I took a tiny sip. "I gave birth in November, signed the adoption papers. I had almost enough credits to graduate, so I stayed in my bedroom until January. Then my school let me take a couple of classes at the local community college so I could skip freshman English in college and go right into a sophomore honors class. And in September, off I went right on schedule, pretending I was just another college co-ed."

"Did you hold the baby?" Jan asked.

"Jan," Harmony said.

"No," I said. "They whisked it away so fast I didn't even get a look. Nobody even told me whether it was a girl or a boy, but I heard one of the nurses say *she's perfect, poor little thing*. And I think I somehow knew it, *she*, was a girl anyway."

I took a ragged breath. "Kimberly. I never would have named her Kimberly. The final season of *Bewitched* aired the year I had her, and I used to daydream about naming her Tabitha. And calling her Tab for short. I've thought about her every day since she was born. And every time I opened a can of Tab I thought of her more."

"Tab?" Jan said. "Tab? Clearly you were not ready to keep a baby."

Chapter 19

I met Kimberly that summer. She was getting ready to head across the country for her sophomore year of college. She'd lived most of her life barely a half hour away from where I gave birth to her, just about an hour away from where I lived now.

Our paths could have crossed so many times—at Logan airport, shopping at the good mall or even the not-so-great mall, on some random street somewhere—and we wouldn't have even known it. Or maybe we both would have felt it, like when you're walking along and you hit a cold patch of air and it's like some ghostly presence has just entered your force field.

She'd written a return address on the envelope and a phone number at the bottom of her Mother's Day card, clearly putting the ball in my court. So I waited until the following Saturday morning when I figured any self-respecting college student would still be sleeping.

I made sure my big tan cordless phone was charged, pulled out the antenna, carried it to the corner of my apartment where I got the strongest signal, took a deep breath, punched in the number.

A motherly voice answered on the third ring.

"This is Glenda," I said. "Gardner."

"Thank you for calling," she said, as if I were the babysitter or the Avon lady.

"Thank you for letting her send me a card." I almost said Mother's Day card, but caught myself just in time.

A long beat of silence followed.

I heard the rustle of paper. And then she suggested a date and a time and a place for lunch.

"On my calendar," I said like an idiot.

"Looking forward to it," she said, which wasn't much better. It wasn't until we hung up that I realized I didn't even know Kimberly's mother's name.

We met at a restaurant on Cape Cod. It was nowhere near where I lived or where they lived. Maybe it felt like neutral territory to them. Maybe they thought it would be easier to ditch me in a crowded tourist area if I turned out to be a nutcase.

Or maybe they were on their way to the Cape, or on their way home from the Cape, or maybe it was one of dozens of restaurants that had special meaning to them after 18 years together.

I left extra early, knowing that the inevitable bumper-to-bumper traffic on the road to Cape Cod on a summer Saturday would make my forty-five-minute drive at least double that, probably triple. Which was a good thing, since I accidentally drove around the Sagamore Rotary twice. Because when your palms are sweating and you keep forgetting to breathe, it's easy to miss the right turnoff.

After crossing over the Cape Cod Canal on the Sagamore Bridge, I managed to get off at Exit 1 on the first try. I twisted and turned my way to the foot of the bridge and the Christmas Tree Shop, a Cape Cod landmark complete with a massive windmill and the world's largest thatched roof.

The Christmas Tree Shop carried lots of cheap and interesting stuff, Christmas and otherwise, and you never knew what you were going to find there. It was as good as a trip to Marshalls. If this meeting was a bust, at least I could do some browsing while I was in the neighborhood.

Maybe they wanted to hit the Christmas Tree Shop, too, to get Kimberly all stocked up for school, and they decided to fit me in. Maybe if it went really well, we could all go shopping together. I sang the Christmas Tree Shop theme song to try to soothe myself: *Don't you just love a bargain.* Hearing the shake in my voice made my stomach flip over, almost like a baby kicking.

The Bridge Restaurant was tucked in with some tiny shops at the rear of the Christmas Tree Shop parking lot. I'd never been there, never even noticed it before. When I opened the door, it looked like the kind of charming little gem of a restaurant tourists might pass over on the way to Chili's. There were two tiers of tables with fresh flowers, soft lighting, antique fixtures throughout.

I picked them out right away. Kimberly's mother stood up, waited for me to join them.

"Alice," she said. "Alice Sullivan."

Kimberly stood up, too. Seeing her would have been gut-wrenching if I wasn't so numb.

And then she threw her arms around me. If I could have, I would have stood there hugging her forever. Her long blondish hair was freshly washed. She smelled like Gap Dream, a young and pretty perfume, a smell as uncomplicated as I wished my own teenage years had been.

"Kim," her mother finally said.

"Kimberly," she said. And it was enough to break our hug.

We sat at the small round table, equidistant from one another.

"Thank you for letting me meet you," I said, carefully making eye contact with both of them.

"Thank you for letting us adopt her," Kimberly's mother said.

"Thank you for having me." Kimberly rolled her eyes, making fun of us both.

Female servers were still called waitresses then and ours came over and handed us menus, poured our water. I tried to read the menu, which seemed to offer dishes from all over the world, each one explained in smaller print below. The words were way too much for me to process so I just closed the menu. When they both ordered Sinigang, a fish stew from the Philippines, I did, too.

"It's excellent, isn't it?" Kimberly's mother said. "All that swordfish and shrimp and scallops and scrod over jasmine rice?"

"You two can split my scallops," Kimberly said. "They creep me out."

I reached for my purse, pulled out two small wrapped boxes, slid them both over to Kimberly.

She ripped the paper off one of them like it was her birthday, opened it. It was a black velvet choker adorned with a single puffy silver heart.

Her face lit up. She tied it right on over the tattoo choker she was already wearing. It went perfectly with her blackish metallic lipstick, her tiny baby doll dress, her Doc Marten boots and summer-weight ruffly ankle socks.

"Thank you so much," she said. "It's a wicked nice choker. I'm majorly, one hundred and ten percent in love with it."

I wished I could quit while I was ahead and grab the other box back, but she was already opening it.

It was a delicate teardrop-shaped tawny citrine pendant on a thin gold chain. I'd bought it a few years after she was born, even though I knew it would only make me sadder, and I'd kept it in its little box ever since. Just in case.

"How lovely," Kimberly's mom said. "Your birthstone, Honey."

"Cute," Kimberly said as she tucked it back in the box. "Thanks."

I hadn't relaxed enough to actually taste my fish stew, but at least I managed to get a few spoonfuls down.

Then Kimberly dropped a scallop into my bowl and I almost lost it. All I could think of were all the peanut butter and jelly crusts I hadn't finished from her sandwiches when she was little, the mint chocolate chip ice cream cones I hadn't licked so they wouldn't drip all over her.

"Did you want to keep me?" Kimberly said.

Her mother opened her mouth to say something, closed it again.

"I wanted you to have more than I could give you," I said. "I wanted you to have perfect parents who knew who they were and would be able to keep you safe and support you through scary things if they happened."

Kimberly smiled. "They're not completely perfect."

"Thanks, Sweetie," her mother said.

"To tell you the truth," I said, "I would have loved to have been adopted right along with you. I was 17 and completely overwhelmed and my parents were so, so angry with me."

"My birth father's name wasn't on the original birth certificate," Kimberly said. "Was it a one-nighter or did he bail on you?"

"Kim . . ." her mother said.

"It's okay." I closed my eyes. "It was a drunken high school party. I never told him."

She tilted her head. "He must have guessed it if he went to the same high school. So he was either a poser or a total noob. Do I look like him? Because I don't really look that much like you."

I shrugged, trying to remember, trying not to remember. "Maybe the hair?"

"I might want to know who he is at some point," she said. "Just to see for myself. Or in case I ever need a kidney or something."

"If you need a kidney," I said, "you can have both of mine."

She nodded. "Okay, that should tide me over for now. Is there a spousal unit?"

"You mean when I had you?"

When she laughed and pushed a piece of hair out of her face, I thought I could see the tiniest bit of me around her eyes. And maybe her hands.

"I mean now," she said. "You know, a husband?"

"Not at the moment," I said.

"Kids?" Kimberly said.

"Kim . . ." her mom said.

"Talk to the hand," Kimberly said as she held up one palm in her mother's direction. "If I have half-sisters and brothers, I have every right to know about them."

"Watch your tone," Alice said.

"Sorry," I said. "You're it."

"You're not *that* old," Kimberly said. "It could still happen. Let me know—I might be persuaded to babysit occasionally."

Kimberly unhooked her Jansport backpack from the back of her chair, unzipped it in her lap. She gave her lips another slash of black, pulled out a curvy Spice Girls edition Polaroid camera. It had pink and blue accents and a pop-up flash and SPICE CAM emblazoned on the front.

"It's majorly embarrassing," she said. "But it's the only Polaroid I have."

Once the waitress finished clearing our plates, Kimberly asked her to take our photo. We slid our chairs together with Kimberly in the middle. She took three pictures, one for each of us.

As we sat, waiting for the white-framed snapshots to come to life on the table, Kimberly talked a little bit about her college, the major she'd switched three times, her foggy goals. I said something lame about wanting to look into branded cameras once I got back to work on Monday.

Kimberly's mom said she was thinking of taking some classes herself.

Once our photos were ready, just like that Kimberly was over me. I could tell she was ready to show her snapshot to her friends, give them the deets on her birth mom, hang out.

If she were a few years younger, it might have been different. She might have needed someone to drive her around, take her shopping. Maybe she would have even wanted to run away to my house when she had a big fight with her parents.

But she was way past that point, both of her Doc Martens already dangling out of the nest. Itchy from spending a summer back in her smalltown high school world, probably already scheming about getting a job somewhere else so she wouldn't have to come home for the whole summer next year.

As we stood outside the restaurant, Kimberly handed me a piece of black paper with her dorm address written in the same pink loopy jelly-roll-pen letters she'd used to sign my Mother's Day card.

I handed her an index card. I'd carefully printed my home and work addresses and phone numbers in red pen.

"Call me if you want to meet for coffee," Alice said.

"I'd love that," I said, even though I could tell she was just being nice.

If they'd headed for the Christmas Tree Shop, I might have tried to accidentally on purpose bump into them, just in case this turned out to be my last chance.

Instead I watched their car drive off. Then I wandered up and down the aisles of the Christmas Tree Shop for some much-needed retail therapy.

I dodged tourists and filled my cart with all the things Kimberly might need for another year of school. A Celestial Star Sun Moon reversible comforter and pillow cover. Coordinating extra-long dorm sheets in a navy that was so dark it was almost black. A wooden photo-collage frame. Gel pens and a big fat pad of black paper. A little travel iron. Shampoo and conditioner and soap and deodorant and a cute plastic shower caddy to carry it all to the dorm bathroom. Towels and wash-cloths and a terrycloth robe. Dry erase markers and a white-board. A laundry basket and a couple of plastic milk crates for storage, black of course.

I gave the cart a long look. Then I left it in the middle of the store and walked right out of the Christmas Tree Shop, head held high, shoulders back, tears running down my face.

When I showed my Polaroid to Jan, she said Kimberly was adorable but didn't look much like me, not that I wasn't adorable. Harmony said she was beautiful and she had my eyes and my smile and she would have known she was my daughter from a mile away.

Fourteen years later, The Bridge Restaurant would burn down in a morning fire in 2005. The Sagamore Rotary would turn into the Sagamore Flyover in 2006. And the thatched-roof Christmas Tree Shop with the windmill would close forever in 2023.

But even when the physical evidence was gone, I'd never, ever forget every detail of the first time I actually saw my daughter.

I'd hang in there, too, staying in touch with Kimberly and her mom, careful not to overstep, occasionally sending thoughtful cards and little gifts, saying yes to invitations and not inviting them too often. Not quite family, but family adjacent.

And the day would come, after lots of ups and downs and twists and turns in my own life, that I'd be in the loop when Kimberly's own daughter Delaney was born.

When my daughter's daughter looked at me with her wise hazel eyes, it was almost like looking at myself as a baby. And it was definitely like we already knew each other.

Not long afterward, Jan would pull some strings. And for four and a half magical years I'd take Delaney to work with me and have lunch with her in the fabulous childcare so Kimberly could go back to work.

As The Rolling Stones sang in my theme song for that era, you can't always get what you want in this life. But you get what you need.

Chapter 20

"I can't believe we're in," I said. "We're actually doing this."

For proof, I glanced down at the long-sleeve camouflage T-shirt I was wearing over coordinating camo leggings. Since Evie and I were driving us off island, it was a just a quick glance, but enough to make the whole thing feel real. Or almost real.

Incredible golden marsh views flanked both sides of the causeway. A flock of spoonbills fed at the edge of a tidal pool. Roseate spoonbills are large pink wading birds with distinctive spoon-shaped bills. They're gorgeous from a distance and kind of wacky-looking up close.

You're expecting an elegant pink flamingo and suddenly you're like what *is* that? Spoonbills feed in shallow waters, moving slowly, swinging their heads from side to side, spooning their way through the silt. They get their pink color from eating the local shrimp.

A sprinkling of white ibis and snowy egrets were dining with the pink spoonbills, creating pops of pastel against the green-gold marsh grass. A single line of brown pelicans flew overhead, on the lookout for bigger fish.

Harmony was riding shotgun. She wore a camo jean

jacket and a cute camo head wrap with a bow. She held a hat in her lap.

Jan, wearing a long flowy camo top over leggings and a camo baseball hat, was jammed sideways into Evie's practically nonexistent rear seat.

"I'm all about electric vehicles," Jan said, "but next time you pick out an EV, you might want to consider the bendability of your backseat passengers."

"That's right," I said. "She's my car, but it's all about you."

I gave Evie a reassuring pat on her steering wheel. "And I'd appreciate it if you choose your words carefully. Evie likes to think of herself as my forever car and she's extremely sensitive to backseat shaming."

"Aww," Harmony said. "Remember backseat sex?"

Harmony sighed. Maybe Evie did, too.

"Not in this backseat," Jan said. "I don't care how bendable you are."

At the end of the causeway, a sign said WELCOME TO BRUNSWICK.

We took a right on US 17. Harmony leaned over and turned up the volume. We sang "Respect" with Aretha Franklin and "I Am Woman" with Helen Reddy and "Run the World (Girls)" with Beyonce.

"Great job on the female empowerment playlist, Honey," Harmony said.

"It's good, right?" Jan said before we dove into "Man! I Feel Like a Woman!" with Shania Twain.

Evie and I turned left on Chapel Crossing Road. We drove until we came to a modest sign for the Federal Law Enforcement Training Center and pulled into the registration office parking lot.

I rolled down Evie's windows. Harmony turned up the volume even higher and we blasted out the rest of "Came In Like a Wrecking Ball," singing along at the top of our lungs with Miley Cyrus.

"The perfect entrance song," I said. "They'll know we're coming."

"Just so they don't lock the doors fast," Jan said.

Harmony and I got out of the car, looped our matching camo waist packs, which we were old enough to know were really rebranded fanny packs, over our chests like crossbody bags.

We leaned back in, grabbed Jan's hands, eventually managed to pry her out of Evie's backseat. Jan reached back in for her matching camo fanny pack.

I hit my key fob to lock Evie. Harmony handed me my hat. It was a full coverage camo sun hat with flaps covering the neck and a roll-up face drape.

I put it on, rolled the face drape up to my eyes.

"Good call not driving in that thing," Jan said.

We took a moment to brush the driving wrinkles out of our camo clothes.

"Isn't it just amazing," Harmony said, "what you can find in resale stores when you've got a good eye."

All three of us wore military-inspired combat boots with chunky lugged soles. Ankle straps on our right boots held our stainless steel water bottles.

We checked each other out.

"Too much?" I said.

"Never," Harmony said.

"We'll blend right in like chameleons," Jan said.

We pulled out our phones and started taking selfies together. We struck a pose. And another. And a few more, because the truth is that once you hit midlife and beyond, taking a great photo is all about the ratio of the good angles you still have left to the number of pictures you take.

And just in case you're collecting camera tricks, another good one is to hold the phone high to get the most flattering, non-jowly look.

The FLETC registration office turned out to be a

completely non-intimidating room that could have almost
been a bank lobby.

We made our way to one of two lines of average-looking
people heading toward the same kind of plate glass windows
bank tellers stand behind.

"I expected more somehow," Jan said. "We didn't even
have to go through a metal detector. We could be packing
anything."

"Right?" Harmony said.

A few people turned to look at us, checked out our full
camo wardrobe.

I pointed at a big sign with an arrow that said WEAPONS
CHECK.

"Got it," Jan said. "It's the honor system around here."

"That's so nice," Harmony said. "I truly believe people
will step up if you just give them a chance to be trustworthy."

When it was our turn, a woman behind the window with a
FLETC insignia on her shirt took our driver's licenses, found
our names on the clearance list, wrote down Evie's license
plate number.

The woman handed us identification badges attached to
blue and white FLETC neck lanyards.

"You don't happen to have anything in more of a camo
print, do you?" I said.

We drove slowly toward what looked like a cross between a
turnpike toll station and a fortress.

A huge sign spanning two guard stations said FEDERAL
LAW ENFORCEMENT TRAINING CENTERS.
FEDERAL-STATE-LOCAL-TRIBAL-INTERNATIONAL.

Two lanes in and no lanes out. A high fence blocking off
any other access.

In front of the glassed-in guard stations stood massive

cement planters that even a tank wouldn't have been able to plow through. The hulking planters were filled with tastefully chosen plants, but that didn't make their purpose any less clear.

"Yikes," Jan said. "This is getting real. Legit, bona fide, boot-shaking real."

I rolled down my window and held up my lanyard for the FLETC insignia-ed guard. Harmony and Jan passed me their lanyards and I held them up next.

The guard gave us a long look, checked off our names on a list, let us pass.

I tapped Evie's radio on again. Gloria Gaynor started to sing "I Will Survive."

"No irony there," Jan said.

Harmony turned the volume way down.

We drove and drove and drove through acres of wooded roads.

"Are we still in Brunswick?" I said. "Or have we crossed into an alternate universe?"

"Actually," Jan said, "we're in a place called Glynco now. All FLETC. Eighty-two thousand residents, literally its own zip code."

"This feels kind of like one of those scary movies," Harmony said. "You know, right before you get lost in the woods and the spine-chilling music starts."

"Knock it off," Jan said. "This is probably the safest place in the universe. I mean, basically you throw a rock and you hit a federal agent."

"Who then locks you up for the rest of your natural life," Harmony said.

"Whose freaking idea was this anyway?" I said. "I had a perfectly nice life back at the townhouse. And Chickpea is too much of an extrovert to enjoy being home alone."

Harmony looked down at her phone. "Okay, it should be coming up. Take the next right and park."

Chapter 21

We stood on the sidewalk outside a wreck of an old house.

Layers of peeling paint, screen door falling off, broken window patched with cardboard. The front yard was littered with discarded Mountain Dew and clear nip bottles.

Against my better judgment, I'd rolled down my face covering. Jan had her baseball cap on backward. Harmony was still wearing her camo headband.

"I thought drug testing us in the meth house was a nice touch," Harmony said.

Jan shook her head. "All that worry about peeing in a cup and they went right for the swabs. I have to admit I still breathed a sigh of relief when we all tested clean."

Two fit, well-built 50ish men, wearing chinos and tucked-in polo shirts with official-looking insignias, stepped off the sidewalk to pass. They glanced over as they circled around us.

"Be still my heart," Harmony said.

"It's like we died and went to hot guy heaven," I said.

"I was expecting more uniforms," Jan said. "There's nothing like a man in full uniform. Or a woman. Or a gender-unspecified person."

"Maybe they put the uniforms on later," Harmony said. "You know, depending on the exercise."

"I hope so," I said. "Otherwise, I'm going to have to run around and pull everybody's shirts out of their chinos. Those full tucks are just not doing it."

"True that," Harmony said. "Full tucks only work with culottes, wide legs and trouser pants. A half tuck might be acceptable, especially a French tuck. But a full tuck with regular chinos is just a stylistic no-no."

"Agreed," I said. "Somebody around here needs to call the fashion police."

"They're probably already training them," Jan said.

"Then they need to raise the style bar," Harmony said.

We turned to check out some other role players clustered around a battered picnic table on the meth house front yard. Average-looking people ranging in age from early 20s all the way up to us. In T-shirts and jeans or pants or sweats.

I unzipped my fanny pack, pulled out a camo lip gloss. Put some on, smacked my lips.

"Do you think we should share our camouflage resale sources," I said, "or just let them figure it out on their own?"

Jan, Harmony and I were hanging out in a seedy reproduction biker bar with the rest of our role players group. I was pretty sure a group of FLETC role players could be called a pod or a collection or a herd or a swarm or a cluster or a bunch or a band or a bevy. Or even a party, which is what role-playing video gamers call themselves. During the pandemic, we could have been called a quaranteam.

Apparently Harmony preferred to come up with her own name for us. "Bonkers," she said. "That's what we are. Anybody who would voluntarily sign up to do this is one sandwich short of a picnic."

The bar was dark. You could smell the stale beer even when you casually held a finger up to cover your nostrils. An entire Harley motorcycle was suspended from the ceiling. A stripper pole stood front and center on a low stage.

A sign over the door leading to the outside said OUT OF CHARACTER.

Jan tried hoisting herself up the stripper pole while we waited for the FLETC students and instructor to show up. She kicked up her feet but didn't get off the ground.

Harmony and I climbed up on the stage with Jan. The three of us circled around the pole a few times. The overall effect was less ageless sexy stripper goddess and more "Ring Around the Rosy."

"Hang in," Harmony said to Jan. "Everybody has to start pole dancing somewhere."

"I'm not feeling the click," Jan said. "I think I'm back to popsicle sticks. Although I might work in a few of these for some mixed media collages."

Jan pulled a bullet out from behind one ear.

Harmony and I gasped.

"Relax," Jan said. "It's just a used casing. I found it on the meth lab lawn."

"They'd better be recycling those," I said. "Brass is absolutely a recyclable metal."

Harmony pulled out her phone. "Brass casings can be reused a number of times," she read.

"Not if Jan steals them," I said.

"It's art," Jan said. "Think of it as upcycling if that helps."

"Ooh," Harmony said, still looking at her phone. "Listen to this. Researchers at the UMass-Dartmouth Center for Innovation and Entrepreneurship created a prototype that can disassemble ammunition. They recycle the metals—"

"See," I said. "I told you."

"—and," Harmony said, "the gunpowder is then reused as garden fertilizer. It's brilliant. If we have to let everybody keep their dang guns, we just take away their bullets. And feed the whole world from ammunition-fueled garden patches."

"Genius," I said. "It warms my pacifist heart."

"You'll have to convince me about the ammunition-flavored salads," Jan said. "In the meantime, I think I'll stick with collages."

A role player looked up from the pool table where she was playing a game with another role player. She glanced out a window.

"Heads up," she said. "Here they come."

We all took a seat and folded our hands in front of us like we were back in high school and the teacher was coming.

A big burly instructor came into the biker bar with a group of students. The students stopped just inside the door.

The instructor reached up and flipped the sign over so it said IN CHARACTER.

He eyed the role players, then handed us each a dog-eared laminated card stock script.

USE OF FORCE DRILL it said in big letters across the top.

The role players read our scripts.

Jan sighed. "'Sit at table and do nothing.' Apparently I've been typecast already."

"Ditto," I said.

"Ditto plus one," Harmony said.

We sat together at one of the sticky little tables in the sunken restaurant area.

Acting out their scripts, two of the other role players attempted a game of pool. A few others sat at the bar. A 40-ish male role player in sweats took an enthusiastic spin around our stripper pole.

"He's not *that* much better than we were," Jan said.

"Except for the fact that he got off the ground," I said.

A couple of role players left the building with the instructor.

Outside the biker bar, loud gunshots rang out. Some of the role players screamed. Lots of yelling followed. We heard more gunshots.

Harmony, Jan and I dove under our table.

"Don't look up," I said. "So. Much. Gum."

There was more yelling from outside, followed by more gunshots.

"Wait," Jan said. "We're supposed to sit at the table and not move."

"We're improvising," Harmony said.

A male role player ran into the restaurant waving a gun. Even though we knew he was one of us, we all screamed our heads off at the sight of him.

A group of gun-toting students ran in, spread out around the biker bar.

The gun-brandishing role player grabbed a female role player sitting at a table around the neck, screamed at her.

Everybody froze. The role player with the gun let go of the female role player's neck, made a dash for the restroom. Shots rang out.

One of the students pointed to the door, made a circling motion, pointed to the back of the building. Two other students ran out the door. Two more students walked over and stood on either side of the restroom door, guns pointed up in the air.

Nobody moved. Nobody breathed.

Finally, a student came back in with the runaway role player, his hands cuffed behind his back.

"We caught him sneaking out the bathroom window," the student said. "Just like on TV."

"Exactly," the instructor said. "That's where lots of these goofballs get their ideas. Okay, make sure you Mirandize him now that he's in custody, rather than risk forgetting about it when you start interrogating him, which is when you're legally obligated."

The instructor walked over to the door, flipped the sign back to OUT OF CHARACTER.

"Good work, everybody," the instructor said.

Jan, Harmony and I climbed out from under the table.

Harmony straightened her camo headband, fluffed her hair. "No wonder that job application asked if you had any heart issues."

I rolled down my face covering again. "Note to self. Bring earplugs."

Jan nodded. "I'm not sure we'll be able to use any of those particular skills on Butt, but hey, you never know."

Chapter 22

After Harmony, Jan and I had been back in the same orbit for a year or two, whenever I spent time with them it began to remind me that they had actual lives and I didn't.

I knew I was stuck. I knew I needed to get unstuck. Connecting the dots between the two was the problem.

It didn't help that everybody at work was always trying to fix me up.

"Do you know how embarrassing that is?" I said to Jan and Harmony on one of the rare occasions all three of us managed to grab a quick cup of coffee together. "I mean, just because I'm currently a single person in a coupled world—"

"Don't rub it in," Jan said. "Oh, to be childfree and single long enough for Calgon to take me away with a lavender and honey bubble bath." She stirred another packet of Sweet'N Low into her coffee.

"That stuff is going to kill you," I said as I poured more half 'n' half in mine.

"But what a way to go," Harmony said. She opened the box she'd bought to take home to her kids, popped a chocolate Dunkin' munchkin donut hole into her mouth.

Jan and I reached over and grabbed munchkins, too.

"Don't eat all the chocolate ones," Harmony said. "My kids will kill me."

Because she worked in Human Resources, Jan had access to all the private employee files, so she'd been scoping out the promising possibilities at work for me.

"What about that last guy you went on a date with?" Jan said. "You know, the one in Sales with the blingy address and the embellished resume? I mean, there had to have been a spark if you picked him from the last five personnel files I illegally Xeroxed for you."

"That's the problem," I said. "I think my picker is broken."

"Fine," Jan said. "Next time I'll move beyond prescreening and pick a winner for you myself."

"Maybe you should try answering a personal ad in the paper," Harmony said. "You know, test the classified waters."

"No thanks," I said. "I'd probably show up for a blind date and it would turn out to be one of my ex-husbands."

On the long flight from Boston to Las Vegas for a trade show, the guy in the seat next to me and I started to chat.

The NO SMOKING signs on airplanes had been permanently lit up in red for a couple of years now. He pointed at the one hanging over the aisle in front of us.

"At least we don't have to put up with that anymore," he said.

"What a relief," I said. "And the smoking sections weren't much better than when the whole plane was puffing away. You know that old saying—a smoking section on an airplane is like a peeing section in a swimming pool."

He laughed a manly laugh, deep and rich, a little bit flirty. He would have been good looking even if he wasn't wearing a stylish business suit with roomy pleated pants and a crisp white shirt and paisley tie. I checked out his left hand discreetly—he wasn't wearing a wedding ring.

At least I'd taken the time to fix my hair and makeup before I got on the plane. I was wearing my power suit again, partly because people still dressed up for flying back then and also because I needed it for the trade show and was hoping it wouldn't get as wrinkled as it would have in my suitcase.

He asked me why I was going to Las Vegas and I told him about my job and the trade show while we sipped our Cokes.

The stewardesses, who had yet to be upgraded to flight attendants, rolled the trolleys down the aisles and pulled our meal trays from the slots. We chowed down on some kind of lunch meat and mashed potatoes with a little center crater filled with gravy. Plus a single limp lettuce leaf and a roll and two pats of butter and a fruit cup. With real stainless-steel silverware, no less.

When a pretty stewardess removed our TV dinner-like trays, he didn't even flirt with her. He was a good listener, and he kept asking me questions and we kept chatting. When I asked him, he said he was going to Vegas for a little bit of business and a little bit of pleasure.

When I tried to pin down the details, he flipped the attention back to me. A little part of me realized I was probably oversharing, but it was such a refreshing change to have a guy actually interested in what I had to say, instead of waiting for his turn to talk about himself.

He edged his arm closer to mine on the armrest between us. I casually moved my hand to my lap. Then his legs did a man spread and he pressed his thigh into my knee.

And that's when I got the first niggling feeling. I swiveled both knees in the other direction, tried to take up less space in my seat. I told myself it didn't mean anything—he was just stretching out, just being a guy.

And then I took a good look at his hand where it extended out from my half of the armrest. I was pretty sure I could see the hint of a tan line where his wedding ring had been.

I pulled out the magazine I'd bought back at Logan, gave

it my full attention. Wished I'd picked up something like *Better Homes and Gardens* instead of *Cosmo*. Angled the magazine away from him as I flipped through. Turned the page fast when I came to "514 Hot New Sex Tips You Must Learn Tonight."

"Have a nice trip," I said dismissively when we finally landed. I reached for my Gitano Floral Tapestry Weekender duffle bag in the overhead compartment. He edged by me and grabbed my bag by its leather straps. With his other hand he grabbed his own manly travel bag, which was squished in way too close to my bag.

"Thanks," I said as I tried to take my bag from him

"I've got it, Glenda," he said. His voice was soothing. And it made my skin crawl.

"No, *I've* got it," I said. And I yanked it away.

I tried to wiggle my way in front of an older man who was just pulling his suitcase down, but the aisle was packed and I couldn't do it. So I had to stand there, inching forward with the crowd, the guy standing way too close and literally breathing down my neck.

As soon as we got off the plane, I practically flew up the jetway.

I ducked into the first ladies' room I saw, happy for the first time in my life to see a long line to the toilets. When it was finally my turn, I stalled in the stall as long as I could. When I came out, I pretended to fuss with my makeup, play with my hair in the mirror.

I told myself that it was probably nothing, that I was over-reacting, that it was just a long flight and I was tired.

When I finally walked out of the ladies' room, he was leaning back against the wall directly across the milling crowd from me. He smiled.

I ignored him, merged with the people following the black and white signs that said BAG CLAIM back then in what was still McCarran International Airport. The wiggly pattern in the mauve, gray and pink carpets made me dizzy. Huge bronze and steel fake palm trees that looked like feather dusters on steroids stretched up everywhere. I caught little strips of myself in the shiny chrome disco ball-like mirrored ceilings.

I ducked into a store, circled back out, walked quickly and purposefully in the opposite direction, ducked into another ladies' room.

When I came out, he was leaning back against the wall again. Smiling at me.

I spotted the nearest telephone booth, thought about dashing inside, calling the police. To say what? A man was smiling at me? And then I pictured the guy with his smiling face pressed against the glass, leaning up against the folding door, trapping me in.

I had to get out. And first I had to pick up my checked trade show suitcase, so I started following BAG CLAIM signs again.

I passed under a WELCOME TO LAS VEGAS sign, scampered down some stairs like I was being chased by a pack of spotted hyenas. Like a nervous twitch, my brain reminded me that a spotted hyena is also called a laughing hyena and a pack of hyenas is called a cackle.

I stood next to another single woman waiting for her luggage, struck up a conversation. Her boyfriend came over to join her, and she turned away from me.

I looked up and the guy was standing on the other side of the luggage carousel. When he smiled this time, I was close enough to see what was wrong. It was the smiling with the mouth and not the eyes that was a dead giveaway.

My suitcase finally clunked its way out and circled around to me. I grabbed it, ran for the taxi line. I waited endlessly, inching toward the front of the line, staring straight ahead.

When it was finally my turn, the taxi driver opened the

trunk, jumped out and put my suitcase in. I held on to my duffle bag and climbed into the taxi. Maybe I thought it would feel safer to hold it in my lap. Maybe I thought I could use it as a weapon if I needed to. Maybe I was being ridiculous.

Just as I was closing the door, the guy came out of nowhere. He pushed his way in beside me, pressed his body close to mine.

"I'll wait for the next one," I said as I reached for the door handle on the other side.

"Where to?" the taxi driver said as he took off.

I tried to imagine a world where I could make a Vegas taxi driver back up in a crowded airport terminal, let me off at the curb while my suitcase magically popped out of the trunk and landed at my feet. Then I tried to think of the name of a hotel on the strip where I wasn't actually staying, but my heart was beating so fast I couldn't think of one.

"The Excalibur," the guy said in a low, soothing voice. "Right, Glenda?"

The two miles to The Excalibur Hotel & Casino probably took ten minutes but felt like ten centuries. I thought about jumping out of the cab while it was moving. Then I thought about jumping out when it stopped and leaving the guy to pay, but that seemed even scarier, like I might owe him something. Plus, I needed my suitcase.

So when the cab pulled up in front of the white castle-like hotel with the orange and blue and red and yellow family-friendly turrets, I handed the driver some money. I waved off the baggage porter when he tried to take my suitcase.

The Excalibur had opened a year or two before. It was the largest hotel in the world, with over 3,000 hotel rooms. It was a mullet of a hotel, bright and cheery like a cartoon on the outside, all dark and sepia and medieval-themed like a bad dream on the inside.

Inside it was the kind of place you wanted a valiant knight

to ride in on his mighty steed and challenge the guy who's harassing you to a jousting match. Or at least a duel.

Sadly, I knew it wasn't going to happen.

The lobby was packed with families and gamblers and couples and groups of friends and everything in between.

When the guy slid in beside me while I was standing in the long line to check in, I looked right at him.

"Why are you doing this?" I said.

"Because I can," he said. His eyes were too shiny, too something.

"Leave me alone," I said. "Or I'll get security."

"One drink," he said.

If you're ever being chased by a spotted hyena and want to make it run away, spread your arms wide and wave them around. Make yourself as big as possible. Look threatening and aggressive. Act like you're about to attack. Shout or scream.

I pretended he was a spotted hyena and that's what I did.

"Security," I yelled louder than I'd ever yelled anything in my whole life.

By the time a less than impressive uniformed security guard made his way over to me, the guy was long gone. But that didn't stop him from ruining trade shows for me. I spent the next couple of days looking over my shoulder. I triple-checked the locks on the door of my hotel room at night, slid the desk chair over and jammed it under the doorknob. Balanced the ironing board and iron on top of the chair, as if he might iron himself to death on the way in if he managed to get that far.

A guy from the company had flown in from another trade show to work the booth with me. I gave him a heads up on what had happened in case the guy showed up again.

"Don't worry," he said. "I'll take care of you." He gave me a playful punch in the shoulder. "You can bunk in with me."

And then he winked.

All by way of saying that when my first ex-husband called me not long after I got home from Las Vegas and I saw my old phone number on my cordless phone's Caller ID like a fuzzy blast from the past, he caught me in a weak moment.

And I answered the phone.

Chapter 23

Today the three of us were wearing terrycloth hoodies and sweatpants with sneakers.

We were also leaning back against a wall across from a door that said FORENSICS.

"I'm still fuming," Harmony said, "about that little email they sent us saying our camo clothes were too distracting."

"Jealousy," I said. "Plain and simple. We were rocking those clothes."

"Exactamundo," Jan said.

"Thanks for weighing in, Fonzie," I said to Jan. "I used to love it when he said *exactamundo*."

"Aww," Harmony said. "*Happy Days*. Maybe we should just get out of here and see if we can find it streaming somewhere."

"I mean," Jan said, "if you've got something to say, have the balls to say it to our faces." We'd known one another for so long it was easy to follow the conversation from camo clothes emails to Fonzie to streaming and back to camo clothes emails again.

An instructor came out of the forensics room, flipped the sign over the door so it said IN CHARACTER. He was maybe late 60s or early 70s, fit, broad shoulders. Light blue long-sleeve button-down shirt rolled up over muscular forearms. Navy chinos.

"That tucked shirt isn't half bad on him," Harmony said.

"The nice ass makes it work," Jan said.

The forensics instructor turned around. He had a full head of salt-and-pepper hair. When he smiled, he even had dimples.

"Come on in," he said.

"Oh, we're coming," I said.

The three of us walked into a classroom-sized room along with two male role players.

It was clearly a drug scene. A dark dingy living room with trash all over the place, plates of half-eaten food crawling with fake insects on every available surface.

A dummy cadaver dressed in a flannel shirt and sweats was passed out in a beat-up armchair. On a side table next to the chair, a beer bottle was lying on its side, a crack pipe nearby. What I could only assume was rainbow-colored fentanyl spilled out of a candy pouch on the floor below the table.

The three of us walked right up to the dummy cadaver, leaned over it.

"Wowzer," Jan said. "For a minute there I thought that was a real dead person."

"Where do you find something like that?" Harmony asked the forensics instructor. "It would be nice to have one on hand for Halloween."

"Dapper Cadaver," the forensics instructor said.

"You're not pulling my leg, are you?" Harmony said.

"They do a good business," the forensics instructor said.

I flipped my hair to catch his attention.

"I was thinking more like AbraCadaver," I said in my flirtiest voice. "You know, where the magic happens?"

The forensics instructor grinned at me, walked away.

"Cadaver magic?" Jan whispered. "Seriously? You might want to consider scheduling some more practice time. Your flirt muscles are starting to atrophy."

The forensics instructor grabbed the scripts, handed them out to the role players. I felt a little jolt of electricity when his hand grazed mine, but played it cool. Or at least coolish.

"'Sit in chair next to crack pipe,'" Harmony read from her script.

She walked over to the arm chair, hoisted the dummy cadaver, sat down with it on her lap and started bouncing it like a baby.

Everybody cracked up. The instructor walked over and took the cadaver from her, jammed it into a closet.

"Thank you," Harmony said. "That dummy's heavier than you'd think it would be."

"They always are," I said.

"'Pass out on sofa,'" Jan read. She eyed the ancient plaid sofa, pulled up her hood for protection, flopped down full length on the sofa.

"'Lie on back on floor,'" I read from my script in a sexy voice.

I caught the instructor's eye. "You don't happen to have a mop and some disinfectant, do you?"

"Floor's cleaner than it looks," he said. "Here, I'll help you down."

"Sure." I reached out and held his hands. "Although I'm still pretty nimble."

"I bet you are," he said.

The forensics instructor helped me get settled on the floor. He leaned over me. I whispered something not entirely original about how we have to stop meeting like this. We both laughed, face-to-face. His breath smelled like Starbucks After Coffee Mints. Either that or the residual part of me that wasn't quite over men wanted to go out for coffee with him.

He left the room. We waited. And waited.

"Maybe that was it," Harmony said. "Do you think we can just put the cadaver back in his chair and take off?"

"I don't think so," Jan said. "And we can't afford another email reprimand."

"I'm not going anywhere," I said.

Jan lifted her head up from the sofa and looked around the room. "What I'm trying to figure out is exactly how we can adapt this scenario for Butt. I think it has potential."

The forensics instructor came back in with a group of students. The students split up and went right for the role players, checking our pulses.

Harmony looked up at her FLETC student. "How 'bout we skip the mouth-to-mouth and just say we did it."

When I answered the phone not long after getting back from Las Vegas knowing it was my first ex-husband, I didn't bother to say hello.

"How did you get my number?" I said instead.

"Perks of being one of the bigwigs," he said. "You listed the agency on your resume under previous employment. When the outfit hiring called to check up on you, somebody made a note of it on your permanent file. My infinitely resourceful secretary tracked down your home phone number for me from there."

I started to say something judgy about confidentiality, flashed on all the personnel files of potential dates Jan had illicitly Xeroxed for me.

"What do you want?" I said.

He laughed. "I missed you, too, Hon."

"Don't ever call me that," I said. "You lost the privilege a long time ago."

"I'm sick," he said.

"Poor baby," I said with all the sarcasm I could muster. "Does woo hurt and have a temperature?"

"Testicular cancer," he said. "I'm scared and alone and I could really use some company."

"Hire a new intern and sleep with her," I said. "Easy fix."

"I deserved that," he said.

"And so much more," I said.

It would have been the perfect line to hang up on, but I missed my chance.

Dead silence stretched between us.

"Is that a maybe?" he finally said.

I burst out laughing.

"Listen," I said. "Sorry you're sick but there's no way in hell I'm going to play nursemaid for you. I'm assuming you're calling because you've burned through another marriage, but what about your kids? You know, the adult ones who despised me?"

"I'm sure they'll get back to me any day now with an invitation to stay at the homes I helped finance," he said. "And you might have been right when you called them spoiled and self-absorbed."

"Say that again," I said. "Louder and with feeling."

"What if I stay at your place?" he said. "Just until my chemo's finished? I'll sleep on the couch. It's terrifying to be alone right now."

I looked around my pathetic little apartment, my second-hand couch, my two hot pink beanbag chairs.

"Ha," I said. "You wouldn't last five minutes here."

"Challenge accepted."

Chapter 24

He was at my door in just over an hour, carrying a bouquet of flowers and a bag of bland but upscale groceries. At his feet was the leather racquetball bag I'd given him for his birthday, just after we got married. It was a really nice bag, and I'd thought about taking it with me when I left. I remembered being filled with rage that I'd had it monogrammed, as if even his initials were his fault.

The fourteen-year age difference between us had never seemed like a big deal to me. He was brash and bold and vibrant and handsome. But now I was stunned to see him. He looked old and frail. The full head of hair he was so proud of had gone flat, his roots were gray, little hunks of hair had already divorced themselves from his head.

"Shit," I said.

"You're telling me," he said.

It was an odd feeling to sit on a secondhand sofa with your first ex-husband, the one who broke your heart, and listen to him tell you that he'd already had an orchidectomy on his affected testicle. I knew that meant that they'd removed his testicle, but it still sounded like something you'd do to orchids.

"You should have asked," I said. "I hated you so much I would have sliced off both of your balls for free."

He laughed so hard tears rolled down his cheeks. "See. That's why I needed to be here."

And then he excused himself, went into my tiny bathroom and puked his guts out.

He came out eventually, patting his freshly washed face dry with my hand towel. When he rubbed the towel across his forehead and over the top of his head, a clump of hair stayed with the towel.

He looked at me like a scared little boy in an old man's body.

"Did you bring a razor?" I said.

He nodded.

I pulled out a rickety kitchen chair from the little table Harmony had rescued from the side of the road on trash pickup day and helped me refinish.

My first ex-husband turned on his razor, handed it over, sat in the chair, hummed a few bars of Madonna's "Crazy About You."

"Don't," I said. It was the song we always used to sing to each other while we slow-danced before sex, musical foreplay really. The line about touch me once and you'll know it's true still gutted me whenever it took me by surprise on the radio.

"Oh, whatever," I said. And I sang the line about how it's all brand new. "It's a good song—just don't take the lyrics personally."

Even as we sang the words we could remember, even as I shaved his perfectly shaped head with his shiny chrome Philips Philishave cordless razor, a part of me knew. That if I was the one who had cancer, he wouldn't be shaving my head. He wouldn't be anywhere near me. And he would have been the last person on the face of the earth I would have thought to call.

When I finished, I handed him his still-buzzing razor.

He turned it off, looked up at me like a puppy waiting for praise.

"Not bad," I said. "If we find you some lollipops, maybe you can be a stunt double for Kojak."

"Who loves ya, baby," he said.

"Don't start," I said.

I yanked open the tiny hallway closet door that always stuck, found my raggedy Cinderella broom.

He stood up, reached out a hand for the broom, started sweeping up his own hair. As he should have.

He only threw up one more time before bed.

"If you have to get testicular cancer," he said when he came out of the bathroom, "my timing wasn't bad. A new antiemetic, an anti-nausea drug called ondansetron, was just approved. Before that, the median number of vomiting episodes with cisplatin-based chemotherapy per day was 10.67."

"Wow," I said. "That point-six-seven of a puke must have felt like a walk in the park." I knew it was a stupid thing to say, but I couldn't think of anything else.

He shrugged. "Anyway, this is only the third or fourth time today, I think. It all starts to blur after a while and you lose count."

"How much longer?" I said.

"Just the rest of the round," he said. "I'm almost there. Five-year progression-free survival rate is 82% and five-year overall survival rate with my prognosis is up over 86%."

I nodded.

"Apparently," he said, "neither my sex life nor my ability to father children will be affected."

"Like I care," I said.

He grinned. "They offered me the option of a prosthetic testicle, but I don't think I'm quite that vain."

"Of course you are," I said.

"About one in fifty people will get a second new testicular cancer in their remaining testicle," he said.

"You always land on your feet," I said. "You'll be fine. It's your next wife I worry about."

When I woke up the following morning, he was lying on the floor next to the couch, the couch cushions spread out like a mattress, a throw pillow under his head and a ratty old blanket pulled over him.

He stayed in my crappy apartment for an entire month, although he did have his secretary drop off a nice new air mattress and bedding. I used up all my sick time, then called my boss and said I was helping a sick relative and could I work from home for a couple of weeks. Long before working remote was a thing, that's what I did.

Jan would show up at my house with a fat manilla envelope, ring the bell to my apartment. Sometimes when I opened the door, I'd have a flash of déjà vu, like my life had come full circle. I was a pregnant high schooler again and Jan was dropping off my homework.

"Thanks," I'd say when I opened my door. "Even though I know you just offered to do this so you could sneak in a quick trip to Marshalls."

Jan was Executive Director of Human Resources now, so the truth was she could walk out the door anytime she wanted to. I was just trying to make her laugh.

Jan wouldn't even smile. She'd just hand me the envelope.

"At least come in for a second and catch me up on the company gossip," I said one day.

"No," she said. "And let me voice my disapproval one more time. When is that scumbag in there leaving?"

I stepped into the hallway, pulled the door closed behind me.

"It's just for a little while," I said. "He'd do it for me."

Jan rolled her eyes. "Not in your wildest fantasy is that true. And you freaking know it."

"Love you, too," I said.

While my first ex-husband sat in his chemo chair for hours, I sat in a chair next to him. Nurses came in and out while brightly colored liquids pumped into his IV. Once something happened to his IV and his hand swelled and burned for days.

I dug up the rectangular, original Sony Walkman I'd had since college, and he found some old mixtapes I'd made for him in the glove compartment of his car. My Walkman had a second jack so that two people could plug in and listen at once, but instead I'd just put in a cassette and twist my old headphones so we could each listen with one.

I could read the waves of anxiety and depression on his face, and when they got really bad, I'd loop the headphones over his head so he could listen with both ears for a while. Sometimes he'd reach out to hold my hand and I'd let him.

His worst symptoms came the day after chemo. Three or four days later, he'd still be tired and weak and nauseous, but he'd be better. We'd make soup together, something we never did once when we were married, chopping up garlic and onions and potatoes and squash and carrots and leeks and apples, adding beans and corn and peas.

His assistant dropped off a boombox and some cassettes. So we'd chop vegetables and sing away to the soundtrack from *The Big Chill*. We'd blast out "My Girl" and "Good Lovin'" and "Joy to the World."

When "A Whiter Shade of Pale" came on, sometimes we'd put the knives down and slow dance around my tiny kitchen, singing softly to each other. We both loved the Bach-like organ parts, the inscrutable, nonsensical lyrics, the mesmerizing dreamy mournful mood of the song.

And we laughed. And we talked and talked, crushing oyster crackers and saltines into our soup. The way we used to talk for hours way back in the beginning, but without all the drama. We were happier, more tender. Even when he was hurting, he had this way of making you feel like you were the most interesting person in the world.

It was the perfect bubble.

He proposed to me from the passenger seat of my car after his final chemo session, before the worst of his symptoms started to kick in.

"Don't be ridiculous," I said.

"Listen," he said. "I love you. I'm truly and deeply sorry I hurt you. It's not like I even enjoy my own infidelity that much. I'm wracked with guilt the whole time. I might be reenacting my father's serial cheating on my mother. Or it's frozen childhood trauma and I'm trying to feel something. It's possible I'm waiting for something to go wrong, so I betray before I get betrayed."

"Somebody's had some therapy," I said.

The truth was, he'd never been a gaslighter. He never undermined my reality by insisting that he wasn't screwing around on me. He never made me feel like I was losing my mind. Somebody told me, he owned up to it right away, and he left me for her.

"Admit it," he said. "This last month has been great. Even with the chemo. Even in your shitty little apartment."

I looked at him. Maybe age and wisdom and all the mistakes you've ever made changed everything. Maybe when it came to marriage and me, the third time really was a charm.

"If you give me a second chance," he said, "I won't let you down."

Chapter 25

It took three days to get a marriage license in Massachusetts. We stayed in my apartment while we waited and he vomited. On the fourth day, we met a justice of the peace on a warm early fall weekday morning on a quiet corner of the beach in Marshbury and she married us.

I wore a white slip-like sundress from my closet. He wore the clothes he'd shown up at my apartment in, a white button-down shirt untucked over black pants. We picked some wild blue chicory flowers by the side of the road on the way to the beach for my bouquet. We left our flip-flops at the top of the beach and walked barefoot in the sand. His head was freshly shaved for the occasion, and my still-brown hair was loose and free and wild.

Massachusetts doesn't require witnesses to be present at wedding ceremonies, so we grabbed two people walking by to take a photo with the Nikon Smiletaker camera we'd bought as a wedding present to each other. I threw my bouquet over my shoulder to the ocean.

Afterward, we had lunch outside at a sweet little café overlooking Marshbury Harbor. Then I packed two suitcases and we moved to his place.

I'd lived there with him when we were married the first time, but it wasn't the kind of place you ever really got used to. It was a stunning, fully restored Beacon Hill townhome he'd inherited from his parents.

Built in 1855, it was set back from the street, with black shutters and window boxes and arched windows on a tall red brick facade. Granite steps flanked by custom wrought iron railings led to a huge double door topped with transom windows and a spectacular arch.

It had a basement, five bedrooms, six fireplaces, two parking spots, a fully renovated kitchen. You were still allowed to call it a master suite back then, and it had a spectacular one.

Every inch of the townhouse was steeped in history and dark wood accents. It was just a short walk to the Public Garden and Boston Common and a host of cozy restaurants, bakeries, pubs.

I threw my suitcase on the bed and he pulled me in for a kiss. His whole body still had that chemo smell but it was fading away.

"Let's go back to my place," I said.

He laughed.

"I mean it," I said. "I feel like we've returned to the scene of the crime of our first marriage. Plus this house is way too bling-bling. Maybe you should sell it and buy eight normal houses and give seven of them away."

He laughed again. We stayed. But I kept my job, reverse-commuting against the traffic from Boston to work in an office park in the middle of the South Shore bedroom suburbs. He went back to work at his ad agency, tried to get me to come aboard. I stayed where I was, managed to snag a promotion to Vice President of Marketing that ensured I'd never have to attend another trade show.

And for a while, things were good. Really good. He got healthy and strong and smelled like himself again.

We cooked dinner together on weekends. He picked up takeout during the week because I was the one with the long commute. Sometimes he'd head south after work and we'd sleep in the Plymouth lake house for the night, because even though that meant a tough commute for him the next morning, it was a much shorter one for me.

We stayed in bed on Sundays, making love and drinking coffee and trading fat sections of *The Boston Sunday Globe*. When we finally got up, we took a long walk and grabbed something to eat when a restaurant called out to us.

We had a belated honeymoon in Acapulco, which was the place to go for a beach getaway in the '90s. Tourism was booming in Australia on the coattails of *Crocodile Dundee*, so we took an amazing trip to see the Outback, too. We also stayed in a trendy Chilean hotel in the Atacama Desert, which was as red as I'd imagined the planet Mars.

And then one night after dinner he had to run back to work to finish something he'd forgotten for a pitch he was spearheading for a prospective client the next morning.

"Take a ride with me," he said. "I won't be long."

"No thanks," I said. "I've got a good book calling my name."

Not long after he walked out the door, the phone rang.

The little tan Cidco Caller ID box sitting beside the phone displayed his work number and the name of the agency.

I picked up the phone and said, "Wow, that was fast."

And someone hung up.

I knew instantly. When he walked into the living room two hours and four minutes later, I'd skipped the book for a glass of wine and was watching the end of *Splendor in the Grass* on the classic movie channel.

"Though nothing can bring back the hour/" I said, reciting the Wordsworth poem along with Natalie Wood's disembodied voice on the TV. "Of splendor in the grass, glory in the flower/ We will grieve not . . . .."

"Good memory, Hon," he said from the other side of the cavernous room. In one hand he carried the racquetball bag I'd given him, probably filled with decoy work papers he didn't really need.

"Apparently not good enough," I said.

I looked over at him as the movie credits rolled. "You piece of shit."

He didn't try to deny it. Instead he looked at me with sad eyes. And then cliché that he was, he actually said, "It's not you, it's me."

Short story even shorter, I grabbed the keys off the kitchen counter and moved into the Plymouth lake getaway. This time around, Harmony helped me find a good divorce lawyer. Even though this marriage to each other hadn't even lasted as long as the first one, I got the lake house in the settlement.

"All discarded lovers should be given a second chance," Mae West once said, "but with someone else."

If "Crazy About You" was the theme song for the beginning of my relationship with my first ex-husband, who also became my third ex-husband, then Bonnie Tyler's "Total Eclipse of the Heart" marked the end of us.

More days than not, winding through the backroads of Plymouth on my way to or from work, I blasted out the cassette in my car. I'd sing the lines about how once upon a time I was falling in love and now I'm only falling apart as loudly as I could sing them.

Then I'd roll down the windows and yell, "I am never going there again," to the sugar maples and the pine trees. And once to a sweet female deer that was just trying to safely cross the street and get on with her life.

It was a lovely house with a peaceful view of the lake, but once I officially owned it, I sold it and bought a tiny renovated cottage a stone's throw from a Marshbury beach.

On a good day I could smell the salt air.

Chapter 26

Jan, Harmony and I clumped together in an incredibly realistic mock airport terminal. FLETC instructors in polos with TSA insignias and FLETC students and role players milled around everywhere.

All the airport things were visible. A row of ticketing and baggage check stations, security checkpoints, travel document checker stands, passenger waiting areas.

Plus luggage X-ray machines, walk-through metal detector screeners, advance imaging screeners, curtained-off physical search sections, baggage carousels, a lost baggage claim area.

Long luggage conveyor belts connected the various sections to one another.

We'd been assigned to a group of role players near the luggage screening section. For the occasion, the three of us wore long-sleeve tunic-length T-shirts over sweatpants, plus slip-on sneakers over athletic socks.

"At least we remembered to read the email alert about this exercise," Jan said. "It would be such a hassle to have to keep tying and untying our sneakers."

"And my germaphobe feet don't even want to think about

walking on these floors without a pair of thick socks," Harmony said.

A mixed bag of hot instructors from assorted federal agencies walked by. The three of us checked them out until the last set of broad shoulders disappeared from sight.

Jan sighed. "I'm just glad we found that online role player message board so we know those TSA students get all up in your business on the physical searches."

"I've got three layers of full body shapewear on," I said. "If the overachievers get grabby, I won't feel a thing. I don't mind a good pat down now and then, but my guess is they don't let you choose your own TSA agent."

"I thought I threw out all my Spanx years ago," Harmony said. "But I found a couple of thigh-length numbers. I just hope I don't have to try to smuggle anything through security. My poker face wouldn't fool a polecat on a casino cruise."

"I'm all set in the shapewear department, too," Jan said. "And I layered in a few surprises."

"Oh, please," I said, "not the whoopie cushion. It's so embarrassing when you break that out."

"Boy mom," Jan said. "What can I say."

Our TSA instructor approached our group of role players. She escorted us over to a row of carry-on bags in front of a wall. We waited while she pulled a tag off a bag, read the tag. She eyed the role players, handed a carry-on to Jan.

"Tell me if I'm getting warm," Jan said, "but we're not allowed to open our carry-ons to see what we're taking through, right?"

"Bingo," the TSA instructor said.

Once all the role players had carry-ons, the instructor brought us over to a wardrobe rack filled with sweaters and jackets. Next to it were shelves holding everything from filled quart-size baggies to wallets and digital devices and coolers and picnic baskets and pet carriers and jewelry.

"So the female instructor gets wardrobe duty?" I whispered. "Nothing sexist there."

"Maybe she picked it," Harmony said, "so she can borrow the occasional outfit. You know, like the mock airport version of Rent the Runway?"

We each grabbed a jacket, a baggie, a few more things. All three of us reached for pieces of jewelry.

I looped an ugly necklace over my head. "If we knew we were going to have to accessorize, it would have been nice to be able to bring our own."

"Agreed," Jan said. "I purged again before I moved down here, but I still don't wear half the things in my closet."

We took off our slip-on sneakers and placed them in a gray plastic bin. We folded our jackets neatly and put them in another bin, added our ugly jewelry.

Jan held up her quart-size baggie and examined the contents. "I've been meaning to try this new coconut dental floss. Do you think anyone would notice if I gave myself a five-finger discount?"

"Honey," Harmony said, "if you think coconut dental floss is worth going to federal prison for, I say go for it."

"It might be," I said. "I hear it gets your teeth crazy clean."

Harmony went first. She pushed her plastic bins toward the rubber-toothed entrance of the X-ray machine. Lifted her carry-on up on the conveyor belt. Put a wicker picnic basket down behind that.

She walked over to the metal detector screener and placed her sock-covered feet on the footprints, waited for a TSA student to motion her in. She walked through like nothing at all.

"Yes!" Harmony said with a two-handed fist pump.

She strutted proudly to the other side of the conveyor belt so she could collect her things. Another TSA student behind the conveyor belt held out a gloved hand to stop her.

"Ma'am," the TSA student said. "I'm going to ask you to stand right there and not touch your items."

"Was it my poker face that gave me away?" Harmony said.

Watching Harmony for sudden moves, the TSA student slowly opened the picnic basket, rummaged around inside. Took out a rubber chicken, laid it on the conveyor belt.

The TSA student reached inside the rubber chicken and pulled out a handgun.

Harmony gasped. "It's not mine. I swear it's not mine. Somebody must have planted it."

Jan and I looked at each other, rolled our eyes.

It was Jan's turn to go next. She pushed her plastic bins toward the X-ray machine. Lifted her carry-on up on the conveyor belt.

Jan placed her sock-covered feet on the footprints, waited for a TSA student to motion her into the metal detector screener.

A red light flashed immediately, accompanied by the single-pitch sound of an alarm.

The TSA student motioned Jan to step out and try again. She did. The light flashed red and the alarm sounded.

Another TSA student holding a hand scanner came over.

"Step forward please," the TSA student said.

"Oh, please no," Jan said. "Not the hand scanner."

Jan turned. She leaped out of the screening machine, ran a few big steps in our direction. She hesitated, stopped.

Jan reached into her sweatpants, pulled a metallic padded bicycle seat cover out of her crotch. Holding the seat cover in one hand, she turned around again.

She lifted both arms over her head to surrender.

"*What* were you thinking?" Harmony said to Jan.

Jan shrugged. "A little extra padding seemed like a good idea in case I got hand-searched. I mean, none of these rookies have a good sense of the geography when they're getting all touchy feely. I simply neglected to factor in that a metallic bicycle seat cover involved actual metal."

"You win or you learn," I said.

"No kidding," Jan said. "And these are the hard skills we're going to need as supersheroes."

"Metal bicycle seat cover skills?" Harmony said.

The TSA instructor gestured to me that it was my turn.

I pushed my plastic bins toward the X-ray machine. Harmony started to lift my carry-on up on the conveyor belt for me.

The TSA instructor waved Harmony off. Harmony and Jan stepped just out of the way. I hoisted my own carry-on.

I walked over and placed my sock-covered feet on the footprints, waited for a TSA student to motion me into the metal detector screener.

A red light flashed immediately and the alarm went off.

"Here we go again," I heard Jan say. "I wonder what she put down there."

"In the future, Honey," I could hear Harmony saying way too loudly to Jan. "Just order a camel-toe pad online. Comfy as all get out, and believe you me, nobody's getting near your nethers through that baby. I'll text you a link."

Back at the metal detector, I whispered something to the TSA student.

"Ma'am," the TSA student said. "You're going to have to speak up, ma'am."

"I said," I yelled, "I have titanium hips. Two of them!"

Chapter 27

Two TSA students escorted me to a square curtained-off area.

A TV-like monitor inside caught my eye immediately. Mostly because it showed Jan and Harmony standing on their tiptoes, looking around anxiously for any sign of me.

"Friends of yours?" one of the TSA students said.

"Time will tell," I said. "So, what, you have cameras everywhere?"

"Pretty much," the other TSA student said.

"Don't you think you should post signs warning us?" I said. "I mean, what if we were doing something we didn't want you to see?"

"That's kind of the point, ma'am," the first student said.

"I can't believe they just took Glenda," Harmony was saying on the monitor. "Anything could be happening."

"She's all alone," Jan said. "Without any witnesses. True superheroes would never let that happen."

"Wow," I said. "The sound quality is surprisingly good."

"Right?" one of the students said. "You wouldn't believe what we pick up in here."

Across from where Harmony and Jan were standing, a low

conveyor belt filled with luggage was inching slowly around the room in the direction of a baggage carousel.

Harmony pointed past the carousel and almost directly at me. "I'm pretty sure that's the physical search area over there," she said.

"You mean the handy dandy area," Jan said.

They both shuddered at the thought.

"I, for one, resent the implications," one of the TSA students said.

"My sensibilities are beyond offended," the other one said.

We watched Harmony and Jan cross their arms, tap their feet, pace.

"I apologize for my friends," I said. "As long as you don't make me take off my clothes and show you my surgical scars."

"*Shh*," one of the TSA students said. "They're talking again."

"This is taking way too long," Jan was saying.

"They're probably just having a hard time feeling for contraband through three layers of shapewear," Harmony said.

"They better not be asking her to take off her clothes and show her surgical scars," Jan said.

"Dude," one of the TSA students said. "Do you always think the same things at the same time?"

"Pretty much," I said.

"That would be inexcusably demeaning," Jan was saying. "As well as true discrimination against joint replacement recipients everywhere."

"Lighten up, lady," the other TSA student said to the monitor.

"Not to mention time consuming," Harmony was saying. "Do you have any idea how long it would take to remove three layers of shapewear?"

We watched Harmony and Jan work their way up to the long conveyor belt filled with luggage.

They looked to the right. An instructor was talking to a group of role players.

They looked to the left. Another instructor was talking to a group of students.

"The only way out is through," Harmony said. "I love that saying."

"It's a poem," Jan said. "Robert Frost. Actually, the line was 'the best way out is always through.'"

"Actually, Honey," Harmony said, "who cares? We need to stay focused on saving Glenda."

"What can I say?" I smiled at the TSA students in our little curtained-off area. "They love me, they really love me."

We watched Jan and Harmony step closer to the conveyor belt.

"Okay," Jan said, "so we're going to take just enough luggage off so we can crawl over the conveyor belt and surreptitiously make our way to the private screening place."

"What do we say if anybody asks what we're surreptitiously doing?" Harmony said.

"We just tell them we're role players doing a drill," Jan said. "I mean, there's so much going on here at once, it's impossible to tell what's real and what isn't."

"Good point," Harmony said. "Okay, what's the name of our drill? All the drills have names."

"How about the 'Hurry Up You're Driving Me Nuts' drill?" Jan said.

"That'll work," Harmony said.

Back in the physical search area, one of the students opened a bag of pretzels, offered it around.

We munched away, eyes glued to the monitor, like we were eating popcorn at a movie.

Jan looked over her shoulder both ways, reached out. She struggled to pull a big suitcase off the conveyor belt. By the time she got it onto the floor beside her, the conveyor belt had moved and she was fully blocked by the suitcases again.

Harmony was already struggling with another big suitcase. Jan jumped in to help her. When they eventually managed to wrestle that one to the floor, the gap in the suitcases was gone again.

They repeated this again and again. Each time they succeeded in getting the suitcase off the conveyor belt, the gap in the line of suitcases disappeared before they could climb over the conveyor belt.

"I think I've seen this before," one of the students said. "Damn, what show was that?"

"*I Love Lucy*," I said. "Once you get to a certain age, your whole life is one big *I Love Lucy* episode if you have the right friends."

Harmony and Jan jogged a few steps to chase the most recent suitcase gap. An instructor and some students glanced over at them. My friends went into full wide-eyed innocent mode, walked casually back to where they'd been.

"We're just going to have to be more decisive," Jan said. "You know, pick up the pace. Grab, yank, go. Grab, yank, go. Come on, say it with me."

"Either that," Harmony said, "or we could slow this belt thingie down. I think it's that little red button right over there."

Harmony crossed behind Jan, took a few steps in the direction that the conveyor belt was moving. She leaned over to get to the control button tucked under the conveyor belt.

"Grab, yank, go," Jan said. "Grab, yank, go. Grab, yank, go."

Jan grabbed a suitcase, yanked, hurled it behind her. She began climbing over the conveyor belt.

At the exact same moment, Harmony hit the button.

The conveyor belt sped up with Jan on it.

"Epic," one of the students said.

"It's like the perfect mix of headass and Gucci," the other one said.

"Where are they?" I said. Harmony and Jan had completely disappeared from the monitor. I wasn't sure if I was more worried about my friends or more afraid I might miss something.

One of the TSA students pushed a button, then another. The other student grabbed the remote from the first one.

They kept pushing buttons on the remote, trying to find the right camera to pick up Jan and Harmony again.

"Get me off this thing," Jan was saying when we finally found her on the monitor again. Harmony came into view, grabbed Jan's hand.

They both yanked. Harmony ended up squished in beside Jan on the conveyor belt.

The conveyor belt was really moving now.

"Oh, no," I said. "We're going to lose them again."

"Not to worry," a student said. "I'm pretty sure this is the camera that tracks the belt."

Sure enough, the camera stayed with them.

"Your 'grab, yank, go' technique could use a little refinement," Harmony said.

"You were supposed to slow it down, not speed it up," Jan said.

"The print on those switches is way too small," Harmony said.

"Ageism," I said. "Plain and simple. Maybe I could put in a request for bigger fonts while you've got me here?"

"Don't push your luck," one of the students said.

Jan and Harmony each hugged a big suitcase as they looped through the mock airport on the conveyor belt.

People glanced over at them as they passed, assumed it was just another role-playing exercise.

"This is actually kind of fun," Jan said.

"Once you get past the sheer terror," Harmony said.

Ahead of them the conveyor belt climbed steeply, circling

around and around and around toward the high ceiling, then bumping the luggage down again.

"Thoughts?" Jan said.

"Prayers might be more relevant," Harmony said.

In the nick of time, their conveyor belt came to a junction and veered off sharply in another direction.

"What a rush," Jan said. "So refreshing. Almost like a quick trip to Disney World."

"Glenda," Harmony said. "We need to stay focused on Glenda. And getting off this thing."

One of the TSA students crumbled the empty pretzel bag into a ball, arced it into a wastebasket.

"Nice shot," I said.

"Come on," the other student said. "Let's finish this up and get back on the floor before some idiot writes us up."

I stepped out of the private screening area, fluffed my hair.

With perfect timing, a curve in the conveyor belt sent Jan and Harmony heading right for the screening area.

"Glenda," they yelled. "Over here."

Instead of yanking them off when they came by, I grabbed their hands and seat-hopped on. Harmony and Jan shoved some suitcases over to make room for me on the conveyor belt.

Just in case anybody was watching the cameras, I twisted my wrist back and forth in a queenlike wave.

"Are you okay, Honey?" Harmony said.

"They didn't do anything to impact your positive self-image, did they?" Jan said.

"No," I said. "They were great. We just hung out, watched some TV, talked titanium for a while."

The conveyor belt took a turn to the left and we all leaned with it.

"It was a little bit triggering though," I said. "I met a blind date on the beach once and the guy brought his metal detector."

Jan and Harmony patted me on the back.

"We were on our way to rescue you," Harmony said. "We just found ourselves taking a teensy little detour."

"Like you always say," Jan said, "life has a way of getting all lifey on you."

"I never doubted for a moment you'd be there if I needed you," I said. "Eventually."

"Supersheroes that we almost are," Jan said.

When we looked over, we saw our TSA instructor on her phone. Looking right at us and glaring.

Dash sat behind a massive desk wearing a long-sleeve shirt with an official FLETC insignia. He looked really handsome. And really mad.

Harmony, Jan and I sat in chairs across from him as if we'd been called to the principal's office. Which we kind of had.

Dash gave us a stern look across his desk.

"We're sorry," Harmony said.

"So sorry," Jan said.

"I barely even got on it," I said.

"Nice," Jan said. "Throw us under the conveyor belt. I mean, we were only trying to rescue you."

All together, the three of us crossed our arms, leaned back in our chairs.

Still in synch, we crossed our legs. Then crossed them the other way.

"Listen," Dash said. "I'm the one who put in a good word for you, remember? My reputation is at stake here."

"Really?" we all said at once.

"Nah," Dash said. "Just stay out of trouble from now on, okay?"

"So, so difficult," Jan said.

"But not impossible," Harmony said.

"We promise they won't do it again," I said.

"And if your mother comes to visit you at the townhouse," Jan said, "we even promise we won't try to corrupt her."

"Actually," Dash said, "the three of you might be a good influence on her. My mom could use some more fun in her life."

Chapter 28

Back when Jan's three sons were teenagers, she woke up in the middle of the night when her husband rolled into her back.

"Don't even think about it," she said.

Then she heard a gurgling, gasping sound behind her, a sound she'd describe so many times that I'd start to think I'd heard it, too.

Jan turned over in his direction. Even in the dark she could tell he was in serious trouble.

She grabbed his shoulder and shook. "What?" she said. "What is it?"

He snorted once and went silent.

She sat up in bed, turned on the light. "Call 911," she yelled to her sons.

Then, because they were sleeping teenagers, she grabbed the bedside phone and called 911 herself.

A 911 operator's calm voice talked Jan through checking for breathing and a pulse. She was fairly sure her husband didn't have either.

By then her sons had come into the bedroom in their underwear, rubbing their eyes, looking scared. Jan relayed the instructions from the 911 operator as her sons lifted their dad with the bottom sheet and lowered him to the floor.

Her oldest son began compressions.

They'd all had CPR training, Jan at work and the boys at school. Up until that moment, they hadn't realized they'd all been trained to do CPR to the beat of the classic disco song "Staying Alive."

So that's what they did. For twelve long minutes that felt like an eternity, they all sang "Staying Alive." Their voices cracked and became hoarse. Swallowed tears soothed their scratchy throats. They took turns counting. Thirty compressions, two breaths, thirty compressions, two breaths. When their arms got tired, they switched off.

"We got it, Mom," her oldest son said when Jan moved in to take a turn.

She ignored him. "Stay alive, goddammit," she yelled as she pressed and pressed and pressed. She felt a rib crack under her hands, possibly another.

Two paramedics arrived and took over the CPR. A blur of defibrillator-CPR-defibrillator-IV-oxygen mask-CPR-stretcher and ambulance followed.

Jan rode in the ambulance while her oldest son followed with his brothers. The paramedics took turns performing CPR the whole way.

Not long after they arrived at the hospital, Jan's husband was pronounced dead of sudden cardiac arrest.

"I think he was dead the whole time," Jan would say later. "But we were all trying so hard to change the story. In the movies, it seems like CPR gives you maybe a 75% success rate. In real life and real death, not so much. It's like 6%."

But first was shock and disbelief, a bad dream she couldn't wake up from. The house filled with casseroles, family flew in for the funeral. Harmony and I picked people up at Logan Express and the Hingham ferry, drove them to the house or their hotel. We sat with Jan when she needed it. Stayed out of her way when she needed that.

"But he'd just had a check-up," Jan said. "He was fine. I mean, he had a bit of a Dad gut and he needed to drop a few pounds, but he didn't have any underlying conditions. His kidneys and liver were even healthy enough to donate."

"You did everything you could, Honey," Harmony said. "The boys did, too."

"I'm just trying to be there for them," Jan would say.

"We're just trying to be there for her," the boys would say when Harmony or I dropped off some takeout or a bag of groceries or just stopped by to check up on them all.

Later we listened to Jan's heartbreaking story of going through the things in his closet with her sons and how they'd wanted to keep them all.

I knew he was a nice guy, but when he was gone I realized that even though I'd known him for years, I hadn't spent much time with him. We weren't really couples friends. We didn't do group holiday meals or vacation together with our significant or insignificant others. We went out to dinner a few times over the years, but it always involved the three of us sneaking off to the ladies room at some point to talk amongst ourselves while the guys shook their heads and said *there they go again*.

Our friendship was many things, but maybe most of all it was a vacation from the rest of our lives.

Jan stayed numb for a long time. It was just too big a loss to process. She cycled through Elisabeth Kübler-Ross's five stages of grief—denial, anger, bargaining, depression, and acceptance—not in a straight path but in a tangled maze of ups and downs, bad days and not quite so bad days.

Then she circled around the grief board again and landed squarely on pissed off.

"I can't believe," she'd say, "he left me with three teenage boys to raise by myself."

"I don't think he did it on purpose," I'd say.

"You don't know that," she'd say.

Her sons were going through loss and grief in their own ways, which involved lots of sullen moping around and copious amounts of acting out. She grounded them, took away their cars and phones, curled up in the family room and watched their dad's favorite movies and cried with them. They planted a tree in the yard for him, rented a boat and sprinkled his ashes in the ocean.

Jan ordered four identical silver cremation pendants and saved just enough of his ashes to split four ways and fill them. She left them wrapped under the Christmas tree with gift tags from Santa. They all cried when they opened them. Then they wore them while they watched *Home Alone* together, like they always did on Christmas Day, and cried and cried some more.

And eventually all three of Jan's sons were off to college and beyond, out of the nest at least temporarily. And that's when we started worrying about her.

"You don't have to date," Harmony said, "but you need to get out, Honey."

"I have my work," Jan said. "I have my friends."

"Your work sucks," I said. "And Harmony and I can only take you so far."

We tried to talk her into joining a grief group. She refused, but signed up for a painting class instead.

"I'll go once," Jan said. "But if they turn out to be a bunch of whiners, I'm out."

Chapter 29

It took us a while to notice. Harmony was busy expanding her personal business empire and going to her kids' gymnastics meets and hockey games. I'd leapfrogged my way from Vice President of Marketing to Senior Vice President of Marketing, and the work never ended. Plus I was dating a guy that I thought I might just be optimistic enough to let myself fall in love with.

Whenever I'd grab a quick coffee in the company cafeteria with Jan, she'd casually mention something she'd just done with a woman in her painting class. A garden tour, a visit to a museum, an open-air painting session in a nearby park. All very non-Jan things.

One night, while I was driving around with Harmony to water office plants for old times' sake, she said she'd been hearing about the woman, too.

"Jan told me she's awesome and so much fun," Harmony said as she trimmed back some errant growth on a green garden wall. "And they're part of a group that paints graffiti and murals on buildings for free. Something about bringing joy to the community."

"Jan?" I said as I dumped water on a Boston fern. "Our Jan?"

"I'm a teensy bit crushed she didn't invite us," Harmony said. "To any of them."

"I know, right?" I picked up some yellow leaves that had fallen from a Ficus tree. "*We're* awesome. *We're* fun."

"I think we might be losing her, Honey," Harmony said.

"Never," I said. "We just have to strategize. We'll pull her new friend into the fold. Once Jan sees her standing next to us, she'll know we're the true awesome ones. And if that doesn't work, then we can all hang out together."

We tried. Hard. We invited Jan for coffee and told her to bring her new friend so we could meet her. Repeatedly.

She made up multiple excuses. Then she ignored us. Then she said yes.

And she showed up alone.

"Where is she?" I said before she even sat down.

Jan shrugged. "Something came up at the last minute."

"Stick out your tongue, Honey," Harmony said. "So I can see if you're lying."

Jan laughed. "My mother used to say that when I was little. I was so afraid the black mark on my tongue would show that I'd always keep my mouth closed and mumble whenever I lied. Hindsight 20/20, it was a fairly obvious tell."

"Don't try to change the subject," I said. "Why don't you want us to meet her?"

We waited while the server poured our coffee, took our first sips.

Jan clunked her mug down on the table. "Don't be ridiculous. Pull out your phones and let's get a date on the calendar for dinner."

About a week later, we met at a trendy charming restaurant a few towns over.

Jan's new friend was as charming as the restaurant.

"Let's order sweet potato fries for the table," she said. "And just keep ordering them with different dipping sauces."

So that's what we did. No salads. No entrees. Just an explosion of sweet potato fries.

Jan's new friend was a portrait photographer and she entertained us with stories about her crazy clients.

"The dogs are the easiest," she said. "And the pot belly pigs are the most photogenic."

She was funny and kind. And pretty in a soft, laid-back, not-trying-too-hard kind of way. She was also way younger than us, by at least a decade, maybe a decade and a half.

When Harmony and I got up to go to the ladies' room at the same time, Jan didn't even make a crack. She and her new friend just leaned over the latest batch of sweet potato fries and kept talking.

"Shit," I said as Harmony and I washed our hands at the sink. "I'd pick her over us in a heartbeat, too."

"Don't you dare talk about us like that, Honey," Harmony said. "We have shared history. And huge deposits in Jan's emotional bank account."

"She's so young," I said. "Remember young?"

"It's all one big tired ol' blur." Harmony's eyes crinkled at the corners when she smiled. "Going back to that age would be about as much fun as riding a muskrat ass-backward through a prickly pear forest."

"But you don't know what you don't know back then," I said. "You still think anything can happen. And her eyes are so wide open. Physically I mean, not metaphorically. The exact opposite of ours."

"We just have to hang on tight and not let go," Harmony said.

"Agreed," I said. "That's our Jan plan."

We kept trying. Jan kept drifting away from us.

Finally Harmony and I descended on Jan unannounced for a friendship intervention.

Once we had her sitting down at her kitchen table, I opened my printed-out script first.

"Jan," I read. "I love you. I've stood by you through thick and thin, year after year after year, and you've done the same for me. While I fully support you having other friends, I fear you're heading down a path that will leave Harmony and me alone and bereft."

I nodded at Harmony. She opened her script. "Jan," she read. "I love you to forever and back. And I know deep down in your heart you love me, too. But I want you to put that heart back on your sleeve where it belongs and be our old friend Jan again."

Jan crossed her arms over her chest and tilted side to side like she was rocking a baby.

"Ohmigod," I said. "Are you dying on us?"

"I'm fine." Jan smiled. "Better than fine. I just don't know how to do this. I mean, I never thought I'd be here. It's all new. I've never even thought about a woman this way before. Well, maybe a little incident back in junior high, but I think we were mostly getting in some practice for boys."

"Wait, what?" I said.

I was pretty sure I could feel my jaw drop. Maybe Harmony's, too.

"That's it?" Harmony said. "That's it? Oh, Honey. We don't care who you sleep with—"

"We just care who you friend with," I said.

Jan's cheeks were pink when she grinned at us.

"I love you meeces to pieces," she said. "I guess I was afraid it would change things."

"Like, what, we wouldn't want to be alone in the ladies' room with you?" Harmony said.

Jan shrugged. "She makes me happy. I think it's her, not her gender. I think I'd want to be with her whatever she was. I was so uptight—I think I thought lesbians were these mystical, otherworldly creatures, and I'd never even heard the term pansexual."

Harmony pulled out her phone to google it.

"She's just so relaxed about the whole thing," Jan said. "She thinks sexuality is a fluid continuum and it's all about connection. And she doesn't like labels, all the straight vs. gay vs. bisexual vs. curious stuff. She says she identifies as all of the above."

"Wow," I said. "You are right on trend. Late-blooming lesbianism is a thing, with more and more women who have previously been in long-term heterosexual relationships moving into same-sex relationships. If you think about it, it's a brilliant adaptation. Single women massively outnumber single men at our age, and most of the straight men who are still available are either dating younger women or aren't worth it. Or both."

"What's that old saying," Harmony said, "about a woman without a man is like a fish without a bicycle?"

"Don't ruin it for me, you guys," Jan said. "Just let me think it's special."

And for a couple of years, it was. Two of Jan's sons weren't the least bit rattled by their mom's new relationship, and the third one got used to it. Even after they were married, Jan hung out with Harmony and me about as often as she did before.

And then Jan's wife wanted to have a baby. And Jan was out.

"I can't do it," Jan said to Harmony and me as we sat out on the cozy little back deck at my cottage. "I love being a mother. But I can't go through all that again. I'm just starting to figure out who I am post-mom, you know?"

"I get it," Harmony said. "One more year and both of mine are off my credit cards. Then I just have to figure out how to take them off my worry list."

"But," I said, "we could have lunch with the kids together,

now that Kimberly is letting me take Delaney to childcare. That wife of yours is going to have to pop that baby out fast though, because Delaney only has two more years before she's in school fulltime."

"I love how your eyes light up when you say their names, Honey," Harmony said.

"It's such a gift," I said. "I can't believe I got this lucky."

"Perfect," Jan said. "And then everyone can think we're both grandmothers."

"I'm an exceptionally young and good-looking grand-mother," I said. "But yeah, that could be awkward. Although think about it, guys have babies at 80 like it's nothing at all."

Jan shook her head. "She said she'll do all the baby stuff herself. Right. I take one look at the kid and I'm up to my elbows in dirty diapers again. I'd never be able to compart-mentalize like that."

"So what are you going to do?" I said.

"Split up," Jan said. "I know her—she's a force. She'll move on to someone who wants to co-parent before the divorce papers are dry. But at this stage of my life, I'd rather be alone than stuck in a life that isn't a good fit."

I should have taken the time to write that down. It might have saved me a fourth marriage to a third husband.

But hope springs eternal and all that. And he was perfectly fine while we were dating and I was just kicking the tires. But once we got married and I had a chance to take a good look under the hood, in a nutshell, it never should have happened.

If I had to pick two reasons from a plethora of possibili-ties, I'd have to go with an invasive porn habit and incessantly leaving the toilet seat up, which I was only marginally sure were unrelated. The story of that marriage was so short I could tell it in a haiku:

Seasons have taught me
That love is overrated
Honestly I tried

I once heard Cher say in an interview that her mother was always telling her to settle down and marry a rich man. Cher said she viewed men as a luxury, like dessert. Her response to her mother: "Mom, I am a rich man."

And eventually I came to the same conclusion as Jan did. Maybe Cher, too. Alone can be a gazillion times better than the alternative.

Chapter 30

When I looked around my townhouse, I could almost forget that a group of entitled vacation squatters had made a mess of it not so long ago.

The movers had finally delivered my personal items, at least the stuff I hadn't donated or recycled in my never-ending quest to simplify my life. I'd even done my own version of Swedish death cleaning, which sounds morbid but manages to be both practical and freeing.

Basically, you get rid of the stuff you don't need anymore, so that you notice the stuff you keep. And mostly so that no one else has to do it for you when you kick the bucket.

Even with my scaled-down possessions added to the mix, my townhouse still looked practically identical to Jan's and Dash's and Harmony's.

A wood-topped beige stoneware dog-bone-embellished canister that said CHICKPEA sat on the middle of my dining room table.

My purple handheld weights were crisscrossed over one of the seafoam green throw pillows on the white slipcovered sofa. Not only did they look good, but they also had screw-off ends and extra weight bars so I could continue to build as much bone density as possible. Even though it was too late for my poor hips, my goal was to hang onto all the rest of my original body parts.

I also had a set of resistance bands with non-slip handles, adjustable ankle straps, a padded door anchor. But I didn't love the band colors and I could never seem to find the right door downstairs to make it work. So I kept the whole set upstairs in a guestroom that had a well-positioned closet door and tried to remember to use the bands.

A dog print-covered sign over my living area sofa said ALL YOU NEED IS A DOG AND THE BEACH. I wasn't sure I was all the way there yet, but I thought I might be on my way to believing that sign.

Across from the sofa, Chickpea was stretched out on a white slipcovered dog bed that looked exactly like my sofa but smaller, complete with tiny seafoam green bone-shaped throw pillows. If I could manage to find a tiny pair of purple pawheld canine weights, my doggie décor would be complete.

Harmony and I were hanging out in my small kitchen area in our yoga pants and T-shirts, leaning back against the counters.

"Listen," Jan said as she came out of my powder room. "Every time we come across a toilet, we have to squat, hover just above the toilet seat, and stand without using our hands. Ten times. Before or after using the toilet, depending on the level of urgency."

Jan took a deep breath, launched into pitch mode. "It's a functional exercise that targets your upper thighs and buttocks muscles as well as the bone density in your hips and spine. It builds lower body strength and total body stability. It works the core, calves, quads, hamstrings, glutes, abs, and hip flexors."

Jan took a breath and dove back in. "If you do your kegels at the same time, it's a total win-win. And if you factor in the number of times we pee a day as we age, we'll be supershero strong before we know it. And also never have an issue with climbing into a car or getting out of a chair."

She was good. Harmony and I didn't even wait until we ran into a toilet. We both grabbed onto the edge of the kitchen island and started to squat and stand right there.

"Duly noted, Honey," Harmony said. "My hindquarters thank you kindly for the boost. And while we're at it, let's pinky swear that we won't start sliding into old person ramble-itis."

"Garrulity," I said, pulling up a word from my memory banks. "Excessive talking is called garrulity. As people age, they have more info and acquired wisdom stored in their brains. But they find it harder to choose which bits to share with others and how to avoid unnecessary details. It's also easier to get distracted and go off on tangents."

"That's it, Honey," Harmony said. "That's exactly it. There's this lovely woman who catches up to me while I'm taking a walk around the neighborhood. Yesterday she listed off every present her former neighbor's two-year-old grand-daughter got for her birthday. Then a white car passed us and she told me all about the three white cars her dead brother used to own. After that she gave me a blow-by-blow of the results of her lab tests from her annual checkup, with a detailed comparison to last year's."

"Maybe you can jump in," I said, "and say something like 'let's put a pin in that for now and enjoy the sound of the birds singing?'"

"Right," Jan said. "And then she'll tell you all about the pincushion her grandmother let her play with when she was five and how she let her keep the pins. And then she'd give you a detailed descriptions of the forty-two doll outfits she sewed with those pins. It's assaultive, like listening to some-one's extreme stream of consciousness, or being bombarded with a data dump."

"Maybe next time I'll try a gentle 'let's slow our roll,

Honey,'" Harmony said. "'We need a minute to breathe in some salt air.'"

"Note to selves," I said. "We know things at this age. We're practically dripping with wisdom. But just because we remember something doesn't mean we have to say it out loud."

"Take a beat," Jan said. "And think: is this something the other person has any reason to be remotely interested in hearing?"

"We should have a garrulity signal," Harmony said. "In case one of us starts doing it."

"How about this?" Jan circled one finger in a wrap-it-up gesture.

"That's just plain rude where I come from," Harmony said.

"What if we bat our eyes and look over-the-top fake interested?" I said.

"Perfect," Harmony said. "That's exactly how I was brought up. You act sweet as pie all day long around perfect strangers, and then you save all the nasty for when you get home behind closed doors with your blood relatives."

"Batting our eyes as a garrulity buster it is," Jan said.

"Bonus hack," I said. "Blinking decreases with age and especially when you're engaged in near-vision tasks like your phone. So not only is batting our eyes our garrulity buster, blinking twenty times several times a day helps increase the secretion of oil that keeps your eyes lubricated and prevents dry eye."

"Okay," Jan said as we all blinked away. "Moving on to more interesting things,"

"Let's hope," I said. "Or I'm calling the garrulity police. And yes, I know FLETC is probably already training them."

Jan held up an eco-friendly shopping bag that said TWICE BUT NICE. While she was squatting and standing in my bathroom, she'd multi-tasked and put on a bright red T-shirt and a yellow forehead band with a red star on it.

She twirled around so we could get the full effect. The front of the T-shirt had a Wonder Woman torso printed on it and the attached red cape flared out behind her like a garden flag.

She opened the bag and handed identical forehead bands and cape-enhanced Wonder Woman T-shirts to Harmony and me.

"Thanks?" I said.

"I'm not sure these are quite sexy enough for a faux four-some," Harmony said. "We don't want Butt to think we're trying to put one over on him, even if we are."

"Fine," Jan said. "We'll wear something a little less kick-Butt and save these for after we've taken care of him. Which will officially make us full-fledged supersheroes."

Harmony slid a sheet of paper out from under a coffee cup on my island.

She held it up, looked at it. "PROS AND CONS. What's this?"

I snatched it away from her.

Jan snatched it from me.

I snatched it from Jan, crumbled it up in my fist. "Mind your own beeswax."

Harmony and Jan looked at each other. They leaned back against the counter to wait me out.

"My first ex-husband called," I finally said. "His cancer is back. He wants to move down here."

"You mean your first and third ex-husband," Jan said. "But who's counting."

"Here-here?" Harmony said. "In with you? Again? Oh, Sweetie."

"Like he did last time?" Jan said. "Only to leave you again once he was in remission? To move on to his upgrade wife? As opposed to his child bride, the one he left you for the first time?"

"She was so not an upgrade," Harmony said. "Neither of them were upgrades."

"I know, I know." I sighed. "When you put it that way . . ."

"Did you have anything on the pro side of the list?" Harmony said.

"I was still working on it," I said. "It's just that when we were good, we were so good. And maybe I want to feel needed by someone other than Chickpea."

Chickpea looked over at us, tilted her head.

"See," Harmony said. "Even Chickpea knows that man doesn't have the good sense God gave a rock. You'll wait on him hand and foot and then he'll be gone again."

"Or gone-gone," Jan said. "As in permanently. Either way, you're left picking up the pieces, Glenda. It's not fair to you."

I shook my head. "I know. I know."

"Text him right now and just say no," Jan said. "No reason, no excuses. Say you wish him well and you know he'll find someone to help him get through this—"

"Because they always find another sucker," Harmony said.

"And then ghost him," Jan said.

"Ghost him?" I said.

"Well, maybe a get well card," Harmony said. "But that's it."

"Now," Jan said.

I found my phone, typed a text.

Jan grabbed my phone, read the text, held it out so Harmony could read it.

They nodded their approval. Jan handed the phone to me.

I scrunched my eyes shut, opened them. "I can't do it."

I handed my phone to Harmony.

She pulled her hand back dramatically, pressed Send.

"This is why we need to be supersheroes," Jan said. "So we don't hide our shine, make our lives all about someone else. I mean, think about all the positive impact we could have on the world if we focused. Think about what Nancy Drew would do."

"If it was Ned," I said, "Nancy would take him in."

"If it was Ned," Harmony said, "he wouldn't have screwed around on her."

Chapter 31

Harmony was sitting next to Chickpea on the human sofa. I was sprawled out on the doggie sofa across from them.

"Are you sure you're all right down there, Honey?" Harmony said.

"It's actually way more comfortable than the one you're sitting on," I said.

Jan was standing over by the sliding doors that led to my little patio. She'd duct-taped a big sheet of paper to the glass.

Across the top of the paper, big handwritten letters said KICK BUTT GOALS.

Underneath that, in big vertical letters, each one below the next, she'd written S-M-A-R-T.

"SMART," Jan said, "is a mnemic acronym that stands for specific, measurable, achievable, relevant and time-bound."

"I'd like to time-bound Butt all right," Harmony said. "With a thick scratchy hunk of rope—"

"—wrapped all around and around him—" I said.

"—and pulled so tight he turns into an eye-poppin' bull-frog," Harmony said.

Jan cleared her throat, gave us a mom glare over her reading glasses. "As I was saying, before we undertake this escapade, we're going to need a SMART plan that will lead us directly to our Kick-Butt Goals."

"If there's a PowerPoint coming," I said, "I think I just remembered I've got someplace to be."

"I think I just remembered the same someplace," Harmony said. "And I might have to bat my eyes as I back my way out the door."

Jan pulled her marker out from behind her ear, pointed it at the big sheet of paper.

"Stay with me, team," she said. "Now, what are our overall Kick-Butt goals?"

"We want Butt to buy a new accessible pool lift like he was supposed to," Harmony said. "And preferably relocate it so we don't keep stubbing our toes."

Jan turned her back on us, started writing on the paper.

I gave her a minute to catch up before I jumped in. "We want him to recycle for real. And open the pool at 5 AM. And make it friendly-dog friendly."

Jan kept writing.

"Wait," I said. "Even if they're dogs, they should still get to pick who they want to be friendly with. So let's stick with well-behaved-dog friendly. Although once again, why should the dogs have to behave when the humans are jumping around all over the place?"

"Plus," Harmony said, "well-behaved dogs rarely make history."

"Good one," I said.

"Thanks, Honey," Harmony said.

"Focus," Jan said.

"Okay, and we want Butt to stop being dishonest," Harmony said. "And disgusting."

Jan stopped writing, turned around to face us.

"We're superheroes," she said. "Not miracle workers."

The big sheet of paper duct-taped to the slider was completely covered in messy writing that went every which way. Jan was back sitting on the sofa again.

"That's it," Jan said. "We've got our specific, measurable, achievable, relevant and time-bound plan."

"We're so SMART," Harmony said. "Okay, who's going to send him the text with the faux foursome invitation?"

"Not me," I said. "I've already sent one painful text today."

"Fine," Harmony said. "I'll do it. Even though I was the one who pushed Send for you."

Harmony pulled out her phone, walked up to the sheet of paper on the slider, tried to make out the words and type a text.

"I can't read this and type at the same time," Harmony said.

"Stay with it," I said. "It's a good brain-strengthening challenge."

"Oh, hush up," Harmony said. "My brain is just fine. It's Jan's handwriting that's a challenge."

Jan stood up. She reached out a hand and pulled me up from the dog sofa.

We joined Harmony at the slider.

"Okay," I said. "Type this: 'Beau, How about a naughty little party, just the four of us?'"

"Got it," Harmony said. "Ugh, I'll never be able to look at my phone the same way again."

"Okay," Jan said, "Now type this: 'Don't dress up. We'll bring the toys.'"

"Then just put the faux foursome date and time," I said.

"RSVP or not?" Harmony said.

"We don't need one," Jan said. "He'll be ready and waiting. Now sign all three of our names and add some red heart emojis."

"I think we need something sexier than red hearts," I said,

"so he can't possibly miss the sex part. How about a winking face, a blowing a kiss face, a tongue, an eggplant, and a sweat droplets emoji?"

Jan turned to look at me. "How come you know all those and I don't?"

"Husband Number 4 was an emoji guy," I said.

Harmony was still tapping away. ". . . eggplant, sweat droplets. Got 'em. Okay, one of you has to press Send because I. Just. Can't. Do. It."

She held out her phone. Jan and I read the text over, checked for typos. And emoji glitches, because emojis are just so tiny it's easy to pick the wrong one. Like hitting the laughing face when you meant to hit a crying face because you just got a text that someone died. Or accidentally sending the poop emoji instead of the eggplant emoji. I did a triple-check on the emojis, just to be sure.

"Are you sure we should really go through with this?" I said. "I need a full loofa scrub after just getting this far."

"Of course we're going through with it," Jan said. "We follow the plan, we hit our goals. *Then* we take showers, dry off, put on our supershero cape shirts. And we use the bonus time we're so damn lucky to have to be a force for good in the world."

Jan put her hand on top of mine. Harmony put her hand on top of Jan's.

We pressed Send.

Chapter 32

When COVID-19 hit, Jan, Harmony and I had lots of time to think about what we wanted the rest of our lives to be. We also had plenty of time to let our roots grow out and our hair go pandemic gray.

Leveraging our manufacturing capabilities and distribution knowledge to help meet the overwhelming demand for personal protective equipment, Jan's and my company ceased all regular production. And then we pivoted to round-the-clock production of face masks, gloves and hand sanitizer.

We donated massive quantities to hospitals and other frontline workers, struggled to keep up with online orders from everyone else. All the employees who could, from regular workers right up to the big bosses, double-masked and put on face shields, got to work assembling and packing and shipping everything out.

Along with our masks and face shields, Jan and I wore knitted hats to cover the skunk-like roots in our hair while we worked. It was such a bizarre time in the world that nobody questioned it, or probably even noticed. There were way more important things to worry about.

Until supply chains started to catch up, the company was

all in. It was like time-traveling to another era. A simpler time, a time when we were all focused on the same cause, something bigger than ourselves.

Harmony's work world changed, too. She watered plants during the day in empty office buildings. Her winter rental tenants hunkered down and stayed in their beach houses longer. Or she replaced them with new long-term renters so she didn't have to deal with cleaning and sanitizing for short-term vacationers, especially since most of her same-time-next-year customers had already cancelled.

We all had our groceries delivered to us, sprayed the bags with rubbing alcohol to disinfect them and left them sitting outside or in the garage as long as we dared.

Harmony coached us on regrowing kitchen scraps on window sills and in planters on the back deck. We planted the cut-off ends of romaine and Boston lettuce, plus celery and carrots and beets and green onions. Supply chain issues were making it hard to find decent produce, and pandemic food anxiety was a thing.

There was also just so much death swirling around that our little victory gardens gave us some semblance of control, and it felt good to bring even a tiny bit of new life into the world.

The three of us Zoomed together practically every night. Jan and I would yank off our knitted hats with a dramatic flourish, grab our measuring tapes and compare the length of our roots.

Harmony didn't have to wear a knitted hat. Her dark blond hair was just filling in with more and more lighter streaks and slowly turning to white around her face. She hadn't even bothered to have her hairstylist do foils or balayage in over a year.

"It's like an optical illusion," Harmony said. "Because my hair is already lighter, there's not as much contrast between the gray and white like there is with darker hair."

"That's amazing," I said. "People would pay big money for those streaks."

"Yeah," Jan said. "I'm surprised you haven't figured out a way to cash in on that."

Jan's and my skunk roots kept getting longer. While we were ditching dye, we decided to ditch sulfates and silicones and drying alcohols and parabens. During long pandemic nights we binge-ordered healthier hair products online. If they didn't work for us, we'd drop them off on one another's doorsteps. We quit heat styling, too, and let our hair grow as long as it wanted to.

Then Jan started ordering cruelty free temporary hair dye filled with ingredients that were actually good for your hair. She colored her hair Flamingo Pink and Cool Blue and Minty Mermaid, streaked it, ombre-ed it, dyed her whole head.

Harmony and I couldn't resist. So we all started passing around the temporary hair dyes and playing with them. It was like we were kids again trying to color our dolls' hair with Jolen Creme Bleach and Candyball Cherry Jell-O.

It was a time in the world when you could do things like dye your hair crazy colors. And if you were lucky, you'd realize you could actually do things like that anytime. You just had to decide you wanted to.

Eventually we ditched even the temporary dye and let our hair do its own thing, because we decided we liked rocking our own silver best of all.

"When our hair grows in completely," Jan said one day when she and I had just finished measuring our roots, "and the pandemic is finally, finally over, I'm taking my retirement package. I don't want this to be the rest of my life."

"I'm in," I said. "One hundred percent."

"I'm ready to cash out, too," Harmony said. "Richie's never going to go for it, but I think I have to do it anyway."

And that's when we hatched our plan for taking over our townhouses.

Delaney and I FaceTimed together at least once a day. In a non-pandemic world, I knew this never would have happened. But she was stuck at home and bored, and I was the lucky beneficiary.

She still called me Gramda, the name she'd invented as a toddler to differentiate me from her other two grandmothers. During the years when Kimberly let me take her to work with me, Delaney and I would have deep conversations over lunch in childcare.

First we'd trade sandwich halves, sharing her peanut butter and jelly on white, my turkey with sprouts and grated carrots on whole wheat. I'd split my tangerine with her, counting the segments out loud. Delaney would fold her fruit roll-up exactly in half and tear it right down the center.

When Delaney was four and we'd just finished gobbling down our lunches, she said, "Gramda, I want to spell everything in the whole wide world."

"And someday you will," I said. "But let's start with your name."

"It's too many letters," she said. "Let's do cat."

"Cat it is," I said. I took her by the hand to my office so she could sit at my desk and write cat over and over again.

"Who was the very first artist?" Delaney asked one day when she was maybe six.

"I don't know," I said. "Let's find out."

So we finished eating and off we went to my office. She sat in my computer chair and I leaned over her while she took over my mouse. We searched the internet and finally agreed that the first artists were the cave people. And we both spent most of our lunch time that week drawing our own cave pictures on computer paper and taping them up on my walls like the most beautiful wallpaper in the world.

Somehow Delaney was thirteen now. She flat-ironed her

beautiful brown hair and expertly turned her round hazel eyes
into cat eyes with a few flicks of eyeliner, sometimes jet black
and sometimes pink-and-blue glitter. She was brilliant and
beautiful and wise beyond her years. An old soul.

Her questions had changed, but she still almost always
showed up with a good one.

"What a nice surprise," I said when I answered her Face-
Time call. "It's good to see you again. Tell your mom I
said hi."

Kimberly's face appeared over Delaney's shoulder. "Love
you," Kimberly said.

"Love you, too," I said. And she was gone.

I propped my phone up against a book so I wouldn't act
like a dinosaur and accidentally let my hand drop so the
camera only showed my chin. I actually had a kickstand on
my phone case, but the book was easier.

Delaney and I never wasted time on questions like *How
was school?* Especially now that her school day was frustratingly
remote.

"Okay," she said. "Would you rather only eat breakfast or
only eat dessert every day for the rest of your life?"

"Hmm," I said as I considered. "I think I'd rather eat
dessert for breakfast every day for the rest of my life."

"I knew you were going to say that!" Delaney said. "I set it
right up for you."

"Okay," I said. "Would you rather adopt a dog now or
wait until after the pandemic?"

Her eyes got wide. "Seriously?"

"I'm thinking about it," I said.

"Now," Delaney said. "Of course."

So we spent a happy stretch of days emailing each other
links to shelter dogs at all hours of the day and night. When I
found Chickpea, I almost didn't tell Delaney because I wanted
our shared search to go on forever.

But I was afraid someone would scoop her up first and I didn't want to lose her.

Delaney didn't even reply to my email when I sent Chickpea's link. She called me instead.

"YAAS," she said. "She's fire and I'm totally vibing with her already. And she's old enough that you don't have to potty train her and young enough to still be fun."

"I'm still fun," I said.

"I'm serious," Delaney said. "It's dope that she's part pitbull. It's a completely misunderstood and underappreciated breed. And the chihuahua side has that rizz, you know, snack charm."

"Right," I said. "And she's small enough that I can pick her up."

"You mean *we* can pick her up," Delaney said.

And we did. I called the shelter immediately to make sure she was still there, gave them all my information so they could check up on me. The next day I made the trek to get Delaney at her house. She came running out to the car, all masked and ready to go. My own mask was already on, and I rolled the windows down to get extra air flow.

"What do you think of her name?" I said to Delaney as we drove to the shelter.

Delaney thought about it. "It's good, like a baby chickie mixed with a peanut. Plus, she's probably already been through a lot and we wouldn't want to add to her separation anxiety by changing her name on her."

Chickpea *had* been through a lot. A nice volunteer at the shelter told us she'd been found tied to a dumpster by the side of a busy road. She'd spent the whole night there, kept herself from freezing to death by pressing herself to the ground and wiggling her way under the dumpster.

"Goals," Delaney said. "Way to be a rock star, pupper."

I bent down to scratch Chickpea behind her ear. "What a brave girl you are."

It was love at first sight for all of us. But I decided to foster Chickpea because by that point in my life I was so gun shy about commitment.

I didn't even last a whole day. Less than twenty-four hours later, Chickpea officially became a failed foster. And once I dropped her off to be spayed and get her shots and paid the adoption fee and signed all the paperwork, we belonged to each other.

Chickpea jumped right into my Zoom world, thoroughly entertaining Jan and Harmony, who immediately started online shopping little diva doggie outfits for her and having them delivered to my house.

Chickpea licked the phone repeatedly whenever I Face-Timed with Delaney. Delaney would pick out one of Chickpea's new doggie outfits and I'd dress her up in it. I taught her to stand up on her hind legs and pirouette around so that Delaney could get the whole view.

Delaney taught her to sing "You Need to Calm Down" along with Taylor Swift. Chickpea got all excited every time the oh-oh, oh-oh parts came on, barking away to the beat. When Taylor and Delaney sang the you need to calm down, you're being too loud parts, Chickpea howled away like she not only understood the lyrics but thoroughly agreed with them. I laughed and laughed and sang along with them.

The best part of my life was Delaney. But even after the pandemic wound down, the world had changed forever. And even with the lure of Chickpea, most of our communication was by phone and FaceTime and Zoom.

So at her sixteenth birthday party, I gave Delaney a silver necklace with her name spelled out in cursive. And an IOU for a round trip flight to visit me whenever it worked for her.

Not long after that, Chickpea and I hit the road.

Chapter 33

We rolled as slowly as possible down the townhouse road in Jan's electric Volkswagen ID.Buzz, which had the awesome retro hippie vibe of the original VW bus.

"Have I told you that Edison's official color is Energetic Orange?" Jan said.

"At least once a day since you bought him?" I said.

"Them," Jan said. "Their pronoun is them. And even though their interior color is a bit muted because of their taupe accents, you have to admit that outside and in, most of my Edison is the exact color of a Golden Isles sunset."

"And this is why I packed up and moved down here to be with you," Harmony said. "Because I knew the conversation would always be so dadgum scintillating."

I started batting my eyes at Jan in our garrulity signal.

Jan ignored me. Harmony giggled.

Jan was driving, of course, and I was riding shotgun. Harmony was sitting in one of the middle seats.

The three of us were wearing robes over sheer, long, flowy black negligees.

"Who knew I'd get more use out of those Spanx," Harmony said. "And so soon."

"I've got all three layers of my shapewear on, too," I said. "Just in case."

"Don't think I forgot my padded bicycle seat," Jan said. "Although I have to admit it makes it a little bit awkward to hit the brakes."

"Let's make this quick," I said. "Life is too long for uncomfortable underwear."

"Somebody write that down," Jan said.

I took a small spray bottle out of the pocket of my robe and gave the air over my shoulder a spray.

Harmony made a sputtering sound. "Thanks for that. Is there something you're trying to tell me?"

"That better not be directed at Edison," Jan said. "Their hygiene is exemplary."

"It's a pre-spray for Butt," I said, "since we're going to have to spend so much time in close proximity with him. In case he has old man smell."

"Don't you think that's a teensy bit harsh?" Harmony said. "I don't think repulsive necessarily comes with a smell."

"Actually," I said, "old person smell is a real thing. As people age, they develop a specific body odor that the Japanese call kareishu. It's from a chemical called nonenal, this grassy, greasy odor from the oxidation of fatty acids that our skin starts producing as early as our 40s. It's a tough smell to get rid of because the fatty acids aren't water soluble, so it transfers to clothing and bedding and it doesn't wash off in the shower."

"Wowzer," Jan said. "It's like senior cooties."

"Doesn't that just beat all you've ever stepped in," Harmony said. "I knew I should have died young and left a good-smelling corpse."

"Hey, spray some of that in this direction," Jan said.

"We're fine," I said. "We eat plenty of mushrooms and we put dried mushroom powder in our buddha bowls—something in mushrooms keeps you from developing the smell. The chlorophyll from all the greens we eat also helps, as well as exercising and drinking lots of water to help dilute the fatty acids."

"Why don't they just lead with that when they're trying to make you get healthy?" Jan said.

I gave the bottle another spray. "I DIYed a solution with persimmon extract and green tea because both help break down the fatty acids so they can dissipate more quickly."

"Why does it smell like lavender?" Harmony said. "Not that I'm complaining."

"Oh, right," I said. "I added a few drops of lavender essential oil because it decreases anxiety and stress, just in case we need it. And not that I think it'll take much to get Butt's attention, but the scent of lavender is also arousing."

"Great," Jan said.

"But it's only the twelfth most arousing scent," I said. "So I think we'll be fine."

Three hot young shirtless FLETC guys jogged toward us, waved.

We waved back, sighed.

"Speaking of arousing." Harmony leaned between our seats to get a better glimpse of the hot FLETC guys. "If I had my druthers . . ."

"Not an option," Jan said.

"On so many levels," I said.

A gray-haired bobblehead doll with a sign that said WORLD'S BEST GLAMMA was nodding its head on the dashboard in front of us.

Jan grabbed it, wiggled the suction cup loose and handed the bobblehead to me.

"Put her in the glove compartment," Jan said. "I don't want her seeing any of this. Just give her a quick spray first."

"Just asking," I said. "So the vehicle is a they and the bobblehead is a she?"

"Keep up," Jan said.

We passed another driveway with a big truck backed in, front facing the road.

We rolled by two women walking in our direction, who might or might not have been eyeing our outfits as they waved to us. We waved back.

"What if this gets out?" I said. "You know, what if Butt blabs about it to the whole island?"

"Who cares?" Harmony said. "If people are still talking about us at our age, I say that's a good thing. Let 'em flap their jaws right off."

I tried to sing Bonnie Raitt's "Something to Talk About," but I only got as far as the let's give them part, and then my voice fizzled away from nerves.

Jan put on her blinker and pulled slowly into Butt's driveway.

Before she even put her EV into park, Butt opened the door.

He stepped out on his tiny front porch wearing a white sleeveless T-shirt. His golf shorts had hot dogs printed randomly all over them. Each hot dog was tucked into a roll and had a drizzle of mustard on it.

"What," Jan said, "he couldn't find anything more phallic than that?"

"They must have been out of eggplant emoji shorts at the golf store," I said.

Butt waved far too eagerly.

"Should we be alarmed that he's wearing a wife-beater?" Harmony said.

"I'm pretty sure you're finally not allowed to call sleeveless T-shirts that anymore," I said.

"I think," Jan said, "we should actually be more alarmed about how it looks on him."

Harmony, Jan and I got out of Jan's bus, stood side-by-side in the driveway. We opened our robes just a little, shimmied our shoulders, gave Butt sly little waves.

All three of us were wearing sneakers, the better to make a quick getaway.

"Let's do this," we all said at once. We didn't want to tip him off with a fist bump, but it was implied.

Butt's townhouse layout was identical to Jan's and Dash's and Harmony's and mine. A big glass fishbowl filled with golf balls squatted on an ugly dining room table.

The open living area had been taken over by a black leatherette sofa and a bulky black leatherette recliner. Matching seriously outdated orangey-brown end tables flanked the sofa, and a third identical table sat next to the recliner.

A weathered sign over the couch said, MAN CAVE. WHERE I DO MAN THINGS. I gave my spray bottle a discreet spray in that direction.

A square black leatherette coffee table in front of the sofa looked big enough to have sex on. Which might well have been the point.

"Have a seat, girlies," Butt said, "while I get all y'all a stiff drink."

"I'm assuming you keep your Viagra upstairs in the bathroom off the primary bedroom?" Jan said.

"Whoa," Butt said, "you broads get right to it."

"Be right ba-ack," Jan sing-songed.

I tiptoed up the stairs behind Jan, looked over my shoulder to make sure we weren't being followed.

"I bet Buttbrain still calls it the master," I said as I walked into the ensuite bath. "I mean, the shift to primary from master was way overdue. Talk about racist and sexist implications. Although it's just the tip of the iceberg, so it's not like the gatekeepers should be patting themselves on the back for—"

"Concentrate," Jan said. She'd already found her stash tin and placed it on the counter between the double sinks.

She scanned a row of pill bottles, grabbed a prescription bottle, took out a Smurf-blue pill, flushed it down the toilet.

I caught her eye in the mirror, raised my eyebrows.

"Viagra," she said, as if I'd never seen a Viagra pill before. "In case he counts them. You know, like carving notches on his bed post."

"Diabolical," I said. "And yuck."

Jan did one-potato, two-potato to choose another bottle, opened it, fished out a white capsule. Then she opened the stash tin and took out a blue raspberry gummy edible.

She looked up toward heaven. "I'm sorry, Mellie, but it's for a good cause."

Jan began squishing the blue edible around the white capsule.

"What's that in the middle?" I said.

She shrugged. "Whatever."

"We don't want to have to worry about any drug interactions," I said. "It would be a pain in the Butt to have to take him to the ER."

I reached into the pocket of my robe, pulled a capsule out of a baggie.

"Just to be on the safe side," I said, "try this instead. It's an empty gelatin capsule. I use them to disguise the taste of pills for Chickpea. I also brought some of her pill pockets. I use those when she gets bored with the taste of the gelatin capsules."

"I want to come back as your dog," Jan said.

"You should be so lucky." I scratched Jan behind one ear.

Jan swapped out the capsules, finished shaping the blue

edible around the empty gelatin capsule into the distinct
diamond shape of Viagra.

She held it up. "The good news is that it takes the same
amount of time for both Viagra and these edibles to kick in."

Our eyes met in the mirror. I tried not to gulp.

"So in approximately one hour," Jan said, "Butt still won't
be able to get it up but—"

"—he won't care so much!" we both said.

Jan and I clomped down the stairs. Harmony slid out from
under Butt's arm, crossed over to meet us.

"Take your time, why don't you," Harmony hissed.

"Easy tiger," I said to Butt. "We have plenty of time for all
that. And so much more."

Harmony, Jan and I circled around Butt, wiggled our hips
suggestively. Hip lubrication took a bit longer these days, but
once we got going, we still had the magic.

Jan held the fake Viagra pinched between her thumb and
forefinger.

"Open wide, Mr. President," she said.

Butt opened his mouth. Jan teased him with the fake
Viagra, whisked it away.

The three of us kept wiggling, added some sexy arm
movements to our hip action.

"We like to do it this way," Harmony said. "It's part of our
ceremonial Viagra ritual."

"Wowza," Butt said. "You skirts are all kinds of kinky."

Harmony and I put our hands on top of Jan's pill-holding
hand.

"Are you ready, Mr. President?" I said.

"So ready," Butt said.

Butt closed his eyes and opened his mouth wider.

Jan popped her concoction into his mouth, pulled her

hand away quickly, wiped it on her bathrobe. I knew she was far less concerned about a residual gummy contact high than she was about catching Butt cooties.

"Down the hatch," Butt said. He puckered his face. "Hey, what'd you do to it?"

"We like to add a special erotic flavor to enhance the experience," Harmony said.

Butt ogled her. "I'd like to enhance your experience, darlin'."

Chapter 34

Now all four of us were riding in Edison, Jan's electric VW ID. Buzz.

Jan was still driving. The two middle seats were empty. Butt sat in the third seat between Harmony and me. I gave the air in front of us a quick spray while Butt was looking the other way.

When he leaned forward against his seatbelt, his legs disappeared under his stomach, making him look like Humpty Dumpty being held back from a fall.

"What I still don't get," Butt said, "is why we can't do it at my place. That coffee table of mine would probably hold all four of us without breaking."

"Nothing more awkward than sitting around on a date waiting for that little blue pill to kick in," I said.

"So," Harmony said, "we thought you might enjoy a little pre-foursome sunset tour around the island in the meantime."

"You know," Jan said, "be a tourist in your own town?"

"You dames are so gosh darn considerate," Butt said. He landed two beefy paws on Harmony's and my knees. I could feel us both trying not to cringe.

We drove along the short causeway toward East Beach. The sun was low, getting lower.

Snowy egrets had taken over the branches on a wax myrtle tree at the edge of a gorgeous expanse of golden marsh. They looked so calm it was all I could do not to jump out of Jan's retro bus and climb up the tree to join them.

Jan did a slow loop of the East Beach roundabout, took the third turnoff toward Gould's Inlet.

"I gotta tell you," Butt said, "this vehicle we're riding around in is giving me flashbacks to the VW buses of my younger days. Buddy of mine used to have one. We'd pick up a couple of cute little chickies, drive 'em down to the beach to watch the submarine races. Hope we got lucky."

Jan looked at us in the rearview mirror. "That's exactly where we're heading. To watch the submarine races."

"You're going to get lucky," Harmony said.

"So, so lucky," I said.

We drove around the island until Jan finally pulled into Gascoigne Bluff Park. She found a secluded space between two live oak trees dripping with Spanish moss.

An expanse of marsh stretched out in front of us. Beyond that the Frederica River meandered out to the open ocean.

Over another swathe of marsh on the other side of the river, a fat orange sun was setting.

"Looook," Butt said. "It's like this great big pumpkin. With all this rainbow sherbet dripping and twinkling around the edges."

Jan turned around. Harmony, Jan and I raised our eyebrows.

"It almost feels like it's taking me with it," Butt said. "The lower it gets, the more I'm changing . . ."

I reached over to open the sliding door. "Come on, let's get you out for a closer look at that rainbow sherbet."

Harmony and I helped Butt out. I steered him until we were standing in front of the EV, kept a tight hold on his arm so he didn't end up in the river.

When I turned around to see what was going on, Jan was opening the rear hatchback. I watched her swivel out a black box that looked like a flight equipment case, open the top to reveal a two-burner stovetop.

"We're cooking for him?" I heard Harmony say. "I didn't sign up for that."

"Nah," Jan said. "Edison just likes to show off their stovetop."

I started to signal them to keep it down, but Butt was completely oblivious. He was busy swaying side to side with his arms extended as if he were dancing with the tall marsh grass.

Jan slid out a cooler and dropped it on the ground next to the stovetop. She opened the cooler, held up a container of pink liquid and a stack of cups so I could see them.

"Mocktails," Jan stage-whispered. "Just act like they're really strong."

The next time I peeked, Harmony had lined up the cups around the back ledge of the opened bus and was pouring drinks.

I jumped at the sound of Jan flipping the middle seat down on itself.

Butt didn't even notice. He was pointing and bending his knees as he sank lower along with the sun.

Harmony came to join us holding two mocktails.

I grabbed a mocktail. "Thanks," I said sweetly. "Your turn."

I ditched them to join Jan. Jan and I put our drinks down and grabbed a folded foam mattress tucked in beside the stove top. We walked it to the side of the bus, folded down a built-in bed, slid the mattress on top of it.

"If this thing had a bathroom," Jan said, "I'd probably just move in and rent out the townhouse. Edison and I could be very happy together."

We pulled out the striped beach bag with our supplies. The two of us put fresh sheets and a faux fur throw on the bed. We added a pair of pink faux fur handcuffs and a cute little matching whip.

Jan climbed into the front seat, swiped her finger along a vertical panel near the rearview mirror. Above my head, a sunshade started to open, exposing a huge panoramic sunroof and the sky beyond.

"That'll do it," Jan said.

It was almost dark in the park now. Jan, Harmony and I sipped our mocktails and followed Butt, who was lumbering through the trees.

Butt stopped suddenly. He looked up.

A face was carved into the side of a tree.

Butt reached up, traced his finger over the face.

"It's like it's me," Butt said. "But not me."

Even in the near dark, we could tell we were all rolling our eyes.

We followed Butt some more, occasionally dodging a garland of Spanish moss draping down.

Butt pointed to a basket hanging from a live oak tree.

"Frisbee golf," he said slowly. "Who. Brought. The. Frisbee?"

"I think you just have to feel the frisbee and it will appear," I said.

Butt opened his mouth to say something, got distracted, turned in the opposite direction.

We followed him to a stand with a big wooden box filled with painted rocks.

Butt stopped, read the sign over the box.

"KINDNESS ROCKS," he said. "Do you think this has been here all along? Like since they made this island?"

"Or maybe," Harmony said, "it built itself because it knew you were coming, Pumpkin."

Butt reached in, picked up a brightly painted rock. He held it arm's distance away, squinted at it.

"YOU ROCK," Butt said. "Wow. Just wow."

Butt was sound asleep on his back on Edison's bed, snoring away under the golden glow of an old-fashioned-looking LED camp lantern. One hand clutched his painted rock, which was pressed to his chest.

A pink faux-fur handcuff dangled from the same wrist. My spray bottle was almost empty, and the air in the retro bus smelled like lavender and Butt.

Harmony, Jan and I sat side-by-side on the rear seat, watching him.

Butt stopped snoring. He stopped breathing, then took a big gasp of air.

"Not to diagnose," Harmony said, "but that sure sounds like sleep apnea to my ears."

"I saw the CPAP machine in his bathroom," I said. "I didn't even think to bring it with us."

"He'll be fine," Jan said. "We can just give him a shove in the shoulder if he needs it."

"Yeah," I said. "That's what I used to do with my fourth husband."

"Okay," Jan said. "Who's going to reach into his shorts pocket?"

We all shuddered. Then we did rocks/paper/scissors. Harmony lost.

"Why me?" Harmony said. "Why is it always me?"

Harmony scrunched up her face, reached into Butt's pocket, slowly pulled out his phone.

I grabbed Butt's thumb, pressed it to the phone's touch ID pad. The screen opened right up.

Jan grabbed the phone from me. "Got it," she said when she found Butt's contact list.

"Okay," she said in no time. "We've signed our townhouse community up for actual recycling with his email."

"Good job, Honey," Harmony said.

Butt mumbled in his sleep.

"I was talking to another Honey," Harmony said.

I tilted my head back to watch a sky full of glimmering stars through the sunroof while Jan focused on Butt's phone. I tried to find a constellation, almost wished I'd paid more attention while some date or husband was mansplaining astronomy to me.

"Now," Jan said, "we're sending emails to the rest of the HOA Board and CC-ing the management company, in case they're the ones that reprogram the key fobs. The first one says that owners Glenda Gardner, Harmony Lewis and Jan Rivera now have 24/7 pool access. Due to their status as official FLETC role players."

"Ooh," Harmony said. "That's good."

"Oooo," Butt mumbled. We ignored him.

"Okay," I said. "The next email should say that pre-approved dogs now have pool access and the signs should be changed accordingly. Then say that Chickpea Gardner has already been pre-approved."

"Done," Jan said. "So how should we phrase the part about the accessible pool lift?"

"I think we should let that one go for now," Harmony said. "Maybe we can just accidentally-on-purpose leave the cover off the lift one night so that someone else figures out that Butt didn't really buy a new one."

"Good call," I said. "That way we can just thank him for the sweet favors he insisted on doing for us after our totally mind-blowing foursome."

Jan tucked Butt's phone next to the painted rock and the pink handcuff. "Okay, now we've got to rough him up a little."

"Do we *have* to?" I said.

"There's no way around it," Jan said.

Harmony reached into her bathrobe pocket, took out a bright red lipstick.

She dabbed some on Butt's mouth. She reached back into her pocket, sprayed two quick puffs of perfume on him.

Jan leaned over Butt to get a better look. "His belt has to be under here somewhere, but I don't see it."

"Just yank out his shirt," Harmony said. "He'll figure he got too excited to take off the belt."

Jan and Harmony yanked out Butt's sleeveless T-shirt.

I rubbed a scarf up and down my arms, tucked it under my robe and rubbed it around some more. Handed the scarf to Jan, who did the same.

Jan handed the scarf back to me. I peeled the fluffy throw blanket down, rubbed the scarf over Butt's arms, across the shirt formerly known as a wife-beater, around on his head.

Harmony pulled the throw down lower. I did a lightning quick pass of the scarf across Butt's thighs.

We all stared at the crotch of his golf shorts.

"I can't," I said. "I. Just. Can't."

Butt was lying on his back, just beginning to stir.

All three of us leaned in. I grabbed the other side of the pink handcuffs, gave them a little tug.

"Hey there, Wild Thing," I said.

Jan picked up the cute little whip, circled Butt's face with it. "You were masterful," Jan said. "Just masterful."

"Wait." Butt squinted up at us. "We already did it?"

Harmony dragged a fingernail down his chest. "We sure did, Sugar Britches. I've never seen one man give three women so much pleasure. And by the looks of it, I'd say the feeling was mutual."

We helped Butt sit up in bed. He was still cradling his painted rock.

"Speaking of reciprocal pleasure," Jan said, "that was just too kind of you to insist on fixing our pool fobs and making sure Glenda's emotional support dog could stay with her at all times."

"You're a good man, Mr. President," I said.

Chapter 35

Harmony, Jan and I stood at the pool gate. Chickpea sat on the ground beside us. In honor of trash day, a jagged row of trash barrels decorated the townhouses all up and down the road.

I waved my key fob in front of the pool lock. It flashed red.

Harmony waved her key fob. Red.

Jan waved hers. Red again.

"How much longer could it take to reprogram our key fobs?" I said. "It's been almost a week."

"At least we still have Dash's." Harmony waved Dash's key fob in front of the gate. It flashed green and we all walked right in.

We turned to watch a big blue trash truck rolling down the townhouse road, its mechanical arm reaching out and scooping up each trash barrel, dumping the contents into the back of the truck.

"Have you ever stopped to think," I said, "how sad it is that the mechanical arm on that truck is like the AI version of a second trash guy? I mean, somebody lost a perfectly good paycheck."

"It's way too early to wax philosophical about lost

paychecks," Jan said. "Just feel lucky we had ours when we needed them."

"How empathetic of you," I said.

"I'm just passing the AI baton to Gen Z," Jan said. "Let them figure out all that stuff."

"Fine," I said. "As long as they help us save the ocean while they're at it."

That settled, we all crossed our arms, still watching the trash truck.

Under the light of the streetlights, the truck stopped in front of the recycle area. The driver got out, opened the fence gate, climbed back in the truck.

The mechanical arm reached out and grabbed the recycle barrels one after the other, dumped their contents on top of the rest of the trash.

"You don't think Butt's on to us, do you?" Jan said.

The three of us opened our mailboxes with our little keys, pulled out our mail. Mixed in with the junk mail, Harmony and Jan each had a long white envelope.

I had two.

We sat on a bench and tore them open. Fast, like ripping off a waxing strip back when we still tortured ourselves like that.

"The HOA has revoked my pool access," Jan said.

"Same," Harmony said. "And they're fining me for illegal entrance and infraction of the pool rules."

"Ditto," Jan said.

"Me, three," I said. "Plus they're also fining me for illegal dog entry."

"Jerks," Jan said.

"That Butt is about as useless as a screen door on a

submarine," Harmony said. "I can't believe we wasted our precious time fakin' an orgy with him."

"Slimeball," I said.

"And that HOA could start an argument in an empty house," Harmony said.

"Get a life, people," Jan said.

I tapped my finger on the final paragraph. "And look, it's supposed to be paid to the HOA, so we can't even get Butt in trouble for trying to pocket the money."

We sat there, letting it sink in. Our hearts sinking along with it.

When two shirtless FLETC guys jogged by, we barely waved. We didn't even bother to turn and catch the rear view.

We sat on the bench some more, as if we'd been planted there. I took a long slow sip from my water bottle, because hydrating is something you do, even when you don't care, even when you feel like a total loser.

"Oh, this just sucks," Jan said.

"Bigtime," I said.

"It's like being a rooster one day and a feather duster the next," Harmony said. "And you don't even know when the whole thing up and turned cattywampus on you."

I took another sip of water. There was nothing more to say. And now I really needed to pee.

We kept sitting there on the bench, three aging lumps on a log.

"Maybe our best days are behind us," I said. "Maybe the bell curve thing was right and this is what it feels like to be over the freaking hill."

A red sporty-ish car drove slowly down the townhouse road, rolled almost to a stop as it approached us.

Butt lowered his window. When he held up his middle finger, it looked like a Jimmy Dean sausage.

The three of us raised our own middle fingers, but our hearts weren't in it.

"So that's it then," Harmony said.

I sighed. "Three smart women who had so much to offer, and they were bested by a Butt."

"We went for it and we lost," Harmony said. "We can't even use Dash's pool fob anymore. We might get him fined, too."

"Maybe the supershero thing was too big a stretch for us," Jan said.

I sighed.

Harmony sighed.

Jan sighed.

"I guess no matter how old you get," I said, "a part of you is still hoping for that happy ending."

We tried so hard to shrug it off, to forget about the whole thing, to move on.

We ignored the pool and walked the beach. We read books and made buddha bowls. Jan Zoomed with her sons and grandkids, and when I stopped by to drop something off one day, her computer screen looked like a reboot of *Hollywood Squares*.

Harmony got flowers from her husband and talked to her kids.

My first and third ex-husband sent me more texts. I ignored them.

Delaney and I tried to teach Chickpea to paint masterpieces via Zoom, but Chickpea wouldn't hold the brush in her teeth and she didn't like getting her paws in the paint.

So I covered the canvas with a sheet of parchment paper and let her pirouette all over it.

When I peeled off the paper, it wasn't quite the masterpiece we were hoping for.

"She'll get better," Delaney said.

"You think?" I said.

"Maybe not," Delaney said. "Can you send it to me anyway so I can hang it up in my room?"

So after we got off the Zoom, I dipped Chickpea's paw in the paint so she could sign her painting with a pawprint.

Chickpea gave me a look of horror.

"Sorry," I said. "But it'll mean a lot to Delaney."

I cleaned Chickpea up quickly, gave her an extra treat to help her forget the trauma. Then Evie drove us to the mainland to get the painting matted and framed and packed for shipping to Delaney.

After we picked it up, we went to the post office to mail it.

Then we strolled around the St. Simons Pier Village, window shopping. I found an "I Brake For Turtles" bumper sticker. Then I found a window decal that said SSI in lower case cursive, the I for island dotted with a seagull in flight.

We wandered behind the official Visitors' Center to see the live oak tree with a tall carving of a mermaid named Cora, who according to legend has lived in the seas around St. Simons Island for centuries. Cora is the protector of the island's loggerhead turtles. Her melodic humming is supposed to lead the baby turtles out to sea after they hatch on the beaches, guiding and protecting them.

I set the timer on my phone camera, leaned it against the wooden camera stand. Chickpea and I posed for a photo in front of Cora

After that, I only had the rest of my life to fill.

Jan, Harmony and I worked another role-playing exercise at FLETC, but even that had lost its luster. Especially since, although I made Harmony and Jan walk by the Forensics door three times with me, we never once saw the instructor with the salt-and-pepper hair and the dimples.

After the role-playing exercise, Jan picked up a few more empty bullet casings in front of the meth house. When we got back home, she mixed them with seashells and strung everything together with wire to make a set of windchimes. She hung her very taste-specific creation next to the birdfeeder on her little back patio.

"Whatever cranks your tractor," Harmony said when she saw the windchimes.

I snuck over under the cover of darkness that night and put a tiny fake daisy in each empty bullet shell.

Harmony took up the ukulele again. Her husband Richie came to visit for a long weekend. I heard them fighting through our shared wall and tried not to listen.

"You okay?" I said once he was gone and the three of us were rocking away on our little front porches.

Harmony looked at me with tired eyes. "Maybe my expectations need some trimming around the edges. But as our old friend Janis Joplin once said, 'Don't compromise yourself. You are all you've got.'"

"I think," Jan said, "the rest of her quote is, '"There is no yesterday, no tomorrow, it's all the same day.'"

Jan let out a sound that was half sigh, half moan. "I gotta tell you, I'm really starting to feel that. Like it's all one endless, freaking day."

"And not in a good way," I said.

Early one morning we were all sitting in our rocking chairs, bathed in amber from the dusk-to-dawn lights over our front porches, drinking coffee and staring with glazed eyes through the darkness at the vacant pool across the road.

"Come on," Jan said. "Let's go to the beach."

"Now there's something new and different," Harmony said.

I just sighed.

Most of the sky was still dark when we arrived. I tried to take in the spectacular pink light at the horizon.

The compostable food service gloves and our net ocean cleanup bags were still back at the townhouse. Maybe I'd forgotten them, or maybe I was just too world weary to care right now. With all the pollution in the ocean, picking up a few measly pieces of litter felt like tilting at windmills.

We walked the beach in silence. Tourist season was over and the early birds like us had the place practically to ourselves. It felt vast and lonely.

Despite my worst intentions, force of habit and all that made me squat to pick up a white plastic knife that had washed in to the edge of the water.

Harmony found a makeup brush, the ends still stained pink with blush, that must have fallen out of someone's beach bag.

Jan found a turquoise ice cream scoop that would be good as new after a quick run through her dishwasher.

Spontaneously, we all dropped to our knees and started making a sand sculpture as the pink light disappeared and the sun began to rise. We dug and dug with our bare hands, jamming course wet sand under our fingernails.

Part frustration and part creation, we put all our energy into it, as if we could change the whole stupid world one sand-castle at a time. We just kept digging and piling and patting the sand.

Then we began detailing with our found trash-to-treasure tools. We sliced and brushed and scooped.

Without a vote or even a discussion, the slab in front of us started turning into a mermaid stretched out on the sand.

And then somehow it pivoted.

About an hour later we'd created a naked thirsty woman crawling on her belly toward the ocean to save herself with a drink of salt water.

"Dark," a woman said as she walked by with her friends.

We sat down next to our poor sand woman, tried to brush off the speckled sand stuck to our knees, our hands.

"I can't take it anymore," I said.

"There has to be a way," Jan said. "We're better than this."

Harmony let out a puff of air. "I'd say it's high time we squat down on the horse blankets and hammer out all the bits that are finer than a frog's hair."

Chapter 36

Jan, Harmony and I were sitting around Dash's dining room table, playing OceanOpoly with Dash and his mom. Otesha looked exactly like him, except for her long gorgeous silver locs.

I rolled the dice, moved my lobster playing piece five spaces, completely missed the treasure chest and had to pay a $75 diving fee instead. Pretty much the story of my life.

"Otesha is such a striking name," Harmony said.

"Thank you," Dash's mom said. "It's a Swahili word. It means hope, a cause to grow for, a reason to dream."

"Wow," Jan said. "We could use some Otesha in our lives right about now."

"Call me Tesha," Dash's mom said. "All my friends do."

"Thanks," I said. "But I hope it's okay if I hang onto every single hopeful syllable."

Tesha laughed, rolled the dice and moved her seahorse, landed on the manatee, snapped it up for a cool $375.

"I'm the youngest of five," Harmony said. "I think my parents' hope was that my name might inspire the other kids to stop beating the bejeezus out of one another for a few minutes. A hope that turned out to be more aspirational than realistic."

"It's a beautiful name." Tesha smiled, turned to me. "Where did Glenda come from?"

"There are two possible scenarios," I said. "One, that I was named after Glenda Farrell, the smart, sassy, wisecracking actress who was a big star in the 1930s. The other story is that my mother named me after Glinda the Good Witch, but she hadn't watched *The Wizard of Oz* in a while and spelled it wrong. And when she realized it, she made up a better story."

"Good pivot," Dash said. "Almost as good as Walter to Dash."

Tesha gave him a mom glare.

Jan shook her head. "Jan is so boring it doesn't even have a story. It's not even short for Janice or Janet or Janis Joplin. Just plain boring Jan."

"January," I said. "Tell everyone it's short for January."

"Sure," Jan said. "Even though my birthday is in April. Wait, are you just trying to figure out a way to make me age faster than you?"

"Busted," I said.

Our hot game of OceanOpoly continued. Harmony rolled the dice, then Jan.

Harmony, Jan and I looked at one another, nodded.

"Dash, Honey," Harmony said. "Can you do us an itsy-bitsy teensy-weensy favor?"

"You just have to bring the backup," Jan said. "We'll do the heavy lifting. We can't let the bad guys win, you know?"

"The thing is," I said, "when you stop fighting the good fight, all that's left is old."

Dash sighed, rolled the OceanOpoly dice.

"Walter," Tesha said, "help my new friends out."

"How much trouble is this going to get me in?" Dash said.

❁

Harmony's garage door was up. The three of us were sitting side-by-side in chairs facing the opening.

Carly Simon's "You're So Vain" was blasting from a Bluetooth speaker. A string of twinkle lights dangled from the open door.

"Some of my fondest memories," Harmony said, "are of sitting in the garage and waving to the people walking by. I can't understand what this foolish HOA has against being neighborly."

Jan looked at her phone. "'Garage doors must be kept down except during use,'" she read.

"Ridiculous," Harmony said.

"Shouldn't be much longer," I said.

A red sporty-ish car pulled into Harmony's little driveway.

Butt kicked the door open and lumbered out. "Looking to get yourselves another fine, girlies?"

"I dare you to come over here and say that to my girly face," Jan said.

Butt grinned, took a step forward.

The music cut off.

Jan grinned at Butt with her Dracula teeth.

A bright motion-activated light turned on. It lit up a line of burly federal agents standing shoulder-to-shoulder in the back of the garage. They had ski masks pulled over their faces, tight T-shirts tucked into chinos, bulging biceps all around.

The biggest federal agent crossed his arms over his chest.

"Be the solution," he said in a deep voice. "Not the pollution."

Harmony's garage door was closed now. Butt was hanging from a harness attached to the garage door opener ceiling mount in the center of the garage, bicycling his feet.

The three of us and the masked federal agents were taking turns pushing Butt like he was swinging on a swing.

"Who says," Harmony said, "you can't really get away with hanging someone from the ceiling with a garage door opener like you could back in 1980?"

"I stand corrected," I said.

The Beatles broke into "With a Little Help from My Friends." Butt kept swinging and the rest of us sang and danced to the music.

"Okay, we've made our point," Jan said once the song ended. "Lower him."

"Please," Harmony said. "Lower him, please. Just because we've got a man hung up in my garage doesn't mean we can forget about our manners."

A couple of FLETC agents, forearms bulging, grabbed the thick ropes and lowered Butt to the garage floor.

He was shell-shocked enough when he landed that he didn't try to escape as we all paraded him across to the pool. I swiped Dash's key fob, opened the gate.

A woman walking her dog didn't even glance over. A car drove by, then another. Maybe they thought it was official business. Or an HOA meeting. Or maybe Butt had hit on them, too, and they didn't really care who was doing what to him.

It wasn't pretty, but eventually we got Butt strapped onto the cracked seat of the accessible pool lift.

A few button pushes and a loud cranking sound later and he was dangling over the pool.

Harmony, Jan and I gathered around the pool with the federal agents. I held Chickpea, who was looking longingly at the pink flamingo float on the pool deck.

"Ouch," Butt said. "Hey, come on, this crack hurts my butt."

"I'm going to let that one slide right by," Jan said.

"Okay," I said. "We can do this easy or we can do it hard."

Chickpea barked her agreement. A masked Dash looked at us, made a circling motion to tell us to move things along. Beside Dash, a masked Otesha grabbed his hand to make him stop.

Jan pushed a button on the remote she was holding.

The pool lift lowered Butt until he was inches above the water.

"These are our demands," Jan said. "You set up real recycling, make good on the money you've stolen from the HOA, give us 24/7 pool access, order a new accessible pool lift."

Jan handed the remote to me. I pushed a button and the pool lift seat tilted sideways.

"Knock it off with that thing," Butt said.

I rolled my eyes. "Pre-approved dogs in the pool area during non-peak hours. Preferential parking for electric vehicles. EV charging stations."

I handed the remote to Harmony.

Harmony pushed a button and the pool lift tilted in the opposite direction.

"I'm getting seasick here," Butt said.

"Don't think we're cleaning up after you," Jan said. "If you throw up, you're on your own."

"Hey, it's my turn." Harmony cleared her throat. "You approve the installation of a Little Free Library. And a community herb garden. And a collection station for canned food donations for the island shelters."

"Animal and people," I added.

Jan waved a pen and paper. "You sign on the dotted line. Now. Or our masked friends here scrape that sorry butt of yours on the way out of the chair and dump you in the nearest gator-infested swamp."

"And don't think you can wiggle out of it later," I said. "Our new friends know where to find you."

The masked federal agents and Otesha all pointed two fingers at their masked eyes and then at Butt.

"And they live here," Jan said.

The biggest federal agent pulled off his mask and glared at Butt.

"Right next door to you," the biggest federal agent said. "Sign says ACHING MUSSELS."

Butt gulped.

"One more itty-bitty teensy-weensy thing," Harmony said. "You're going to resign from the HOA Board and turn your spot over to the three of us to job share."

"Done," Butt said.

Harmony sighed. "Don't you just love it when the trash takes itself out."

Harmony pushed a button on the remote and tipped Butt backward.

"No skin off my nose," Butt said as he struggled to sit up.

Jan grinned. "But a sizeable slice off your butt, Butt."

Harmony and I shook our heads.

"Sorry," Jan said. "Apparently butt-joke restraint is a limited resource."

Chapter 37

At exactly 5 AM we flashed our key fobs in front of the pool gate sensor, one after another. Then we sat along the edge of the pool, dangling our feet in the water and drinking our coffee, just because we could.

"The world counts you out," we whisper-sang. "But only if you let it. While they're looking right through you. Go for it, you won't regret it."

"Damn, we're good," Jan said. And then we started at the beginning and sang our whole theme song all the way through.

After that, we figured out a hack for our resistance bands.

"Genius," Harmony said as we each wrapped a band around a tall skinny sabal palm, also known as a cabbage palm, in our postage-stamp front yards.

The soft light of our crooked streetlight and our dusk-to-dawn amber porch bulbs were just enough to see as we worked the major muscle groups of our upper body. We unhooked the handles from our carabiners and switched to the ankle straps.

A car drove by slowly, rubbernecking at us in the almost dark.

"What are *you* looking at?" Jan said to the disappearing car.

"The streetlight would probably work as a resistance band anchor, too," I said. "I mean, it's not *that* crooked."

"Maybe," Harmony said, "now that we're on the HOA Board, we can actually get it straightened out."

"Either that," Jan said, "or we can just wait until another SUV hits it from the other direction."

Our bone density increased by another workout, we stopped to watch the Belt of Venus, that gorgeous pink light at the horizon, peeking around the edges of a row of crepe myrtles.

Then we jumped into Ms. Daisy and headed for the beach.

Harmony and Ms. Daisy found WSSI, the classic hits station, just as The Beach Boys started singing "Wouldn't It Be Nice."

We belted out the part about wouldn't it be nice if we were older. And the part about wouldn't it be nice to live together in the kind of world where we belong. We sang it with feeling, really getting into it. Chickpea howled and yowled along.

"Wow," Jan said when the song ended. "I've always loved that song, but the lyrics fit in a whole new way. Like it was written for us now, even though it's been out since we were probably 10."

"I could take a pass on the we could be married line," I said.

"Don't get me started," Harmony said.

"There are lots of good theme songs in the world if you take the time to listen for them," I said. "But they're not half as special as the ones you make up yourself."

❀

Jan, Harmony and I walked along the edge of the ocean wearing compostable food service gloves, picking up trash and putting it into our net ocean cleanup bags.

We were wearing yoga pants and T-shirts.

Jan's T-shirt said LOVE IS LOVE.

Harmony's said LITERACY IS NOT A LUXURY.

Mine said THERE IS NO PLANET B.

One of the true joys of getting older is not caring what anybody thinks about how you look. Which gives you the freedom to turn yourself into a walking billboard about the things that matter to you if you feel like it. Or not.

"We've got bonus time," we sang at the top of our lungs. "So how're we gonna use it. What a gift to find. We can choose it before we lose it."

A couple wearing designer sunglasses and upscale athleisurewear gave us a look as they passed us.

We sang even louder. "Bonus time. Some get it and some miss it. It would be a crime. If we were to dismiss it."

A guy having a loud conversation with his phone on speaker cut in front of us. He glared as he passed us. Like we were the ones causing the noise pollution, not him.

"We're talking bonus time," we roared even louder. "We're rocking bonus time."

"We're actually getting good," Jan said.

"Maybe it's not too late to start a band after all," I said. "I mean, just think, we could have been The Beach Girls."

"Not *that* good," Jan said.

Harmony bent down, picked up a small round disk. It was brown and had tiny hairy bristles around the edge. She splashed a few steps into the water, tossed it in gently.

"The best is yet to come," she yelled to the disappearing sand dollar. "Don't waste it!"

Jan squatted down and picked up a purple beer cozy at the edge of the water. She held it up so we could read the formerly white letters that said RETURN TO SENDER.

"I have this terrible feeling that's one of ours," I said.

"Karma is a boomerang," Jan said.

"And this is why we pick up trash," I said.

We walked a stretch of sand in silence, kicking off our flip-flops, feeling the sand between our toes and the breeze in our faces, taking in the sharp tang of ocean air. A hunk of gray hair broke free from my ponytail and danced in the wind.

"Bad things happen," I said. "People can be total butts. You just have to keep putting one foot in front of the other and you'll get there."

"You build your supershero skills," Jan said.

"You watch for opportunities," I said.

"And then you butt right in and do the work," Harmony said. "And you use your bonus time for as long as you're lucky enough to have it."

I squatted to pick up a crunched beer can, careful to bend from the knees so I didn't throw out my back. I did a couple of extra squats while I was at it, in case we didn't run into a toilet for a while.

"Maybe," I said, "our next adventure could involve starting a circuit training-slash-trash pickup-slash-save the ocean movement."

Jan let out a loud snore.

"We're going to have to come up with something spicier than that, Honey," Harmony said.

"Something that would make Nancy proud," Jan said.

We walked some more. A black skimmer flew low over the edge of the ocean, opening its bill and dropping its long lower mandible into the water, skimming along until it felt a fish, whipping it out of the water for breakfast. The bright orange-and-black beak reminded me of Toucan Sam from the Froot Loops of my childhood.

Once you got to a certain age, pretty much everything reminded you of something.

"As our friend Gloria Steinem once said," Jan was saying

as I watched the skimmer fly away, "'One day an army of gray-haired women may quietly take over the earth.'"

"Maybe not so quietly," I said.

"We've got our first HOA Board meeting coming up," Jan said. "That might give us something."

"I don't know," Harmony said. "I mean, how many flavors of nutty as a fruitcake can one HOA Board have?"

"I guess we'll find out," I said.

"Maybe Tesha will have a good idea for us," Harmony said. "She's thinking about moving down here. I told her we'd keep an eye out for a townhouse for her."

"If it's Tesha's idea," Jan said, "we're going to have to cut her in on the supershero action. I'm fine with that, as long as we can find her a T-shirt with a cape. She's definitely one of us."

"Absolutely," Harmony and I said at the same time.

"Owe me a Coke," we both said as fast as we could.

We picked up the pace, stretching out our legs, swinging our arms and our ocean cleanup bags.

"Maybe I can ask my date if anything needs fixing over at FLETC," I said casually.

Jan and Harmony stopped in their tracks. I kept walking.

"Dangling dates is not okay," Harmony said when they caught up with me.

"Spill," Jan said.

"Fine," I said. "The forensics instructor texted me. Dash must have given him my number."

Harmony started singing The Captain and Tennille's "Love Will Keep Us Together," punching alternating fists out in front of her in one of our old aerobic dance moves. Jan jumped right in.

"It's no big deal," I said, mostly to make them stop. "We're just meeting up for a walk on the beach."

"As long as he doesn't bring his metal detector," Jan said.

"Funny," I said. "So funny I forgot to laugh."

We walked some more, mineral sunscreen still sitting on top of our skin like the whiter shade of pale of the Procol Harum song. Our diva sunglasses shielding our eyes from the sun. My big turquoise hat creating a circle of shade around me.

"Where were we?" Jan said.

"We've established the fact that we've still got it," I said. "And now we're answering the age-old question of what are we going to do with it?"

"We have time," Harmony said. "It takes a lifetime to figure out what you really want. I think if you could boil it down to any one thing, it's having a goal, a purpose, something that might just make a damn bit of difference. Preferably with a healthy dose of fun thrown in."

"Maybe," I said, "it's simply a matter of finding our next wrong to right. I mean, we know we'll always bring the fun."

"I can see it," Jan said. "The three of us wearing our supershero shirts with the attached capes, driving over the causeway looking for adventure, the golden marshes lit up by a golden sunset."

"The whole world might be going to hell in a handbasket," Harmony said.

"But age is just a number," Jan said.

"And we're taking names and kicking butt," I said.

Thank you so much for reading **Bonus Time!** If you enjoyed it, I'd be so grateful if you'd take a moment to leave a kind review so that other 40-to-forever women readers like you can find it.

To be the first to hear about Glenda, Jan and Harmony's next adventure, make sure you sign up for my newsletter at **ClaireCook.com**.

Must Love Dogs series

While I'm cooking up the next book in the *Bonus Time* series, I hope you'll enjoy the following excerpt of *Must Love Dogs*, my bestselling novel-turned-romantic comedy movie starring Diane Lane and John Cusack, which is now an 8-book series.

Must Love Dogs

Chapter 1

I decided to listen to my family and get back out there. "There's life after divorce, Sarah," my father proclaimed, not that he'd ever been divorced.

"The longer you wait, the harder it'll be" was my sister Carol's little gem, as if she had some way of knowing whether or not that was true.

After months of ignoring them, responding to a personal ad in the newspaper seemed the most detached way to give in. I wouldn't have to sit in a restaurant with a friend of a friend of one of my brothers, probably Michael's, but maybe Johnny's or Billy Jr.'s, pretending to enjoy a meal I was too nervous to taste. I needn't endure even a phone conversation with someone my sister Christine had talked into calling me. My prospect and I would quietly connect on paper or we wouldn't.

HONEST, HOPELESSLY ROMANTIC, old-fashioned gentleman seeks lady friend who enjoys elegant dining, dancing and the slow bloom of affection. WM, n/s, young 50s, widower, loves dogs, children and long meandering bicycle rides.

The ad jumped out at me the first time I looked. There wasn't much competition. Rather than risk a geographic jump to one of the Boston newspapers, I'd decided it was safer and less of an effort to confine my search to the single page of classifieds in the local weekly. Seven towns halfway between Boston and Cape Cod were clumped together in one edition. Four columns of "Women Seeking Men." A quarter of a column of "Men Seeking Women," two entries of "Women Seeking Women," and what was left of that column was "Men Seeking Men."

I certainly had no intention of adding to the disheartening surplus of heterosexual women placing ads, so I turned my attention to the second category. It was comprised of more than its share of control freaks, like this guy—*Seeking attractive woman between 5'4" and 5'6", 120-135 lbs., soft-spoken, no bad habits, financially secure, for possible relationship*. I could picture this dreamboat making his potential relationships step on the scale and show their bank statements before he penciled them in for a look-see.

And then *this* one. Quaint, charming, almost familiar somehow. When I got to *the slow bloom of affection*, it just did me in. Made me remember how lonely I was.

I circled the ad in red pen, then tore it out of the paper in a jagged rectangle. I carried it over to my computer and typed a response quickly, before I could change my mind:

Dear Sir:
You sound too good to be true, but perhaps we could have a cup of coffee together anyway—at a public place. I am a WF, divorced, young 40, who loves dogs and children, but doesn't happen to have either.
—Cautiously Optimistic

I mailed my letter to a Box 308P at the *County Connections* offices, which would, in turn, forward it. I enclosed a small check to secure my own box number for responses. Less than a week later I had my answer:

Dear Madam:
Might I have the privilege of buying you coffee at Morning Glories in Marshbury at 10 AM this coming Saturday? I'll be carrying a single yellow rose.
—Awaiting Your Response

The invitation was typed on thick ivory paper with an actual typewriter, the letters O and E forming solid dots of black ink, just like the old manual of my childhood. I wrote back simply, *Time and place convenient. Looking forward to it.*

I didn't mention my almost-date to anyone, barely even allowed myself to think about its possibilities. There was simply no sense in getting my hopes up, no need to position myself for a fall.

I woke up a few times Friday night, but it wasn't too bad. It's not as if I stayed up all night tossing and turning. And I tried on just a couple of different outfits on Saturday morning, finally settling on a yellow sweater and a long skirt with an old-fashioned floral print. I fluffed my hair, threw on some mascara and brushed my teeth a second time before heading out the door.

Morning Glories is just short of trendy, a delightfully overgrown hodgepodge of sun-streaked greenery, white lattice, and round button tables with mismatched iron chairs. The coffee is strong and the baked goods homemade and delicious. You could sit at a table for hours without getting dirty looks from the people who work there.

The long Saturday morning take-out line backed up to the door, and it took me a minute to maneuver my way over to the tables. I scanned quickly, my senses on overload, trying to pick out the rose draped across the table, to remember the opening line I had rehearsed on the drive over.

"Sarah, my darlin' girl. What a lovely surprise. Come here and give your dear old daddy a hug."

"Dad? What are you doing here?"

"Well, that's a fine how-do-you-do. And from one of my very favorite daughters at that."

"Where'd you get the rose, Dad?"

"Picked it this morning from your dear mother's rose garden. God rest her soul."

"Uh, who's it for?"

"A lady friend, honey. It's the natural course of this life that your dad would have lady friends now, Sarry. I feel your sainted mother whispering her approval to me every day."

"So, um, you're planning to meet this lady friend here, Dad?"

"That I am, God willing."

Somewhere in the dusty corners of my brain, synapses were connecting. "Oh my God. Dad. *I'm* your date. I answered your personal ad. I answered my own father's personal ad." I mean, of all the personal ads in all the world I had to pick this one?

My father looked at me blankly, then lifted his shaggy white eyebrows in surprise. His eyes moved skyward as he cocked his head to one side. He turned his palms up in resignation. "Well, now, there's one for the supermarket papers. Honey, it's okay, no need to turn white like you've seen a ghost. Here. This only proves I brought you up to know the diamond from the riffraff."

Faking a quick recovery is a Hurlihy family tradition, so I squelched the image of a single yellow rose in a hand other than my father's. I took a slow breath, assessing the damage to my heart. "Not only that, Dad, but maybe you and I can do a Jerry Springer show together. How 'bout 'Fathers Who Date Daughters'? I mean, this is big, Dad. The Oedipal implications alone—"

"Oedipal, smedipal. Don't be getting all college on me now, Sarry girl." My father peered out from under his eyebrows. "And lovely as you are, you're even lovelier when you're a smidgen less flip."

I swallowed back the tears that seemed to be my only choice besides flip, and sat down in the chair across from my father. Our waitress came by and I managed to order a coffee. "Wait a minute. You're not a young fifty, Dad. You're seventy-one. And when was the last time you rode a bike? You don't own a bike. And you hate dogs."

"Honey, don't be so literal. Think of it as poetry, as who I am in the bottom of my soul. And, Sarah, I'm glad you've started dating again. Kevin was not on his best day good enough for you, sweetie."

"I answered my own father's personal ad. That's not dating. That's sick."

My father watched as a pretty waitress leaned across the table next to ours. His eyes stayed on her as he patted my hand and said, "You'll do better next time, honey. Just keep up the hard work." I watched as my father raked a clump of thick white hair away from his watery brown eyes. The guy could find a lesson in . . . Jeez, a date with his *daughter*.

"Oh, Dad, I forgot all about you. You got the wrong date, too. You must be lonely without Mom, huh?"

The waitress stood up, caught my father's eye and smiled. She walked away, and he turned his gaze back to me. "I think about her every day, all day. And will for the rest of my natural life. But don't worry about me. I have a four o'clock."

"What do you mean, a four o'clock? Four o'clock Mass?"

"No, darlin'. A wee glass of wine at four o'clock with another lovely lady. Who couldn't possibly hold a candle to you, my sweet."

I supposed that having a date with a close blood relative was far less traumatic if it was only one of the day's two dates. I debated whether to file that tidbit away for future reference, or to plunge into deep and immediate denial that the incident had ever happened. I lifted my coffee mug to my lips. My father smiled encouragingly.

Perhaps the lack of control was in my wrist. Maybe I merely forgot to swallow. But as my father reached across the table with a pile of paper napkins to mop the burning coffee from my chin, I thought it even more likely that I had simply never learned to be a grown-up.

Keep Reading! Go to ClaireCook.com/books to find links to buy all of my books.

Must Love Dogs, the series

Based on the bestselling novel-turned-romantic comedy movie starring Diane Lane and John Cusack!

Dogs, dating, adorable preschoolers, and meddling family in every book.

"Voluptuous, sensuous, alluring and fun. Barely 40 DWF seeks special man to share starlit nights. Must love dogs."

Must Love Dogs (#1)
Must Love Dogs: New Leash on Life (#2)
Must Love Dogs: Fetch You Later (#3)
Must Love Dogs: Bark & Roll Forever (#4)
Must Love Dogs: Who Let the Cats In? (#5)
Must Love Dogs: A Howliday Tail (#6)
Must Love Dogs: Hearts & Barks (#7)
Must Love Dogs: Lucky Enough (#8)

"*Must Love Dogs* has already been a major motion picture, and now *New York Times* bestselling author Claire Cook's hilarious and heartwarming series is begging to hit the screen again."
—*New York Journal of Books*

"With all the stress and hardship in the world, Claire Cook's **Must Love Dogs series** is a perfect respite from it all. It is a wonderful comfort read, one with great humor and heart and substance. I can't wait to see what happens next!"—
Candace Hammond

"Funny and pitch perfect." –*Chicago Tribune*

"Wildly witty" –*USA Today*

"Cook dishes up plenty of charm."
–*San Francisco Chronicle*

"A hoot" –*The Boston Globe*

"Claire Cook has an original voice, sparkling style, and a window into family life that will make you laugh and cry."—
Adriana Trigiani

Acknowledgments

Thank you to my awesome readers who give me the gift of my career by reading my books and telling your friends. I'm beyond grateful to you.

Huge alphabetical thanks to Ken Harvey, Beth Hoffman, Jack Kramer, Pam Kramer, Stephanie Lewis, Maggie Marr and Kathy Muller for helping to make this a better book, each in their own unique and valuable way.

I couldn't have written this novel without the old friends and former classmates who shared memories, as well as the new friends who helped with the SSI and FLETC parts. Thank you.

Thanks to nutritionfacts.org for being such a great resource.

A big thank you to all the amazing people at the other end of my newsletter who look forward to the next one popping into your inbox. Another big thank you to my kind and generous early readers and reviewers. I hope you feel my support as much as I do yours.

Forever thanks to Jake, Garet and Kaden for always being there. And to Pebbles, Squiggy and Sunshine for being the best rescue cats ever.

About Claire

I wrote my first novel in my minivan at 45. At 50, I walked the red carpet at the Hollywood premiere of the adaptation of my second novel, *Must Love Dogs*, starring Diane Lane and John Cusack, which is now an 8-book series.

I'm the *New York Times*, *USA Today*, and international best-selling author of 24 fun and inspiring books for 40-to-forever women. If you have a buried dream, take it from me, it's never too late to shine on!

I was born in Virginia and lived for many years in Scitu-ate, Massachusetts, an awesome beach town between Boston and Cape Cod that's the inspiration for my fictional town of Marshbury. My husband and I now live on St. Simons Island, Georgia, a magical snowless place to walk the beach, ride our bikes, and make new friends.

I have the world's most fabulous readers and I'm forever grateful to all of you for giving me the gift of my late-blooming career.

Join my newsletter list at ClaireCook.com to be the first to hear when my next book comes out and to stay in the loop for giveaways and insider extras.

HANG OUT WITH ME:

ClaireCook.com
Facebook.com/ClaireCookauthorpage
Instagram.com/ClaireCookwrite
Pinterest.com/ClaireCookwrite
Twitter.com/ClaireCookwrite
Goodreads.com/ClaireCook
Linkedin.com/in/ClaireCookwrite